A Novel
by
IVA FORSHEY

Copyright © 2017 Iva Forshey.

All rights reserved. No part of this book may be used or reproduced by any means, graphic, electronic, or mechanical, including photocopying, recording, taping or by any information storage retrieval system without the written permission of the author except in the case of brief quotations embodied in critical articles and reviews.

Scripture taken from the King James Version of the Bible.

This is a work of fiction. All of the characters, names, incidents, organizations, and dialogue in this novel are either the products of the author's imagination or are used fictitiously.

WestBow Press books may be ordered through booksellers or by contacting:

WestBow Press
A Division of Thomas Nelson & Zondervan
1663 Liberty Drive
Bloomington, IN 47403
www.westbowpress.com
1 (866) 928-1240

Because of the dynamic nature of the Internet, any web addresses or links contained in this book may have changed since publication and may no longer be valid. The views expressed in this work are solely those of the author and do not necessarily reflect the views of the publisher, and the publisher hereby disclaims any responsibility for them.

Any people depicted in stock imagery provided by Thinkstock are models, and such images are being used for illustrative purposes only. Certain stock imagery © Thinkstock.

ISBN: 978-1-5127-8844-0 (sc)
ISBN: 978-1-5127-8845-7 (hc)
ISBN: 978-1-5127-8843-3 (e)

Library of Congress Control Number: 2017907836

Print information available on the last page.

WestBow Press rev. date: 5/23/2017

To Dean who has stood by me through thick and thin, and generously gave me the time and space to write.

# Acknowledgements

After months of gathering information, I was given the time and space to put it all together and write this book, with a lot of encouragement along the way. I would like to thank the coordinating and design team, the consultants and editors at WestBow Press, especially Reggie Adams, my check-in-coordinator, who has the patience of Job and his forbearance with me has been phenomenal. Others who gave of their time and were very helpful, were, John Opat, Nikki Mota, Genna Ramos, and Adlee Cooney.

# Chapter 1

JoAnn Cobb pressed her nose against the glass door on the back porch, steaming it up as she watched a blue jay flitting about in the shadows of the nearby maple trees. The nasty but pretty-colored jay reminded her of a name she hated and the thought sent a shiver up her back, causing her to twist her head as if she had just bitten into a lemon! Jay! She had eventually, happily discarded that name sometime into her marriage.

Jay! Her late husband, Louis, had insisted on changing her name from JoAnn, to Jay.

"Jay!" she had humbly cried. "It sounds like a bird or a man's name, and I don't like it." She remembered the argument so clearly. His excuse, by way of exclamation, was, 'When you pronounce the letters JA, they sound like 'Jay'. What's the big deal?' At least that was the story he tried to hand her.

She argued back, "Right. A man's name. When the letters JA are conveyed as a word, not as initials, they do sound like Jay, and I hate it! You are the only one who wants to change it. I fear you have an ulterior motive, and I wish you would be honest with me and tell me what it is."

He never did tell, and so it went. She relented as she had

done hundreds of times, but, she refused to let anyone but Louis call her, Jay. The male-sounding name was actually what he had in mind; however, she didn't discover until years later why he had insisted on the name change. Then she demanded he call her JoAnn, and he did, though reluctantly.

Another name came to her mind now, a name from a long time ago: Jo! It had been a special name given to her by Gabe Holland, one of the sweetest, kindest, most gentle people she had ever met. Gabe Holland, wow! She stepped back from the kitchen door. *Now what made me think about him? Come to think about it, the background and connotation I bring to the situation must make me like or dislike it. Jo, Gabe's special name sounds like Joe with the e, and, that was always acceptable . . .back then.*

Sighing, she turned and took a last glance at the closed-in screened porch, which used to contain cold and hard wrought-iron furniture. Now it was empty. She then walked through the galley kitchen, glancing into the empty den off to the side as she headed into the dining room. The phone rang while she was thinking about the straight-backed, uncomfortable streamlined furniture that used to occupy it. So stiff and formal. She thought the phone had been disconnected, hence, she answered with a ho-hum attitude. "Hello."

"Jo?" the male voice asked.

"I'm sorry, but you have the wro . . .n . . ., did you say Jo?"

"Yes, I did, Jo. This is Gabe Holland."

*Woah! This is too coincidental. I think of him. He calls! After all these years, he calls, just as I am ready to leave this house and head back to his neck of the woods. What could he possibly want?* "Did you say Gabe Holland?" *Of course he did, even if there was something wrong with my hearing, I remember that voice. The thing is that I heard him quite clearly, and a chill is running up and down my spine as I stall for time.*

"Yes, I did," he said matter-of-factly. "I know it's hard to believe, isn't it?" His voice sounded almost as if he were laughing. He probably was if he were the same Gabe of old.

"Gabe, of all people, I wouldn't have thought in a hundred years . . .. I suppose I should have known it was you. It's been years since anyone has called me Jo."

There was assured conceit in his voice. "Of course not, no one ever did and possibly no one else ever will."

"Excuse me."

"Hey, I'm sorry, Jo. This is your old friend calling, but I didn't mean to come on so strongly. I really just called to tell you that I'm glad everything is finally settled about your inheritance, and that I'll be here when you get here, in case you should need help from a friend."

"How did you know?" Her back was up.

"Rusty Owen."

"I suppose I should have known it was Grandpop's old sidekick. Well, thank you, but with the children and Rusty, I think we'll manage." She had just said the understatement of the year. Her voice was cold and empty, like her house, lacking encouragement for any further conversation.

If he heard it, he ignored it. "I understand you are leaving there today, and I don't want to hold you up, just wanted to offer my help if it's needed."

If it is needed! She wanted to shout, I am going to need all the help I can get! Instead, she spoke quickly. "Thank you again. Now I really must attend to some last-minute matters. Good-bye." By quickly holding the phone away from her ear, she all but cut him off from anything else he might have wanted to say. She heard him speak her name before she cradled it. Then she leaned against the counter wondering why she had been so rude to her old companion.

*Gabe Holland! I can't believe it, do not want to believe it, don't want him to be there in Kentucky waiting for me when*

*I arrive. I'm not a child. I am not seventeen or even twenty-one. I am a forty-two year old widow with three children, and have learned with the Lord's help, to take care of myself. I hope I won't be needing him, but at the same time, I'm sure I will.*

    She thought about her life with Louis as she tolerated one last tour of her nearly empty house. A smile played about her lips when she glanced at his closed and locked bedroom door. He had been a good provider, but a domineering, word-abusing husband and father, and something else she couldn't quite put her finger on. At least until after Dana was born, that is, and his friend Roger Eastman boldly came on the scene. Then it was like the end of one repugnant life and the beginning of another, which was just as repulsive. JoAnn no longer existed as a wife, a companion, or a helpmeet. She became his social escort but felt like she had been used as a doormat. From the time her son John asked her of confirmation regarding his suspicions about his father's new life style, it had been downhill all the way, like crashing into one of the many ocean waves she could see from her bedroom window.

    She remembered feeling frozen with immobility, wondering if she would ever be interested in anything again. She had given to and given in to her husband times without number. Then when her children needed her more than ever, had she anything left to give to them? Yes, she did, and she would go on giving to them if she had to tear herself into bits and pieces to do so. She had been whacked hard and sent sprawling, but, somehow, she had picked herself up and maneuvered through the years.

    *If only I had known God then, when everything seemed stripped away, when my back was against the wall, when I hit bottom. I could have taken comfort in the One who saw my plight. He could have taken me up in His capable hands and safely carried me through it all. As it was, the children and I struggled alone. Oh well, no more. Thank you, Jesus.*

Now she settled into one of two straight wing-back chairs in the living room. They were the only comfortable chairs she ever owned. Now, they were the only articles of furniture left in the house, at least the only pieces anyone needed to know about for the present. Their exclusive colonial-style house was beautifully situated near the seashore in New Jersey, in a college town, loaded with educated but sometimes counterfeit inhabitants, much like her parents. Her three children, John, Rob, and Dana, their dog and cat, Mitsi and Samantha, were outside visiting with friends who had come to say a final good-bye. Dana was the only one who would find it difficult to leave the ocean.

Shortly they would head west for Donaldson, Kentucky, to grandpop's old horse farm, where her musings had always fled and her heart had longed to be. Her motives were pure and simple; they had nothing to do with Gabe Holland.

"Do you have anything to do with this Father?" She looked up to the decorative swirled ceiling and asked God, "Was that phone call placed on your timing? I have a promise to keep to Grandpop that has nothing to do with Gabe Holland."

While waiting for someone to come for the chairs, she glanced around the living room. The only thing that had been warm and inviting about it was the fireplace. Even the two remaining chairs, which had graced either side of it, were a tad too masculine. She shook her head when she realized that she really wasn't actively thinking about the room. Rather, her meditations seemed to be coming from a deep well of contemplation, focusing on reflections about Gabe. She hadn't really thought of him since she was married. Nevertheless, she had to admit to herself, that she had occasionally found herself thinking about him ever since the decision had been made to go back to her grandpops farm. The memories carried her back past her now middle-age years into the happy times of youth. They took her to the time when nothing was cluttered or gray. A nice time to remember, a nice person to remember, Gabe Holland.

*Gabe's offer might come in handy. He could lend a hand as he indicated on the phone. I wonder if I can take the chance of receiving his help when it might rekindle old, lost feelings. I'm sure I'll stir up and enjoy old memories as I ride the ranch, but I hope that's all there will be to it. What about any allegiance I have left to my children's father?*

*I wonder what my life would have been like if I had married him instead of Louis? God used Grandpop and Rusty's Friday Night Bible Classes to open our eyes to our need of salvation. I guess Gabe accepted Jesus as his very own personal Savior with his heart and mind, and I with my mind only, and perhaps merely because he did.*

*Under their tutelage, Gabe grew in knowledge and favor with God. Perhaps because I wasn't even really saved and lacked mentoring by anyone, even by my own "saved" but hypocritical parents, I became an agnostic and entered into an earthly bondage to sin, thus Louis.*

A frown, which had spread across her strained face remained there, when Roger Eastman, her late husband's lawyer and intimate friend, timidly knocked, before boldly stepping through the open doorway.

"I hope I'm not disturbing you," he asked, almost apologetically, in his polite silky voice.

She became flustered, then irritated at the sight of her husband's lover. If he had waited, perhaps just another half-hour, she might have been able to avoid him altogether. With God's help she would manage to speak to him, without revealing her inner turmoil.

"No," she managed without getting up and without looking up. "Just waiting for someone from the college to come for these chairs, then we'll be on our way and the house will be yours: lock, stock, and barrel." She kept her voice even as she looked at her watch.

"You are probably anxious to be on your way." He spoke quietly, actually kindly, looking around.

Hearing the smoothness in his voice, she looked directly at him and spoke icily. "Don't do me any favors, Roger!"

It had taken a year of praying and searching the scriptures before she had found forgiveness in her heart towards this man. She read Colossians about forgiveness "through his blood, even the forgiveness of sins". There was no in-between here. Either His death and resurrection triumphed over all sin or it did not over any. Through the Holy Spirit's working, she was able to settle old burdens about Louis and Roger and was able to forgive them, "Lest Satan should get an advantage of us," she read in 11 Corinthians 2. JoAnn gladly took up the peace Christ had so firmly, beautifully, and graciously, offered her.

Even though she would probably never see him again, she did not have to be overly pleasant to her husband's lover. He had successfully solicited Louis's affections, and in winning them, without knowing it, had set her free from a monstrous, artificial marriage relationship. *Father, help me sense your Spirit in me, to demonstrate your peace.*

She still did not stand nor extend him any courtesies. He didn't need them. Roger was so confident that he actually seemed to stand comfortably, possessively in the middle of the empty room.

She wondered if he noticed the involuntary shiver again race up her spine causing her to shiver. Then, she saw how he looked at her and that he seemed to be disturbed, and she knew why. He had never seen her with her dark brown hair cut so short, or dressed so casually before. Therefore, just to irritate him more, she pulled at her size ten jeans and moved her foot to reveal more of her expensive handcrafted boots. Then, she picked up the cowboy hat from the floor and leaning forward, put it on with a deliberate flair, knowing it accentuated her already attractive looks.

"Perhaps you noticed the children and I are dressed similarly. Louis wouldn't have approved, would he?" she asked, looking triumphantly up at him, not waiting for an answer. "Through the grace of God I began to shed him a long time ago, Roger. Now I have completely, it is a marvelous feeling." She spoke triumphantly with a snap of her finger to the brim of her hat, and wished with all her heart that it were true.

He was shocked into silence. If he had expected her to be still mourning after two years, to be meek as she had been in the past, he was clearly disappointed. He stood there in his so-proper vested pin-stripe suit. It fit his rotund body so smoothly and was made from such fine wool that there wasn't a wrinkle in it, although the late May morning was already quite unseasonably hot. His black wavy hair was combed neatly, no, actually perfectly, and his heavy dark eyebrows enhanced his deep green eyes. His pearly white smile turned women on, but was lost to them. His affections drifted only toward his own sex.

The silence in the room threatened to stretch interminably on, when a shout from her son John, told her that someone had finally come to take the last of the furniture.

"Coming," she called happily, relieved to be able to walk out on Roger.

The few pieces she was taking with her, were already packed in the rented U-Haul truck and their own station wagon. The rest had been sold, given away, or would remain. The chairs were the last to go.

So standing up with a deliberate flair, she went to the front door for the last time. The last time for so many things in the house. She was glad, so glad for herself, but sad for the children. JoAnn knew God was helping them adjust to the fact of moving, but when they actually got to the ranch, and the hard work, unpleasantness, and long hours began, what then?

God in his infinite love had begun working in her, and a year before Louis' death, her beloved grandpop had died, and she had inherited his ranch. More importantly, it turned out, was his Bible and a letter it enclosed. Through these, God did His transforming work in her. It took hours and a box of tissues before she emerged from her bedroom a new creation, changed from death to life. She knew her grandpop was rejoicing in heaven with Jesus. With her whole heart, mind, and soul she understood and accepted the entire scope of God's plan of salvation for her life, and recorded the date, June 13, 1972.

Before she had to decide whether or not to leave Louis, or to ask him to move out, or to even pray intelligently about what God would want, he had suddenly become quite ill, and died.

First her grandpop, (her grandma had preceded him by two years) now her husband. Through her pastor, her new Christian friends, studies at church and her own personal study, she became convinced that God is sovereign, that He is in absolute control.

Psalms 103:19 "and His kingdom (sovereignty) rules over all," stayed with her. She was attempting to respond to tragedy in the right way, to see the hand of God in it. She was also finding that His love is not determined by whether or not we feel it; His love is unchanging. She was going to trust the Word, like Romans 8:32-39 and not her feelings. When she hid her feelings, allowing them to twist inside and spoil everything, she was miserable. Now she was a new creature and she felt it, lived it, shared it, and was happy.

Almost immediately upon Louis's death, partly for therapy

and partly because she hoped to have her grandpop's will settled soon and move to the ranch, she enrolled all four of them in the near-by riding stables. She had too long suppressed her love of horseback riding, and she wanted the children to be proficient at riding before they headed for Kentucky. But, as long as Dana had the ocean, she wanted nothing to do with horses!

It was when riding a horse that thoughts of Gabe had first begun to penetrate her troubled mind like a ray of sunshine. She had to wonder why and asked God. "Surely . . ." and she had never allowed herself the privilege of an answer, for such a bitter taste remained in her mouth over Louis, at times permeating her very being. Yes, Gabe had been there at her grandpop's funeral, all handsome and kind, but reserved, and he had been alone.

She found herself talking aloud to God when no one was around. "Unquestionably, I'm not ready to think about men again, Father, certainly not about dating a particular one? What really scares me, is my inability or lack of ability to discern, or will feelings, emotions get in the way again, causing me to make another mistake. "But, now I have you Lord, and in your word in Philippians 4: 6 and 7, you tell me to be anxious for nothing, but with real prayer and thanksgiving, tell you all my troubles. I'm to give my request to you and you will give me your peace, which I won't be able to understand because of its greatness. "So, Father, I lay this problem, this emotion, this "man" thing before you and ask you to guard my heart and mind. In Jesus name, Amen."

Also, she continued working with the students in the literature department and in the college library. She found their vigor and vitality good therapy. What a wonderful opportunity God has given her to witness for Him and what warm, responsive hearts. Walt was one of those students, who now stood awkwardly on the steps as she went to the door.

"Please, come in, Walt."

He grasped her extended hand, "There are many who will miss you." He spoke a little too quickly as he noticed, and then gave a nod to Mr. Eastman, before hastening to pick up a chair. "I guess I held you up. I'm sorry."

"No problem," she spoke sincerely, noticing Rob come bounding up the steps to help him. "It's early yet." Patting Rob on the shoulder, she said, "Thanks, Son."

Extending a helping hand as they cleared the door with the chairs, she spoke quietly to Walt, "Enjoy the chair, it was my favorite." She almost told him it lately had been her dream chair, which made her blush slightly, but Roger stood impatiently by, and she wasn't about to mention it in front of him. Perhaps God had her more ready to think about men than she realized.

"Good luck on the ranch, Mrs. Cobb, and thanks for the chairs and for all your help and encouragement, especially for introducing me to Christ. We'll miss you and be praying for you."

"You're welcome, Walt," she said, as she retrieved her shoulder bag from the inside door knob, and followed the boys outside as far as the stoop. "May God bless and encourage you." *I wonder what you think about that, Roger!*

JoAnn glanced up to the clear bright ocean sky as her two sons, John and Rob helped Walt lift the chairs into his pick-up. Then, she turned back to Roger, who still stood in the middle of the room, his room, his house. When JoAnn had realized how much he wanted the house, she had asked the top dollar and he willingly paid it. That extra money would buy a horse or two.

Slowly, as frigidly as possible, she told him, "The keys are on the kitchen counter. Otherwise, I think you will find something very interesting on the second floor. There was definitely a bit of a grin on her face which she couldn't suppress. Good-bye, Roger."

A bemused smile played about her lips as she shut the door behind her. Everything that had belonged to her husband, everything that the children didn't want; every book, shoe, shirt, piece of his furniture, even his toothbrushes and shoe lacers, had been put into Louis's room following his death. It was there now for Roger or any other of his very intimate friends. He had wanted Louis, well, let him take what was left of him too.

JoAnn almost ran down the front steps to receive more hugs, kisses, and handshakes from the send-off crowd. Then she opened the car door, extracting the keys first, and threw her purse and hat on the seat next to where her thirteen-year old daughter Dana, and the animals waited, impatient to get going.

Before seating herself behind the wheel, she called back to Rob and John and raised her arm and hand with a forward motion. "Westward, hooo!" She felt an exhilaration that was unexplainable as she shut the car door.

When she pulled away from the curb, she pressed the horn, and occasionally blew it again as they drove through the town.

Louis would have hated it so!

"Well, phooey on yoouey, Loouie!"

# Chapter 2

The small caravan began its journey west under the clear blue mid-morning sky. They were hardly away from the city limits, however, when a tire blew on the U-Haul truck. John skillfully maneuvered it to the side of the road, before jumping out to have a look at it. After talking it over, JoAnn decided the thing to do was for her to drive around the area looking for a pay telephone. It wasn't long before she had connected with the U-Haul company who located a garage near their disabled vehicle, and within the hour, they were on their way again.

It seemed the flat sandy tidewater land reluctantly gave way to the great city of Baltimore. From there, JoAnn decided to stay along the Shenandoah Valley and the Blue Ridge Mountains of Virginia, hoping her kids were not only remembering their majesty, but, were once again awed by their grandeur. They drove southwest along the maze of hills and hollows of the Appalachian Mountains of West Virginia, where they took a break at the famous White Sulfur Springs.

The animals were not used to riding in the car, and as soon as JoAnn parked the car and opened the door, Mitsi was out! She and Dana took off after her, while the boys went to head her off another way. A screeching of tires alerted the boys, and sure enough, there was Mitsi in the middle of the road, scared to death, but otherwise unhurt. Rob was able to scoop her into his arms, while John apologized to the driver. Finally, with both animals secured on leashes, they refreshed themselves, peeked into and tested the warm waters of the bathhouses, before starting out once more.

Dana had been her usual quiet self, listening to music, holding Samantha, or just watching the road.

"What are you thinking about?"

"Nothing."

So it went, until they pulled over at another rest stop, where she again chatted easily with her brothers. Then it was back to, "nothing" again. JoAnn was more than a little concerned about Dana, who, although not very talkative, was never this quiet. JoAnn decided to dive into a subject that would appeal to her. "You'll have to invite the twins for a visit after we get settled."

"Maybe."

"You plan to write to one another?"

"Yes."

"That's great!" She smiled to her daughter who was looking out the side window. "You know that's a girl thing. Boys don't usually do that."

Dana finally looked at her mother. "Who will you write to?"

"Shirley Hopkins from the stables asked for my address. The pastor's wife and my Sunday School teacher want to keep in touch."

"No one from the college?"

JoAnn thought Dana sounded disappointed. "Not really. Actually, no. My relationships with them were too superficial." She glanced at Dana and with an upbeat sound, stated, "Now Janice and Joyce are different, aren't they?"

"They're my best friends," she answered, playing with a friendship ring the twins had given her for her birthday.

"You're lucky. I never had a best friend."

"Never?"

"My parents didn't think it was healthy."

"You have got to be kidding! I'm glad they didn't visit often."

"Dana!"

"I mean it." She looked at her mom again. "They never treated you right when they visited."

*When did she get so smart*! As JoAnn returned the look, she saw open honesty and love radiating in those blue eyes so like her own. "They did the best they could." After a moment, "I was an only child. They were afraid I couldn't love them and have affection for someone else at the same time."

For the first time a realization dawned upon her, something she had never allowed herself to dwell upon before. It was her parents who had kept her from developing a serious relationship with Gabe! They had seen she was falling for him that last summer, and had yanked her from the ranch earlier than planned. It was all so clear now, so clear—and that's not all—other things, many other things. *Oh God, help me, help me!* A hurt filled her until her eyes smarted with tears. If they had allowed nature to take its course, Louis would have never had a chance. All those wasted years, those awful wasted years! **But,** I can't dwell on that now. A side-glance at Dana told her she was looking at her. "Dana, you aren't going to understand this, but I need to change the subject."

"Well, I think it strange, especially for two educated people."

"I can't think about it now, maybe later, but not now." She kept her eyes on the road. "I have too much on my mind as it is." She gave Dana a half smile. "I'm glad the twins are your friends and you may invite them anytime you wish."

"Thanks."

*I wonder what child-raising mistakes I have made and what effect they will have on my children's future lives. My few psychology courses gave me just enough rope to almost strangle myself, still, they seem well adjusted and self-confident. I can only trust in You Father and stop trying to second-guess you. Please help me to deal with this new problem at the proper time.*

By the time the sun had well passed its zenith, the family had consumed about a dozen hamburgers, a peck of french-fries, and a case of soda pop. They were all a bit hyper. As the sun lowered in the sky, they entered the mountainous region of Kentucky and began looking for a hotel or motel. In the fading light, they saw patches of tobacco and corn on eroding hillsides so steep that it took your breath away just looking at it. Somehow, people lived there in tiny weathered, patched houses that seemed to step right out of the story of "Christy".

Then finally, the following day, with a quality breakfast behind them, they drove toward the horse capital of the world, the Bluegrass Country. From this great limestone region comes the world's finest breed of racehorses. Acres of fenced serene beauty lined the highways and back roads, behind which grazed famous and prospective champion thoroughbreds.

"In the east, such fine undulating terrain would have been turned into magnificent golf courses," JoAnn said to her quiet daughter, "exactly what Grandpop wanted to avoid."

Tree lined avenues led back to majestic columned houses, and low slung costly and elegant fire resistant barns, capably accommodated the thousands of thoroughbred horses that thrived on the rich pasture of the Bluegrass.

JoAnn thirstily drank in the breath-taking beauty of the scenes before her, and slowed the station wagon sometimes to a snail's pace. She was feeling as exhilarated now as she had felt that summer when she had turned seventeen and had driven alone to the ranch, the summer of Gabe Holland. She found it impossible to drive without her mind wandering.

It had not been difficult to get used to the fact that she was a forty-two year old widow with three children. Most of her married life, she had pretended to love the ocean atmosphere, as well as the college life-style around which marriage to a professor and author had forced her to live. She even pretended to have the perfect marriage. The past ten years had been one big pretense.

The many summers in her growing-up years at her grandpop's horse farm, had never quite lost their hold on her. She had always longed to go back there to live, even if it really had always been just a silly romantic notion, until now.

Dana's quietness as she listened to the radio, allowed her more time for reflection and she thought how quickly one's life can change. Her dear, dear Grandpop was dead and the farm willed to her and not to her father or any of his brothers or any of their children, but to her. How they fought it, even though they were either too old to run it, or didn't need it. She did! Especially now.

She not only loved it but also had often begged her grandpop to let her stay with him. Now she needed it and it was hers. God's timing is perfect. She had intended to sell the house at the seashore anyway, for the children and she had come to the place where they needed a drastic change. It was more than that actually; she felt shackled to a life and people with whom she had never felt empathy. She had lived just as artificial a life as her husband, had listened respectfully to someone else's opinion, with whom she usually disagreed much too often. Their soft life-styles, their exclusive dress code, their intellectual snobbery, had been forced upon her, first by her parents and then by Louis. She had allowed those scales to slough off, as she was trying to shed her husband.

She felt like fortune's child when the will was read. How many people had a dream come true? It would be a challenge and it would be enormously difficult. After much prayer, she at first only insinuated a change to her children. When they discussed the possibility, Dana was the only one to balk, but with the Lord's working, she came around to the way of the majority.

However, JoAnn kept a careful watch on Dana's emotions, ready to deal with any problems she might have as the time drew nearer and nearer; as the house was sold, then the furniture; as John graduated from high school and Rob and Dana played in their last band concert and sang in their last choral concert. Dana seemed to deal with every situation with adult maturity, and JoAnn breathed more easily as the end had finally come. Perhaps she hadn't done too bad a job after all.

Friends and classmates they had known all their lives, schools, theatres, stores, play-grounds, parks, streets, churches, the library and gym, the boardwalk and the ocean, the house in which they had lived all their lives, would all be just a part of their memory. Everything the children had related to with a secure feeling was behind them now. Everything new, different and strange to them, to their thinking and their lifestyle, would need to be learned, and accepted, or rejected. Yet she sensed freedom for them that would never have been possible back in Jersey and certainly not with Louis. This is going to be good; I can feel it in my bones!

So, here they were. All they possessed of this world's goods was packed into her station wagon and the rented U-Haul truck, which her eighteen-year-old son, John Arthur, was driving. New Jersey was far behind them. They had ventured out of their safe haven and had already experienced the unfolding process of their new life.

*Is it stretching things or am I simply being rebellious to want an identity of my own again, to be the woman I am, not the woman I was obliged to be?*

When suave, handsome Louis entered her life, near the end of her senior year in college, her love for him allowed his influence to change her thinking, her life, even her name. In the ensuing ten years, it hadn't really made a difference, not until . . .

When she had gotten her feet under her again, she gradually reverted to things that did count to her, personally, other than her children: her hobbies, friends, books, art, and eventually, church and it's by-products. All positive changes that she hoped would help heal the scars of the past. It appeared to be working.

The transition had seemed easy. Well, actually, not until she was saved and the Lord guided and strengthened her. This is what Dana, Rob, and John saw in her and which led them to eventually want what she had. John was having a difficult time coming to terms with who and what his father was. It wasn't until Christ came into his heart that he fully and honestly forgave his father and accepted him as he had been.

*Well, Louis, old boy, you closed us in, all but locked us up with your money arrangements, thinking you could hold onto the reins of our lives forever. However, you didn't reckon on God!* Roger Eastman's face flashed before her. *Grandpop saw you one better also. I really believe that in God's timing, He freed us in a way you never could or would.*

A youthful image of Gabe Holland replaced Roger's face in her mind's eye. She mentally shook herself, blinked her eyes quickly and shrugged away from under the weight of the heady influence of his image. Half-leaning out the window, she let the wind blow through her layered and feathered haircut, which she could comb with her fingers. She remarked to her youngest child and only daughter, "Fantastic! Beautiful! Have you ever seen anything like Kentucky?"

Dana, with her dark hair newly cut like her mom's, new designer jeans and shirt, and new cowboy boots, which were apparently hurting her feet, for she was trying to get them off, simply groaned, in answer to her mom's question.

"Well?"

"You know I loved living near the ocean, Mom. Nothing can ever take the place of beach combing after a storm, or surfing and floating on huge waves. I just know I would have won in the surfboard competition this summer."

She valiantly smiled at her mother, trying to catch some of the excitement she was feeling. "I see now, that it's spread out just like the ocean. I thought nothing could be like living at the shore!"

"Oh, Honey," JoAnn said, resting her eyes momentarily on Dana, and then reaching to give her tanned hand a quick squeeze. "I'm sorry. I know how much you're going to miss your friends and the water."

After a moment's silence, Dana said, "I have a question."

*Here it comes, the big confrontation.* Nevertheless, she said, "Shoot."

"Why is this called the Bluegrass State? Seems dumb since the grass all looks green to me."

JoAnn could hardly believe her ears. That's all she questions? She answered with aplomb. "I asked Grandpop that same question one time. He said it the grass produces blue flowers in late May, and that if it weren't cut so short, it would have a tinge of blue."

She gave Dana a wink. "But the way it grows! Nothing like it!"

"Look at those horses!" Dana suddenly exclaimed, gazing at the horses grazing behind a fence which was close to the road. "Will Grandpop's ranch look like that one?"

JoAnn looked longingly at the million-dollar country estate nestled among the groves of trees, with miles of gleaming white fencing surrounding it, which probably cost twenty thousand just to paint it. If Dana had been watching her mom, she would have seen an apprehensive look come into her eyes.

"Dana, honey," she hesitated, but had to keep on going. "Grandpop's ranch won't look like that. I've tried to describe it to you and I thought the pictures we looked at back in Jersey would have refreshed your memory."

It had been three years since the funeral, the last time she had seen the Simpson Ranch. Two years of waiting while the adults fought over the will, and hours of listening to the judge and lawyers battle, and just when their case was to go to court, they had decided to quit fighting and let the will stand as written. JoAnn got the ranch!

So now, what would a ranch look like that was built in 1875? Especially when it had been years since there had been anyone who could take a real interest in it, and five years since her grandpop had become ill.

She thought back to Rusty Owens, her grandpop's old friend and caretaker. He had done the best he could with the few remaining animals, the house and cooking for the two of them. Otherwise, the two old cowboys had just seemed to let the days slip lazily, ineffectively by, while, she supposed, the three thousand acres had grown into a mangled growth of briers, thistles, and unwanted trees all of which grew like a wild fire.

She had tried to tell her children that they wouldn't walk into a bed of roses. Now it looked as if Dana was headed for a very real disappointment. At least she was showing an interest. JoAnn wondered what the boys were thinking, what they had been talking about these last two days.

All her words, her descriptions, didn't mean a thing. Childhood memories conjured up castles and shining knights, when in reality, there was just a two storied-house in a grove of ash and tulip trees, an empty bunkhouse and cookhouse, unused pens, barns, corrals and loading chutes, . . . and cowboys? No, no cowboys, no shining knights!

Tears readily surfaced. They would all be so disappointed. Perhaps she had done the wrong thing. Thinking of the boys in the truck behind her, she wondered if she was forcing her will on them? She certainly didn't want to impose her way of life on them as her parents and husband had done to her.

John Arthur, named after his grandfather, was already enrolled at the University of Tennessee for the freshman class. He was tall and ruggedly built in the image of his ancestor and like him, had a love of animals, especially horses. There had always been cats and dogs, and since Louis's death, she had to drag him away from the stables.

Rob, just fifteen, in his outward appearance, except in height, was a carbon copy of his brother. She hoped they were being observant of the land around them, and glancing in her rear-view mirror, picked up speed, noting that John kept pace with her, probably glad to be moving more rapidly toward their destination.

They had driven through large, small, and old towns, past distilleries, then fields recently cultivated and sown with corn and wheat. Once again JoAnn heard a loud noise and noticed John's truck sway, as well as heard his horn. They both slowed down and parked on the berm of the road. Without thinking, she once again opened the door and leaving it open, ran back to the truck. She heard Dana yell something, but didn't turn around or she would have seen Samantha scoot under the car and Mitsi run around the front and down an alley.

"It's another flat tire, Mom," Rob informed her. "Back one this time and no spare."

"Well, I'll have to call the truck company again," she stated, looking around for a gas station or a garage.

"You can see one about half a block back. I'll go this time."

She held up her hand. "No, you stay here and Rob and I will walk on back."

"Well, okay. I'll go ahead and get the hubcap off and fish out the jack and lug wrench."

"Maybe you better wait. The company might only want an authorized person to work on the truck. Perhaps you can go see what Dana wanted."

When she returned with a man who was not dressed like a mechanic, John immediately informed her that she had better go help Dana find the animals.

"Not again! How stupid can I get?" Then she introduced the man as Mr. Reinhart. "The mechanic is too busy and said this man could help us." Turning to him, she said, "I feel like I'm impinging on your time and kindness. We can just wait for the mechanic."

The strapping and tough, rugged looking man just smiled, and when he did, his thick eyebrows seemed to dance. "That could be awhile and I'm no stranger to flat tires." Taking off his jacket and tossing it in his truck, then rolling up his shirtsleeves, he started for the back of the rented truck. "Come on boys, let's take a look."

Shaking her head at her forgetfulness, JoAnn introduced her sons then went to look for Dana and the animals. She found all three sitting on a mound of grass several blocks away.

A cool breeze swept across her back as she approached the trio. One had tears in her eyes.

"Dana, I'm so sorry, so thoughtless."

"There was another dog around here," she exploded looking around her. "It wanted to pick a fight, but a boy came along calling its name and took it home. I just picked up Samantha and got hold of Mitsi, when you came."

JoAnn threw her arms around her daughter, then took off her belt and put it through Mitsi's collar. "Well, come on, we're almost at the ranch."

With the animals secured once again in the station wagon, Dana and JoAnn walked back to the truck, where Rob informed them that John and Mr. Reinhart had taken the tire to the garage to be fixed.

"Mind if I run down to the garage, Mom?"

"No, go ahead, but someone come back with a progress report."

He had just started off, when he returned and said that John and the guy who helped them at the gas station, were on their way back. In no time, they were once again on their way. Mr. Reinhart wouldn't take any money for helping them.

They hadn't traveled far when JoAnn once again pulled off on the berm of the road.

"Why are you stopping in the middle of nowhere, Mom?"

"Get out Dana and come with me," her mother stated kindly. She carefully opened the door this time calling 'stay' to the animals. She swung her long limbs from the car, shading her eyes from the sun with her hand.

John leaned his head out the opened window and asked, "What's up, Mom?"

He didn't recognize the land across the road, apparently Rob didn't either. How easily children forget, how blessed.

"Nothing's up, I just wanted to show you something. Come on, get out. You too, Rob."

Still shading her eyes and scrunching her tired shoulders, she ostensibly scanned the land across the road, and spoke with unbearable pride. "This was your great grandfather's land as far as you can see and then some. He bought and paid for it with his own sweat and tears, the blood of animals and crop failures, during good times and bad. You name it and your great- grandfather and grandpop have experienced it.

"Grandpop had always hoped Dad would take over the ranch, but maybe he was too hard on him. I don't know, for he was turned against ranching long before he graduated from high school. Because of that, I firmly believe we have been given this chance of a life time. We don't want to miss this door of opportunity God is opening wide for us."

She looked from them to the land. "What do you see?"

Rob, quick, always ready with an answer, said, "Nothing! Just grubby land!"

John cuffed him and whispered, "Rob, I warned you."

JoAnn put up a hand to stop him. "That's all right, John. Rob sees exactly what you see, although you're too much of a gentleman to say it."

She was quiet then, just staring across the road. It was a dreadful picture, much worse than she had expected. Just driving by, there was nothing to cause a casual observer to take a second look. She let her eyes roam over the property, her gaze taking in the broken, unpainted fences, the wild unsettled land that had once been rich pasture. She glanced toward the sun as it sent burning rays that seemed to dance on the thickets stirred by a lazy warm June breeze.

It had not always been so carelessly managed, for there was enough limestone underneath the soil to feed strength into the forage and make it a very productive land. It was special to her, and with God and Rusty's help, she would work to make her dreams come true. She took a deep, sweet breath before speaking, almost to herself, choking back tears.

"It isn't like it used to be and I expect the house and barns aren't either; they are over a hundred years old! I just wanted to remind and prepare you for the worst." *To prepare myself too!*

A long faint shudder sent shivers of uncertainty through her. All her hopes and dreams lay in that land across the road. Louis had piled up his own happiness and wealth while she had laid aside her dreams for him. But, in God's sovereignty, hers would come through, she could just feel it!

"Hey! Breathe this air, it doesn't taste like salt," John protectively rescued her. "Makes one feel like a man," he said, stretching his tanned muscular arms and taking in a big gulp of air, then letting out a war-whoop. "I'd like to see us do that back in Jersey without the neighbors complaining."

Dana spoke as much for herself as her mother. "So, who cares what the land looks like, let's move it. I want to see the house."

"I want to see the horses," Rob reminded everyone, as Dana headed for the car.

Just as JoAnn turned to follow her, John's voice stopped her. "Hey Mom!" he pointed, "someone's riding along the fence."

JoAnn shaded her eyes again with her hand as she followed his pointing finger. There was something about that rider on horseback that disturbed her. He sat tall in the saddle, allowing his horse freedom to follow the trail, while he seemed to intently study JoAnn and her children.

The broad shoulders conjured up a cowboy from the mists of her long ago memory, who until recently, had receded to that compartment of her brain where one computes things one wishes to keep but not necessarily to remember. She quickly withdrew her hand attempting to ignore Gabe Holland's wave of greeting. *Why all of a sudden am I being rude to him? Why have I recognized him so easily? Because you have been mentally trying to picture him, and because Dana's simple remark has stirred your heart whether or not you like it, that's why!* She was answering herself. Then she did give a half-hearted wave, acknowledging his presence, afraid to be more enthusiastic.

She spoke a little too quickly to John, "At least someone's using it." Turning on her heels, she spoke over her shoulder as she quickened her steps to the door where Mitsi's tongue was lathering the window. "We'll turn about a half mile down the road. Watch for my signal." She gave a push to the dog. "Stay in there girl."

Pulling at her shirt as she got in, she cried out to God. *Oh, Father, don't let me think about Gabe yet. I've got a ranch to run, and oh, don't let it be too bad, for Dana's sake, for all our sakes, please!*

She found herself glancing around the fields for a glimpse of Gabe, for she was certain that's who is was. Her pulse raced, JoAnn, *get a hold of yourself, so he is still around, be glad for that useful knowledge and shove it into a compartment for future use and forget it and him. Can I really do that? I may need him, and if I ever do, what then?*

At this point, the excitement within her upon reaching the ranch was approaching a point of explosion, as was Dana apparently, for she was sitting on the edge of the seat scanning first one side of the road, then the other, anxiety written all over her face.

# Chapter 3

From the main highway, the dirt road back to the ranch was a tough half-mile and the scenery hard on the eyes. Then suddenly, around a bend of a slight ridge, the landscape changed. The land was cropped as if it had been used for a pasture. Fences were intact and painted, and off in the distance, cattle, sheep and goats moved about, grazing on more of the rich grasses, forage woods, and shrubs, leaving behind them vast tracts of land, ripe for plowing and planting.

"Oh, thank you Rusty Owen, and thank you, Lord!" Dana just looked at her.

Never had she felt so exhilarated as she negotiated the last of the ruts and ridges. The first trip of remembrance over the old road with her parents had been when she was three years old, then every year after that. She was Dana's age when she fell in love with her grandparents and their ranch. The I-don't-want-to-leave kind of love.

"Dana, I don't suppose you remember much about the kitchen. There were so many wonderful family celebrations there, especially the Thanksgivings and Christmases when the whole Simpson and Bennett clans gathered at the ranch. It has a huge fireplace in the kitchen, which was used summer and winter for cooking and baking before Grandpop bought the iron range. It had, still has, a mantle above, crowded with family treasures. A rocking chair! I hope it's still there. You can curl up in it and dream by the warmth of the fire. I believe every woman in the family has sat in that chair at some time holding a child, as I have you." She laughed, "and an old sofa, long gone, under the window with a blanket over the back for a quick cover for a sick person or for warmth on a cold day."

"Is that when the ice man and vegetable vendor came around?"

She laughed at their family joke. "Actually yes. That's where they preserved their food, churned the cream into butter, trimmed and cut up the butchered animals, and rolled out piecrust and cookies. Homework was done there also, and stories read. Imagine all the family gossip that was passed around in that great room. A few tears, some of my own, have fallen on that floor." The memories lay so sweetly on her mind. Oh, no wonder she loved it so. To her it was and always would be her castle, and its inhabitants, her shining knights.

"There it is Dana! Remember that wonderful old sprawling gray stone house? Feast your eyes on those spacious porches, shaded by ancient tulip trees," she was pointing with her finger. "Look, there are still some bent-wood chairs! Ah, a place to perch and get lost in a dream," she smiled at her daughter. "It's one of the pleasures of country life I hope you get to experience often. That one massive chimney on the left, partially covered with vines, serviced that fireplace in the kitchen I was telling you about." It looked, so inhabited, so welcoming.

"Of course, I remember this place. It doesn't look like the horse farms we saw on our way here."

"I should say not! Those were race horses you saw and multi-million dollar estates" *I'm afraid Dana still has on her rosy tinted glasses! I wonder about the boys. I wish I could have heard their conversation in that truck.*

She turned her attention to Rusty Owen who quit digging and looked up at the first sound of approaching company. No matter what job he tackled, he had always been decidedly neat and clean. She often wondered how anyone could stay orderly and ingenious on a farm. Did this man never change? Here he was nearly seventy now, in his clean jeans and plaid shirt. His face weathered even though he was never without his cowboy hat shadowing it, which also covered up a beautiful head of long gray hair. His mouth was never without a pipe, mostly unlit. She saw him hurriedly throw a few shovels more of dirt before he turned to look up to the house, quickly scanning it, his eyes seeming to rest on the large screened doorway as if he were looking for someone. Finally, his short bowed legs took him across the grass to the station wagon.

Rusty had come to the ranch from a neighboring city, and had been with John Arthur Simpson since he was seventeen and fresh out of school. He wouldn't leave him or the ranch, even after John died and his own wages stopped. He not only wasn't born again when he first settled into the ranch program, and he hadn't arrived with a wealth of knowledge either, however he had a single-minded devotion to be a cowboy. Her great grandfather reportedly said that he saw "staying power" in the lad, and stay he did. As far as she knew, he had never married and had given his all to the work of the ranch, learning every facet, eventually becoming indispensable to her grandpop.

When her grandpop began his Friday Night Bible Class those many years ago, which became very popular through word-of-mouth, Rusty willingly joined and was born again in his second attendance. Eventually her grandpop and Rusty jointly led the classes with greater enrichment and power. Rusty took charge when her grandpop reached sixty-five.

JoAnn hoped to resume them for her own sake as well as for the children. Mostly young adults attended the studies, and the churches and community had all been greatly enriched by the moral upstanding citizens they became. They had returned, from all over, by the droves, to pay their respects at his interment. There was truly rejoicing in heaven at that funeral!

"I swear it has a woman's touch," JoAnn reflected, more to herself than to Dana, whose own response of, "it's cute" was hardly noticed as she observed her old friend's approach.

There was something so secure, so stabilizing in seeing Rusty. It was as if his presence signified the rightness of having left everything behind, of pulling up stakes, of uprooting her children from everything they held dear. He had entered into her decision to keep the ranch. His experience would be invaluable: buying horses, lining up stallion services, preparing the fields for pasture, and planting, hiring help, and so much more than she could think of. Equally important, and one area of which he was as yet unaware, would be his spiritual mentoring to all of them.

Rusty stood uneasily as the two vehicles stopped and the family exited. The boys bounded from the truck, pulling at each leg of their jeans, anxious to claim their inheritance. They confided to their mom later, that they felt as if they had come to claim a house and property that still belonged to someone else, namely, Rusty.

JoAnn watched Dana, who expressed again her delightful expectation at the "cute" house, the horses standing picturesquely behind a gleaming white fence. *I wonder if she is feeling what I felt so many years ago.*

As soon as JoAnn and Dana opened the car doors, Mitsi emerged from her confined space in the back seat of the car and tore off inspecting every tree and bush. The Siamese cat,

Samantha, stretched off, not quite trusting her short-lived freedom.

"Mom!" Dana ran around the front of the car and grabbed her mother's arm. "There goes Mitsi and Sam again!"

"I don't believe we need to worry about them this time."

JoAnn's eyes then met Rusty's and she simply couldn't stand his dry welcome. For the first time in her adult life, she felt the freedom to throw her arms around him and kiss him on the cheek. She had never been allowed to even touch another man when Louis lived, not even her grandpop. She had hugged him many times in secret. Indeed, what would she have done if she would have had to face running the ranch alone? But then, if she had listened to the whispers of the devil, she wouldn't even be here.

Rusty wasn't much different in size than when he had first come to the ranch; scrawny, of medium height, but tough. His once dark brown hair was now dry and wiry gray, his skin weathered and dark from the sun. In addition, he was as quiet and gentle as ever, with cautious seeing eyes framed with glasses, and large capable hands. He was knowledgeable about horses, ranchers, and had an "in" with them. She would need him to put all this to work for her.

However, that was not why she was about to go soggy with emotion towards him. She had always been a warm, capable, emotional person. Now that Louis was gone and with her new life in Christ, these qualities were surfacing again. It was so good to be able to express one's feelings with a hug, a touch, or a look without feeling guilty and without looking first to see where Louis was. Secretly her grandpop had often received them.

Collecting herself, she drew her good-looking, well-dressed brood around her, observant of their unnatural shyness. "Rusty, I know you remember my children. This is Dana. I believe she was only ten when you last saw her."

Dana stayed close to her mother, a little in awe of the leathery old man, so typical of what she had remembered that she was slightly astounded.

"And this is Rob. He is fifteen now."

As Rob extended his hand, Rusty took it, gave him a good look-see, and suggested, "You got the makins' of a good ranch hand, young feller."

"And this is John." She waited until they shook hands, then spoke, "He just graduated from high school and wants to be a vet."

A certain twinkle came to her eyes as she explained her children to Rusty. Louis would never have allowed John to become a vet.

"Named after your grand pap, right, Son?" Rusty asked, cupping his pipe in a rough knobby hand, drawing on it as he scrutinized the young man.

John returned the look, respectfully. His mother could see that he liked every remembrance of Rusty, and also, she recalled he anticipated receiving a college education in experience from him. He stretched forth his hand and took a step in the cowboy's direction.

"Yes, Sir," John answered, removing his hat respectfully with his free hand.

"Built like him too, as I recollect," Rusty mused.

JoAnn sensed that Rusty was moved by the memory of John Arthur Simpson. It seemed to ripple through her too. She noticed his matter-of-fact demeanor vanish with the warm exchange. She knew her grandpop had taught him how to run the ranch, keep books, and raise cattle, horses, and sheep. He had taught him how to be a leader, to handle men, when it became evident that his own sons weren't interested, wouldn't be around to take over.

Sometimes God has something different in mind from what we can think or imagine, but she hoped Rusty would mold her boys into good ranch hands and that it wouldn't be too difficult. Running a ranch had changed in recent years, and she was about to find out how much.

Rusty hung an arm affectionately across each boy's shoulder and headed for the house. Samantha had returned and Dana grabbed her up. Mitsi was nowhere to be seen. "You don't think Mitsi will worry the horses do you, Rusty?"

"I don't hear her barkin'. Should be okay."

"I see you were hard at work over there. Planting something?"

"Not exactly."

When nothing more was forth coming, she simply said, "Oh."

"I'd been nursin' a stray calf."

Dana turned toward him with a quick response; "You mean a baby calf?"

"Yep."

Grappling with the unspoken meaning, JoAnn said, "Oh, I'm sorry."

"It ain't the first; won't be the last, either."

Dana again responded. "You mean it died?"

"Afraid so. It had been lost and neglected too long."

JoAnn wanted to get Dana off the subject and suggested they follow Rusty inside, and had stepped one foot on the porch when they heard a horse.

She knew without turning that it would be Gabe.

Rusty turned around and went back to meet him, as if he were expecting him. The children followed closely. JoAnn reluctantly followed.

As Gabe swung down from the saddle, he seemed to be searching for a special face, and when he saw her, gave JoAnn such a look of happiness and pleasure that a tremble of uncertainty sped through her. If she hadn't been praying about him as well as thinking of the possibility of needing an old friend, she wouldn't have been able to join the group so readily.

As it was, his size and good looks annoyed her. She would find it difficult to be around him, a problem with which she wasn't prepared to deal.

Rusty opened the way for her. "JoAnn, do you recognize this cowboy?"

*Do I recognize this man? God help me!* She gave him a nervous glance. "Of course, Rusty, it has only been three years since the funeral." She knew that was not a proper answer. Gabe had grown up to look pretty much like a cowboy in a cigarette commercial. She felt weak with the memories swirling around in her mind. It would be very difficult to be around an "old friend" who had turned out to be as good looking as Gabe had become. *Father, help me. I can't handle this wonderful looking man.*

He helped her by reaching forth his hand, which she felt she had to shake even though she did so uncertainly. She tried desperately to look at him without staring and blushing, without giving away that she had been thinking about him. But how could one not stare. *I had forgotten how good he is to look at! Why haven't I remembered this from having seen him at the funeral?*

"Hello, Jo." Those two words flowed smooth as molasses from his tongue and just as sweet as they had in his phone call. There was too much warmth and obvious delight showing on his face and sounding in his voice. "It's been awhile."

She was actually glad he was here and yet didn't like him being here at the same time, so friendly, so eager, and calling her "Jo", in front of the children and Rusty. She admitted to herself that she liked to hear him say it, but not here, she didn't want to hear it in public, not yet anyway. She took charge, reminding him that he had met the children at one time or another and refreshed his memory as to their names. They looked at him as if they had never seen him before, like he was a celebrity or something. She continued to take charge, but didn't put much thought into what she was saying, she had to get away from his heady influence, from what was so evident in his eyes.

"We were about to go into the house. We are rather tired. Gabe, would you like to join us?" She could tell he wanted to. Probably Rusty had already invited him. Well, he would have to make up his mind without her coaxing him, for without waiting to see his reaction, she grabbed Dana's hand and started to walk back to the porch.

"Another time," he called.

She turned, "Then if you will excuse us . . ."

"Mom!" Rob protested, coming up beside her.

JoAnn quietly stilled his protest. "Please trust me, Son." She turned back in time to see Gabe settle into the saddle and Rusty swat his horse on the rear, helping to send Gabe on his way to wherever. She was certain Rusty had informed him of their potential arrival date, and she should have been more urgent in her invitation to stay.

Rusty caught up with them, and without saying a word gave JoAnn a stiff look, which turned her cheeks red and made her realize that he didn't like her rudeness.

*Rusty you don't know everything!*

However, his voice spoke matter-of-factly, "Reckon you folks are a mite hungry. Marie's been cookin' up a storm all morning."

"Marie?" JoAnn asked in surprise, looking sideways at him, and then followed his eyes up to the front door, unwittingly listening to the sound of the hoof-beats grow fainter.

Then she concentrated on the woman standing inside the screened door. *Exactly who is she? A cook? A friend of Rusty's? She vaguely recalled hearing about a woman friend. Rusty would surely explain."*

Marie stood proud and confident as she held open the door, a good-looking woman. She was younger than Rusty and apparently a woman whose love for the ranch ran as deeply as his, for when JoAnn stepped into the house, it looked much as it had when her grandmother was alive.

She didn't want to take the time to meet this woman. She just wanted to familiarize herself again with the beloved house. The children were antsy as well, nevertheless she introduced each one as they passed in front of Marie, before dismissing them to disperse into the house. JoAnn waited quietly inside until Rusty entered.

Marie was dressed the way her grandma used to dress, with a simple plaid cotton dress, belted in the middle and comfortable but sturdy shoes; her short brown curly hair, with whips of grey running through it, was obviously newly permanent waved. JoAnn noticed an involuntary movement to her ear, probably to turn up her hearing aid. There was a smile on her pleasant, dimpled face as she held open the door for Rusty.

Dana went immediately to where two large sofas sat, with a faded Oriental rug in front of them, and a massive end table in between, with an antique brass lamp that was turned on and helped light up the rather dark room. They did a great job monitored a stone fireplace, which JoAnn had always loved. In one far corner, near a window, sat a small round polished table, which was great for card games or pinochle. It had four ladder-back chairs surrounding it. In another area, Rob and John were testing out the leather chairs surrounding a large leather-topped drum table; probably remembering playing games there in the evenings on their few visits. Louis hated visiting the ranch. What a fabulous room for a family.

From her stance just inside the arched entrance to the living room, a quick glance around brought each pleasant conversation area to her mind; the furniture, the matching oriental rugs worn rather thin in places, from the years of foot travel they had received. Her thought were interrupted by her daughter's distressed voice.

Dana, always concerned about the animals, had pulled back the old lace curtains, mentioning that she couldn't see Mitsi anywhere.

"She won't get lost here, Dana," John tried to reassure her. "We own enough acres for her to be gone for days exploring."

"John!" Dana gasped, her expression was one of begging for a more satisfying answer. "Mom!"

JoAnn went to lay a hand on her shoulder, as she too looked out the window. "It's only been a few minutes, Dana. Give her an hour or so to explore. She's been here before and she will find her way back." With her hand still resting on Dana's shoulder, she urged her daughter to come with her past the floor model radio/ record player, on her way back to where Rusty and Marie stood. "Come on boys," she spoke over her shoulder.

She couldn't help touching it on her way. Oh, the memories the old radio, with over-seas channels and a built-in record player provided, on her summer visits. *I wonder how many times I played the record, "The Old Oaken Bucket" sung by Bing Crosby.* On top of the old radio, stood an old foot high artificial Christmas tree. It still held its place of honor, having been placed there during World War 11, when her father and uncles were serving their country. . . forty years ago! How important the over-seas channels were then! The words on the records played on the built-in record player, about broke their hearts. The radio hugged the wall between two windows, which overlooked the field where the horses stood grazing. What a huge, warm, inviting room.

The stairway off the entry on the right led to sleeping quarters that were rarely used, since everyone preferred sleeping in the newer addition in the back of the house. Years of dogs and cats, and people with muddy boots or feet, of cigarette burns and coffee spills, of scratches and nicks, of family quarrels and hug and kisses, of intent listening groups surrounding the old radio for the latest on the weather or the war, had subdued the room and achieved an atmosphere of comfortable living.

*JoAnn, Jo Ann you have been so rude.* She continued struggling *to* drag her thoughts of; *I think something needs done to these walls,* back to Marie and Rusty who anticipated the family would want to explore before eating, and they were waiting under the archway between the entry and living room. When she finally gave them her attention, she noticed he put his arm around the ample waist of the woman whose height reached to his shoulder.

*So this is how things stand.* JoAnn tried to remember if she had heard about a marriage.

"This is Marie, my wife." He smiled down at her with a look inexpressibly loving, and then looked questioningly to JoAnn. "Hope you don't mind?"

"Mind?" JoAnn answered, completely in control of herself again.

"Well, it's one thing for me ta be liven' here, but ta up and marry an' bring the misses." Rusty spoke apologetically.

"Oh, Rusty," she said sincerely, advancing toward Marie, "you belong here more than I." Then to Marie, she stated, "Please forgive me, us, for ignoring you and your beautiful table. Welcome into the family, and may I say thank you," she spread her hands toward the table, the living quarters, the whole shebang, "from the bottom of my heart for such a pleasant welcome." She took both of Marie's hands and searching her face without being rude in doing so, noticed that there was probably less than ten years difference in their ages. "You'll never know how happy I was to see the house looking so pretty, so much like it used to look when I came here as a teenager."

With that statement, she was suddenly aware not only of the walls, but of the age of the furnishings and wondered if she had enough money to refurbish and replace some of it. The table, covered now with food and place settings for six, not seven, was still not opened to its full length to seat twenty, comfortably. The cherry teacart, hutch, and china cabinet held her grandmothers favorite china, silver, and crystal.

Then turning, she called to the teenagers, re-introducing them and Samantha. The boys had removed their hats and were patiently waiting for the pleasantries to be over, so they could advance upon the table so magnificently set and loaded with food, and within their field of vision. Rusty had always been called Rusty by everyone of every age; Marie said she would prefer the same cordiality.

Some feeling of motherliness, kindness, and immediate love and acceptance permeated the group when Marie smiled. Of course, her words helped a great deal too. "I have a bite to eat ready, if you're interested?"

"Interested!" Rob and John said, almost at the same time. "Lead the way!"

"Whoa, boys. The bathrooms are down the hall through those swinging doors." She pointed to the rear of the living room before turning back to Marie. "I'll be there to help in a minute, Marie," she called over her shoulder, and taking Dana's hand, they followed the boys.

# Chapter 4

She was anxious for a quick look-see into each room of the newer sprawling addition, which contained four bedrooms with two baths, a sitting room, a den with a sofa bed, and an office. She chuckled to herself as she went through the swinging doors and the full realization that newer actually meant thirty years ago, and that the furnishings, mostly antiques with which her family was not accustomed, probably needed upgrading also. She remembered that at the time of the construction, the kitchen also received a face-lift, with the inclusion of two badly needed ceiling fans, and one in every room in the large house as well.

The rooms were neat and every piece of antique furniture was shining. What a load lifted from her heart. *Thank you again, Father.* Their reception was fit for a king. Instead of dust and a musty odor, of covered furniture and drawn window blinds, there was sunlight and a fresh fragrance, sparkling tabletops, and vacuumed and waxed furniture, even though it was old. *Just maybe I could handle these, but can the kids, after being used to very modern? It would help the budget if they could. Humn, where will I place the litter box or should we allow Samantha to run free? I'll have to decide before bedtime.*

There certainly was no reason for her children to express disappointment. How could she every repay Rusty and Marie; and they were afraid she would mind! Of course she did think momentarily about pay for Marie, upon which she hadn't counted.

As was the custom at the ranch, hands were held around the table while thanks was offered for the food. When JoAnn took charge and gave a prayer of thanksgiving, Rusty must have been taken back with surprise

Their bite to eat managed to provide them with baked ham with raisin sauce on the side. Marie knew kids didn't go for that. There was pan-fried chicken, fresh asparagus (she wasn't sure they would like that either but had learned from Rusty that it was JoAnn's favorite vegetable), corn pudding, of course mashed potatoes and gravy, and homemade biscuits. As they were finally all eating, Marie drew their attention to the sideboard where an array of pies and cookies was meant to tempt them.

Conversation flowed throughout the meal; the boys wondered about the horses.

"Of course there are horses. You probably saw all that's left, standin' by the fence as you drove in. Can't have a ranch without horses. Course they're hard ta find these days, alive, that is."

"You still don't have Flora's Girl by any chance?" JoAnn wanted to know, not really thinking of what he had just said.

"Yep. Bill, Bob, an' Lady too," he drawled out. "Course they're old an' a little decrepit an' not used ta a lot of exercise, so's ya need ta go easy at first. Guess you could say they're a lot like me."

"Decrepit? Rusty? Not you," she spoke, unwilling to believe it, as a frown flicked across her face. For a treacherous moment she felt her world caving in.

As she gazed at the old cowboy, she cautioned herself. *Seventy years of age hadn't meant anything to me until now. Was there some hint of meaning behind his words? Was he going to retire and leave me to run the ranch myself? I will have to get down to business sooner than anticipated and find out just where I am heading. I had partly based my decision to return to the ranch on the hopes that Rusty was well and would stay on to be my mentor.*

*He knows it backwards and forwards, inside and out, and any secrets it holds. He loves it too, actually it is the only home he has ever really known. I certainly am not about to make him leave. Perhaps that will be the first thing I need to explain to him. He knows the ranch and loves it as a man; I still love it only as a woman, not as an owner or one with all the responsibility resting on my shoulders.*

*Maybe when I know it as well as he does, I will change my mind, but I am not prepared for disappointment. I have already come expecting the worst; therefore, everything will have to be an improvement. I have already found things looking up. God is good. Rusty must remain, even if in a retired state. I simply must have him nearby.*

Gone was all the dawdling with past memories, good and bad. Everything in the original house was old: the wallpaper and paint, the furniture, mattresses and appliances, the roof, shutters, porches, plumbing, electricity everything. The barns, fences, even the horses were old. What had she been thinking? Where was her brain? What had she led her children into? What had appeared as such a happy experience, full of light and hope, was suddenly filled with darkness and foreboding. Now she was a businesswoman, a would-be foreman, a horse breeder, and a single mom. A failure!

In this contemplative state she thought about the old horses nibbling away in the pasture. They wouldn't be much good for anything, certainly not to plow fields, and in all probability, the machinery was as old and decrepit as they were. Old, old, everything was so old!

She stirred aimlessly at her asparagus before laying the fork down and sitting back in her chair. As she listened to her anxious children's views on riding the horses and scouting the land, she realized that she must be very careful not to say anything to dampen their spirits. Therefore, when they asked if they could be excused, that they were as stuffed as a turkey at Thanksgiving and couldn't eat dessert, but wanted to go riding, they were given permission. "But not until you have helped to clear these dishes away and unload the vehicles."

Rob protested loudly enough for the other two. "Oh, Mom!"

"Thou protesteth too quickly, my son," she told him, managing a grin. "As soon as you finish this fantastic meal, which you have all shown how much you appreciate, we'll decide who gets which bedroom. Then, we'll simply deposit everything in its place and if it's all right with Marie and Rusty, you may take the horses and go for a ride, and keep an eye out for Mitsi."

Rusty noted the relaxed relationship she had with the children. "Think you're Mom's got the right idea. Soon as we're done here, we'll all pitch in. Won't be no time 'tall till you young whippersnappers are in the saddle."

"Hey, what are we waiting for," Rob shouted, pushing back his chair.

"Sure you don't want dessert? Look at those pies," his mother said, giving him a frown over one lowered eye, which was a nonverbal warning that he had stepped out of line.

"No, thank you," he replied, relaxing, glad that his mom never reprimanded them publicly. "No offense intended Marie, but I can't eat another bite."

"Me either," Dana sighed, holding her stomach. "That was a super meal. Thank you, Marie."

"Yes, thank you Marie and Rusty. We weren't expecting a meal. Of course, we weren't expecting Rusty to be married either." Then she added with less enthusiasm, "I wonder what other pleasant surprises God has in store for us."

"You are all welcome and since it would seem you can't eat another bite, why don't we all get busy unpacking that truck," Marie chimed in, to the delight of the children.

John ventured, "You're a woman after my own heart." He looked at his mom for her permission to leave the table.

"Watch it young man!" Rusty kidded, pushing back his chair, which acted like a signal, and before JoAnn could leave the table, the three young ones were headed towards the bedrooms to pick out the one he or she wanted.

"Marie, Rusty, perhaps you would like to help us choose."

"This is your ranch, JoAnn, not ours," Rusty declared.

"Yes, but, I must know where you have been living."

"In my little house. Same as before."

"But . . ."

"Now!" he warned. "You haven't seen it since Marie took over."

"And he means that," Marie conceded. "I'd like to take over here too. I mean, if you wouldn't mind, I'd like to cook for your family and keep house."

JoAnn was stunned. Tears rose in her eyes. Her question was answered before being asked. Isn't that just like the Lord and just when she was feeling down, He picked her up? She almost ran to throw her arms around the two of them. "I was so afraid you might want to go and leave me here alone. I hardly know what to say." She had to wipe her eyes. "God is being so good to me. I don't deserve it."

"Don't say anything," Rusty suggested. "I figure the closer we lived ta God an' ta being a family, the better we'd all feel. Believe me, JoAnn, you're going ta be needin' all the family you can get if you intend to make this into a horse farm like you mentioned in your letters." He put his pipe in his mouth then took it out again. "By and by. I'm impressed with your growth in the Lord. If'n you don't mind me askin', when did you get saved?"

"Thank you and I don't mind at all. It happened right after Grandpop died due to a letter he enclosed in the Bible he gave me."

Just then John called from the hallway, "Mom, aren't you coming?"

"We'll have lots of time to talk about the Lord, right now why don't you go along back and help us select our rooms?"

"Reckon we don't have any choice," Rusty smiled, taking Marie's hand to follow his new boss.

# Chapter 5

There was a central hall with rooms on either side. Halfway down on the left was a break, making a hallway, which led to the outside surround porch. It was to this door John had moved the truck and already had moved boxes into the hall.

JoAnn grabbed Mitsi's collar when she came springing through the open doorway. "Where have you been, Girl? Come with me. You are going to need a good brushing before you roam freely inside." She called to Dana to get Mitsi's leash and meet her on the kitchen porch, where she was sure she would find brushes.

With Mitsi secured on her leash and by working together, in less time than it would take them to saddle-up, the car and truck were unloaded. Rusty then led the boys across the excuse for a lawn, the dirt road that followed the white fence, and on to the corrals.

JoAnn followed them longingly with her eyes and heart, while unconsciously making sure, for Mitsi and Dana's comfort, that the door was securely shut behind them. Most women would have been happy to have a look-see at the house first, leaving the horses, stables, and barns, up to the men. Not

JoAnn, her heart longed to run after the boys, to nuzzle up to Flora's Girl, to breathe deeply of the rich and varied smells. But years of being a dutiful wife and mother first, were so deeply ingrained, that she resigned herself to obeying them for the time being.

"You want to go with the boys?" she asked Dana, as she entered the least masculine room in the house. The sparse furnishings were heavy and dark. The brilliantly pieced wedding-ring quilt was the only bit of color to the otherwise dismal room.

"I don't know how to ride," she reminded her mother. "I know now that I shouldn't have been so stubborn and gone to the riding stable with you."

"Well, we'll take care of that in no time," JoAnn smiled, as she went to give Dana a hug. "Anyway, I'm glad to have you with me. Want to help Marie in the kitchen or unpack?"

"I'll unpack. You go ahead."

"Okay, then you'll have to help me choose a room. What do you say?"

"Sure."

Dana's quiet answer troubled her as she headed toward the dining room where Marie chased her right back to the bedrooms. For a moment, she longed to head out the door where she was standing and join the boys. No one was as anxious as she was to ride the range, to have her own horse under her.

She didn't just want to be around them; she thought she knew her dedication until she began to see things as they really are. She thought it was just the knowledge she was lacking, although she had spent many weeks reading and boning up. It was that all right, and then some. She had expected to concentrate on learning first-hand about feeding, caring, training, breeding, and buying of them. In her wildest dreams, she had not expected to have to worry about the money it would take to care for this aging property. Where's my brain?

What she had read overwhelmed her to the point of desperation. At times she thought there was no way she could run a ranch. The care of the horses, the weather and water, the shelter and numerous potential diseases, the type of material underneath the soil, even pasturing was not a simple decision. Regular services from a farrier and vet were required and costly.

She could not put all this on the children, but God's shoulders were big enough. "Oh, God, you are my God; I will seek you earnestly," she spoke repeatedly, as King David must have done. Gradually she began to focus on God instead of her problems. He quietened her anxious heart and soothed her troubled mind as nothing else did. She would let Him have the reins of her life, and sometimes it might hurt, just as it hurt the horse's mouth when the rider pulled too hard on the reins. She knew she could not be the one in control.

As she had learned to cast her cares on Him, she grew in spiritual maturity and now stood in her own ranch, a demonstration to His sustaining power. Oh, how she loved being back here, no matter the unexpected problems. Already she was certain she had made the right choice to stand firm and wait, and she would not be a pest to Rusty. Neither would she abandon her family for her own pleasures as Louis had done. A long shudder passed through her as she came mentally back to the present and called out to Dana, who met her in the hallway and entered each remaining room with her.

The furniture though sparse, was massive and very plain, even in her grandparent's bedroom. She pictured her grandmother sitting in the big oversized rocker, which must have about swallowed her up, her grandpop standing at the window where he could look out over the nearest corral while he chewed on a stick of gum. He hated chewing tobacco and the unsanitary spitting it required, so he chewed gum.

"This was your grandparent's room."

"Are you taking it? John thought you might."

"I suppose I should."

"If you don't, he will."

"Oh, he will, will he," she kidded, placing an arm around Dana's shoulder. "Tell you what, if I take it, will you help me decorate it to make it look feminine? In fact we could do your room at the same time. God has just made me realize that this furniture is worth money to an antique dealer, so we need to find a way to live with it, but surely there is some furniture around here that we could move around and put in our rooms that isn't so overpowering."

Immediately JoAnn began to see different lamps and pictures, and as she mentally measured the windows for new curtains and the beds for different spreads, color schemes formed in the back of her mind. Would there be time and money to carry through the plans they would make? There would have to be!

"Boy, you can tell no girls lived in this house," Dana said, as she ducked away from her mother's kiss, a much happier girl.

"I think you're right."

It wasn't long before Marie arrived to help empty the closets and drawers in the rooms the boys would probably take.

"I think we'll have to have a homecoming to get rid of these things," JoAnn said, holding up a shirt she knew her father and uncles hadn't worn in years. "But, know what, if they haven't needed this clothing in all these years, they probably wouldn't want them now," she remarked as she lugged an armload of clothes to a large hall closet. "Maybe we should just give them away to a church organization who could forward them to needy people, but as soon as I would do that, I'd get in trouble from one or more of my uncles. Sooo, I guess we better put them in boxes we empty and just store them upstairs."

Breathing deeply from under the last load of clothing being temporarily transferred to an empty room, she wondered aloud as she passed Marie in the hall. "Grandma and Grandpop must have expected their sons to visit more frequently than they did or to stay on here, or else they wouldn't have kept these things in mothballs." She sighed, "At least someone in the family showed Grandpop that they cared, although I never thought he would give it to me."

She paused remembering what she had thought was just as idle conversation. It had come at the end of her last and longest visit before her senior year in college. She had been crying at having to leave. No one else ever cried at leaving the ranch and it always stirred her grandparents and made their parting very sad.

"What would you do with this old place if it were yours, Honey?" he had asked.

She remembered staring across the fields while patting the nose of the horse she always rode. "I'd keep it just like it is."

"You would, would you. How would you manage that, sell off some acres?"

"I'd never sell and Rusty would help me," she had stated with the confidence of a twenty year old. Funny that she should have expected Rusty to outlive her grandpop, but then he was twenty years younger.

JoAnn wasn't aware of it at the time, but her grandpop had asked every family member that same question. She had been the only one with the answer for which he was looking, and the only one who held on to that same dream till the day he died.

"And what would you do for money?"

"I don't know, Grandpop, but I know I would never let this beautiful old place be turned into a housing development or a golf course."

She had been so young and fanciful, to say nothing about being inexperienced at the time, but her desire and attitude had never wavered. Of course, her father and uncles would have turned it into either one immediately, or simply sold the entire property to a developer. Other family members had "cooked their own goose", or so he had stated in his will.

Now here she was, twenty-two years later and the dream she had barely held onto all those years, had come to fruition. She looked at a picture that was sitting on the bureau, of her grandparents. Carrying it to the window, she stared out over the pasture nibbled almost bare by the sheep and pressed it close to her heart. With tears in her eyes, she dedicated herself anew to the dream.

"I'll do my best Grandpop, and if you can talk to God and have Him send people my way to help, t'would be most appreciated."

Marie turned back the covers on the boy's beds, then helped JoAnn do hers. The covers were crisp and white, smelling fresh as all outdoors, probably the only new things in the house. Another of her grandmother's beautiful quilts was folded across the foot of the bed as the final touch. It would be much too warm for it tonight.

"You know what Marie, I think I'll build my decorating around my grandma's quilts."

"I like that idea. May I ask what you did with all your furniture?"

"Sold most of it or just gave it away. Louis, my husband, loved very modern furniture; nothing cuddly or cat napperey. I remembered this house being filled with antique, heavy styled furniture, and I couldn't see the sharp lines and clean silhouettes, brightly colored pieces of ours fitting in. It would have looked so out of place, and just between you and me, was very uncomfortable. Also, I remembered how full this house was already."

There was no regret registering in her voice. "The children kept the pieces they wanted whether or not they fit in with the decor, and we did bring the televisions and stereo units."

Marie gave her a startled look.

JoAnn laughed and laid her hand on Marie's arm. "Not to worry, they know how loud they are allowed to play them."

"Folks got to have a television, and there's plenty of room for everything I've seen." Then surveying the room with satisfaction, she commented, "I think I'll go make a fresh pot of coffee to go with that pie."

"Uhm, does that sound good." She touched Marie's shoulder as she passed her near the door. "I'll check on Dana. At least everyone will have a nice clean bed in which to sleep. They have the rest of their lives to unpack and settle in."

# Chapter 6

When the riders returned to the stable, JoAnn knew Rusty would remind the boys of the proper grooming and feeding procedures before coming into the house. He always had with her. The horses were aging and infrequently used, but they are hardy and good breeds. To cut down on expenses, Rusty had pastured them year round. The pasture he used had fresh, available water and minerals, shelter from the wind and flies, with dry, soft areas to bed down.

In his wise management, he knew the advantages outweighed the disadvantages. There they received natural nutrients and minerals from the grasses, got regular if limited, exercise, and certainly were not bored. Their long winter coats were gone for Rusty had groomed them in preparation for JoAnn's arrival.

She stood on the side porch with Mitsi on her leash, as she watched them ride in. Great pride swelled up within her, along with a wild rush of longing to have ridden with them. She had watched her children carefully over the past years and happily noted that they were growing into normal, natural teenagers. She was not only intelligent and well trained, and had never accepted any responsibility for Louis's life style. Neither had she kept it a secret from the children, nor turned them against him; when they asked, she told. He had been a tough father; a good provider and they loved him, as children love parents. She would not destroy that.

Dana, Marie, and JoAnn were sitting at the table when the men joined them. JoAnn watched in horror as Rob limped into the kitchen. She jumped up and ran to him. "What happened? Did the horse kick you or throw you? Rusty...?" JoAnn asked, turning to him for answers.

Rob pushed her hands off as he hobbled to the nearest chair. "He threw me . . ."

Rusty was apparently aggrieved at Rob's remark, for he spoke rather harshly. "Never say a horse threw you! Admit rather, that you fell off when he shied at somethin'. You're a beginner an' I can see you have a lot to learn." Then he sat down beside Marie without looking at JoAnn.

"Yes, Sir," Rob said, apologetically.

JoAnn still stood behind Rob's chair not knowing quite how to react to Rob or Rusty. It was easier to deal with Rob. "Did you break anything? Your leg or your arm?"

Rob squirmed a bit in his chair. "Nothing broken. My leg hurts a little and I twisted my left wrist."

"Marie?" JoAnn questioned without spelling it out. *Here I am at the outset, depending of this stranger. . . whom I feel I have known forever.*

"I'll get him a pain pill," she said getting up from the table, "then after we eat we'll put ice on it and maybe an elastic bandage to support it."

It seemed JoAnn had to be satisfied with that, so she sat back down and picked up her cup of coffee, watching her son. Rob seemed to be eating without a problem so she relaxed a little and watched Marie and Rusty. Certain looks passed between them as Marie served more coffee, milk and tea.

JoAnn asked, "How long have you two been married?"

Rusty took out the pipe from between his teeth. "About a year an' a half, I figure."

"Were you thinking of getting married before Grandpop died?"

"Yep. He knew. He knew too that I wouldn't leave him."

"Tell me again about the end, if you don't mind. I know you were very close."

"Don't mind 'tall," he declared. "He was mostly active up ta the last month. Helped with the chores an' cooking, rode Bill every day, an' when his ticker gave out, that was it. Nothin' much to tell."

"Was he happy?"

"He was happy in the Lord, could hardly wait to go 'home'. Happy as a man could be who was deserted by his children."

She had to look away then down to the table and spoke quietly, guiltily, "And grandchildren."

Rusty nodded, still with his eyes averted, and said, "He was an understandin' an' forgivin' old gentleman, an' knew times were changin'."

"In everything except with what would happen to his land." Her head came up.

"That's a fact." His head came up as he turned to speak to her. "He sure didn't want no developers gettin' their hands on it."

"But he made no conditions in the will."

"Didn't have ta' JoAnn, now did he?"

"No, Rusty, he didn't have to." She looked around at the children who were all ears. "But you know I wasn't even saved then. Didn't care a hoot what God wanted. I could so easily have changed without him knowing it."

"So I guess you could say he was a trusting an' praying old man too."

"Yes, thank God for that." she sighed, setting down the empty coffee cup. "I know it's late and all of us are tired, but I have a question that's been with me from the beginning."

"Shoot!"

"Where in the world do we begin? You have probably been wondering that yourself. You're aware that we literally don't know beans about ranching. I am really going to depend on you and I hope you don't mind. What do we have to do to get started, Rusty? What are your ideas?"

Now the kids quit eating, all eyes turned to the swarthy old cowboy. He picked up his pipe, and after getting a good grip on it with his side teeth, stated matter-of-factly, "Depends what you want ta do with it."

He was putting it in her ball court.

JoAnn shot him a cautionary glance. "Horses. The children and I have discussed it quite thoroughly, and horses still are the way we want to go."

"That's what I was afraid of."

John hadn't said much since they had arrived. Now he spoke up. "I had forgotten so much about this place. Even though the buildings are old, they are still in good shape. I expect we owe that to you, Rusty. I'm impressed by its potential, and I share Mom's feelings now more than before, about developing it into a horse farm. Nonetheless, from several of your statements, I sense some difficulty about that possibility. Of what are you afraid? To what problem do you keep referring?"

"Ain't nothin' ta be afraid of. Didn't mean that way, Son."

John wasn't so hastily satisfied, but glanced his mother's way for her approval before continuing. "Well, then?"

Rusty took a quick look toward Marie before he spoke. "Now I know John Arthur wanted horses back on the land too, but that was before he knew about Reinhart's business."

"Reinhart?" JoAnn was searching her memory. "That

name sounds familiar. A man with that name helped us fix a flat tire about ten miles from here."

"Don't know of another Reinhart 'round here. Must be the same man. He bought the old Holland place."

"Not Pete Holland's farm?" she exclaimed, momentarily with a feeling of sadness for him, wondering where Gabe had ridden from this morning.

"That's the one."

It seemed information was going to be like pulling teeth.

"I find that hard to believe. I remember it as a very prosperous ranch with a beautiful two-storied home that I would have great difficulty giving up."

"Pete got killed. The story is he fell from a horse on a jump."

"I'm sorry to hear that," she stated sincerely. "Still . . ."

John interrupted by advancing a question. "I don't mean to be disrespectful, but didn't he have any kids who wanted it either?"

"Yep. His son Gabe would have kept it if he could have. You didn't know Pete, Son. All I'm goin' ta' say is, after Gabe's mom died, he'd married a woman never meant ta' be in the country. She was a city-bred girl an' that's where she belonged. Not like JoAnn here. So, after Pete's death, it all went ta' her an' she sold the land ta' Reinhart quicker than you can bat an eye. He put in a meat packing plant."

JoAnn couldn't sit still any longer. She had to know a little bit about Gabe, in order to judge him fairly. "What happened to Gabe then? I mean, where is he living?"

"Stayed on with Reinhart as foreman; lives in a bunkhouse," Rusty answered between ample bites of apple pie. "Comes over right often, too. Seemed anxious to see you again," he said, giving her a funny look, some secret amusement showing.

She flushed slightly then and got up to pour herself another cup of coffee. As she motioned around for more offers of coffee, she happened to glance at John and found him watching her closely.

She had learned to ride a horse on her first visit—which was the first of many. Gabe had been a companion, a friend. They were near the same age, and when his father was occupied with her grandfather, she and Gabe had the run of the ranches. Her knowledge of the people in and around Donaldson was sparse, because, after she graduated from college and married, she rarely visited. She had never expected to return to the ranch or to hear his name again, let alone think about him, see him, and be interested in him. Which she realized now, she certainly had been, until she saw him and the easy influence he could have on her and the children. For some reason it frightened her. For some reason? Louis was the reason!

The Holland land connected with the Simpson. Pete Holland and her uncles and father had been fast friends. They would miss Pete when they visited, as she surely hoped they would. And Gabe? He had been something else, something special. Tall, she remembered with broad shoulders, yet youthfully lean. He had been a playmate and protective riding partner, a teacher, a close summer friend and a summer fling at love. She was wondering how difficult it was going to be to have him so close. Her intentions, with God's enabling, were to steer away from dangerous hazards. Gabe was a hazard. Men were taboo for now, no matter how much they would insist on infringing on her thinking and emotions.

Something else nagged her and she heard John put his finger on it.

"Rusty, what kind of meat packing business does Reinhart run?"

JoAnn watched as a shadow passed over Rusty's face. He was purposely withholding something from them.

His answer was too simple. "He's in the expiration'

business." Then he pushed back his chair, apparently hoping to end the discussion. " 'Spect these boys will have some unfinished business before they can hit the sack."

She let her suspicions pass for now and pointing to her sons, she said, "I think he means you two. Want some help?"

"We'll call you if we do," John volunteered as he and the others reluctantly stood and placed their chairs against the table. "Thanks, Marie."

Rob winced when he tried to do as his brother had. "Marie," JoAnn asked, "could you help me with Rob?"

"Right this way," Marie said, as she gathered up some dishes and headed for the kitchen.

JoAnn wanted to stop and breathe in the sights and smells of this charming, appealing, old room. Right now was not a good time. Instead, she followed Marie to an old medicine cabinet with various medicines, salves, and ace bandages hanging from the wall right inside the back door where it had hung when her grandparents lived there. In no time, Rob's foot and ankle were soaking in Epsom salts and a towel with ice cubes was lying on his arm. By the time the table was cleared and the dishes begun, Rob was ready to be bandaged and he headed for the back hall with the aid of a crutch Rusty found in an out of the way closet. Mitsi and Samantha followed the kids back the hallway.

"I'll look in on you as soon as I help Marie here and don't let Mitsi up on any beds!" she called after them.

"No need to help, JoAnn," Marie said. "Rusty will help, he always does."

"That was before you were taking care of six people, besides, I want to. This has been a long day for you, unless you guys are made of iron." She said, as she began stacking the gold trimmed plates with the little pink flowers around the edge, her grandmother's favorite; here was old again, but this time old was precious old.

After placing the last of the clean dishes back in the breakfront in the dining room, she considered opening the subject of money, as she walked into the kitchen. It had changed since those very early years, always keeping up with the times. It was evident that they had invested a considerable amount, and she wondered where they had gotten the money on which they were living.

She knew that the money spent on the ranch had not come from her Grandpop's inheritance, because the will had only recently been settled, and all the monies handed out to all concerned. She might as well get started, for she planned to deal straight across the board from the beginning.

"Rusty, this food set you back a pretty penny," she began. "And the bedclothes are new, towels and washcloths new, this house in tip-top shape, fences mended for miles and miles," she continued, as she sat the dishes on the counter for Marie to load in the old dishwasher. "I want you to know from the onset, that I expect to repay you for all your expenditures, and since you will be staying on, to put you and Marie on salary and make it retroactive to the time Grandpop died."

Rusty relit his pipe as he leaned against the gas stove, and studied for a minute before he spoke. "Appreciate that. Sure do. But ain't you bitin' off more than you can chew?"

She watched as Marie placed some dishes and silver-wear exactly where her grandmother had always put them, then she eyed him keenly. "Don't give me that. You have all the records I need right there," she smiled, tapping his head, before laying a hand on his arm and wrapping her arms around him for a generous hug, and said, "Tomorrow, we'll get your head and hand together and write up some figures. That is the way I mean to do business, old friend. Goodnight, you two. I guess I don't need to tell you to lock up behind you."

# Chapter 7

When JoAnn awakened early in the strange bedroom, it took her only a second to realize where she was and to jump from bed, rush to the bathroom and back again then hurriedly dress.

For being forty-two years of age, she looked terrific. She was one of those unlucky people who needed to diet and exercise to keep her five-foot-seven frame in shape. Through both, she had gone from a size sixteen to a ten, since Louis's death.

She quickly slipped into old jeans and a short-sleeved cotton blouse. The blouse gave her trouble; always wanting to gap directly in the front, a problem inherited from her mother. *I might just have to switch to knit shirts, even though they are so warm for the summer. Maybe just the next size blouse would do it, though that would be too big everywhere else. Eve never had this problem!* She tucked in the blouse and surveyed herself in the mirror. *Won't stay in anyway, will you?*

After a quick rub-on of lotion, and a swift brush of her great hair style, her blue eyes looked back in the mirror and seemed to say, hurry, get moving, before the family gets awake.

Finally, she slipped from the house with Mitsi on a leash, and headed for the stables.

The land she now owned, at one time, trembled under the feet of thousands of Indians and settlers. Today, a few rabbits struck a frozen position before running into hiding, and her boys would find it difficult to bag their limit if they choose to do so, if there would even be time for such things. She felt that squirrels, woodchucks, and groundhogs wouldn't be easy pickings now either. Now when her dad and uncles lived here...

A blaring naked light bulb guided her toward the stables and tack room. Its glow against peeling paint, did not subdue the delightful apprehension, which had kept her from sleeping soundly, and made her awaken before the rest.

She had wanted, no, needed to be alone at her first go of her buildings and land. During the two preceding years of squabbling, she had walked over and ridden around the ranch a hundred times in her dreams and thoughts. She had remained calm, knowing that her grandpop's will, would not be broken.

Now her dreams were cold reality. It wasn't just the chill of the early morning air, which made her zipper up her light jacket and hug herself for warmth.

Still, as she stepped through the doorway of the barn and pulled it closed behind her, she suddenly felt weak-kneed and let go of Mitsi's leash. She reached out to rest her hand on a post worn smooth with the hands of many others who had stood just inside the door. Possibly her grandpop had stood here to chat, to look at the horses, to discuss the new foal, the pregnant mare, the stallion which was prancing, waiting impatiently to cover a mare. Or perhaps he had simply stepped in from the rain, heat or snow.

Her first order of business was to lift her heart toward the One who had made all this possible. She offered a prayer of rededication of herself, the land, the buildings, her dreams. Before moving, she took a deep breath; the old rich odors were strong in her nostrils.

With the perspective of ownership, she called to Mitsi, took off her leash, and began to explore the old building. It wasn't the largest, with only ten stalls, but it was the oldest in the county. It had been erected the year after the front portion of the two-storied house was completed, and from the same kind of stone. Although rather shabby looking, it appeared to be tight. The oak walls of each stall were satiny smooth, except where they were scarred by chewing or by the hoofs of some high-stepping frightened or excited horse.

The old clay floors she noticed were raked clean, and although each empty feedbox was worn smooth and rather low in the front, they were usable.

The grillwork and latch style steel locks, hidden from the horse's mouths by blocks of wood, appeared to be strong. When she tested one of the sliding doors, she found it still seemed sturdy, balanced, and opened easily. She remembered that the grillwork enabled the horses the enjoyment of seeing one another and helped to calm them; they love to know what is going on around them.

As JoAnn observed all these things, she realized with pleasure that her hours of reading and observation at the riding stable in Jersey were paying off. It had been and still was a functional barn. JoAnn could almost conjure up the animals that had once occupied each stall. From her own memory and the pictures her grandmother and great-grandmother had showed her on her many visits, she had the horses, the carriages and their passengers almost memorized. On her last visit to the ranch, the one item she took home with her, had been her grandmother's picture albums and scrapbooks. Now they too were back where they belonged.

*Now what were these tears for girl? I'm getting misty eyed over everything!*

The barn looked neglected in general appearance, something she never noticed before. She knew it wasn't from the lack of caring, but of flagging energy and old age.

"Still it could be filled to capacity just as it is, and it will be! I've seen worse places, maybe not in Kentucky, but other places. Not that I approve."

Her capital would quickly diminish.

She continued walking down the six foot aisle of old asphalt, peering briefly into each stall, noticing a hook outside each for hanging halters and lead ropes. All was ready for horses.

The tack room smelled of old leather of which quite a bit hung from wooden pegs or draped over worn racks. There was a naked iron cot and a handicapped clock, missing a hand, as well as an old table and chair. Nothing was more than just dusty!

The utility room contained a stainless-steel sink and ten buckets of like metal, which were almost spick-and-span clean. *This room and the aisle must have been paved with asphalt at the same time. Rusty had more than kept himself occupied. He must be a work-a-holic!*

Brooms, tined forks, shovels were hung neatly from hooks along one wall. An old wheelbarrow stood against one wall on its iron wheel, and a manure cart occupied one corner. She found many basic tools as she moved things around; a fresh supply of disinfectant and fly repellant were safely top-shelved.

*You are some special caretaker, Rusty, my good man.*

She stepped from the high airy old barn in time to see first light stealing away the night. She followed a hard clay and gravel path next door to the coach house, which used to house her ancestor's carriages and buggies, then her grandpop's cars, and now Rusty's pick-up. She knew his cottage was located next door to it, and supposed he was up also.

The newest barn, which, like the addition to the house, wasn't new anymore by any stretch of the imagination. It was more conveniently located close to the bunkhouse, which stood north of the house. To reach it, she followed the dirt road from the coach house and around the corral.

It had an eight-foot aisle and twenty-four stalls, as well as a second floor loft for storing hay and bedding straw. All it would need could be found in a big paintbrush and gallons of whitewash mixture. That at least wouldn't tax her purse strings too much.

The barn was empty. Sparrows nesting in every nook and cranny had just awakened. Its asphalt flooring was dry but cold, sending goose bumps to race up and down her body.

"Better get out of here," she said to Mitsi who had stayed close to her.

When she did step outside to the slight warmth of the early morning and tied the dog to a hook, Flora's Girl come trotting from the paddock to the fence to meet her. She held out her hand as the horse approached. After stroking her muzzle and talking quietly for a few minutes, JoAnn threw her arms around the horse's neck and laid her face lovingly against her damp hair, and cried.

Then wiping her eyes, she greeted Bill and Bob who had joined them, and finally, Lady, lazily made her way over. "I think you will be the perfect horse for Dana," she decided. After greeting Lady, she led Flora's Girl through the gate and to the barn where she saddled up. A glow had spread in the sky, awakening all the birds, which quickly filled her morning with song. What a welcome!

# Chapter 8

JoAnn allowed Flora's Girl her head to walk the old post-and-rail fences. Mixed feelings fluttered through her as she appraised the deteriorated, seedy looking bunkhouse and several open-fronted implement sheds. A quick glance revealed a vintage tractor, a plow, and a disk. It was apparent that as her grandpop's needs lessened, so had his supplies and machines.

She was suddenly grateful for such a meticulous grandparent. There would be little to dispose of: no junk trucks, cars, or implements, but, little to use also. She dismounted to take a look inside the bunkhouse. The doors were locked, but through the windows she could see that great care had been taken to cover and store the furniture, which she was sure was of little value. No need to worry about mice with all the cats around. *Dana will find plenty of pets to occupy her mind, but, I think we better keep Samantha an inside cat or we'll have to spend a fortune on deworming her.*

Back on a trail, she reigned in as the sun made its incredible, awesome appearance. Even the birds seemed momentarily hushed. A feeling swept over JoAnn, such as she had never experienced before. It wasn't the early ride, meeting the sun in the face, for she had often ridden early when she had visited in the past. It was something else, something personal, something stirring, trying to be released from deep within her.

This was the first time, ever, she had related God to his handiwork and it was an exhilarating understanding. It was God! He ordered the turning of the earth on its axis, the sun and moon exactly where they belonged every morning, every night. The moon willingly reflected the light of the sun.

*Dear Lord, I have no inherent light of my own; I don't emit an eerie glow. Without You I'm just another cold, dark human. Help me to reflect you as the moon the sun, to be a light on this ranch, in this community. May I be a reflection of you, a clear mirror shining for You.*

*Thank you for helping me understand what I have seen this morning and yesterday, the good, the bad. I'm not disheartened, challenged perhaps, if anything. Help me in handling my money, not to run ahead of common sense. I have a lot of book, head knowledge! It's a little frightening to think of the tremendous needs and care these animals require, all of which I took for granted before. My grandpop was truly a wise, knowledgeable, and patient man.*

*Thank you for Rusty and Marie, and my dear children. Guide us all as we work together. May we honor and glorify your name in all our dealings. May the Simpson name continue to be held in high esteem under your direction. In Jesus name, amen.*

Then she rode on as the early summer morning reluctantly warmed with the sun. "Just like old times, girl," she commented, reaching up to pat her horse on the neck.

She unzipped her jacket, unaware that in the near distance sat another lone rider, who remembered her penchant for early morning rides. Suddenly, off came the hat. How she hated wearing it. Her hair though short, was darkly shining, and she shook her head, lifted her face to the sun to breathe deeply of the clean earthy smells before resettling the hat and urging her horse on.

Then JoAnn noticed the rider ahead urge his horse on so he could approach her in full view. She slowed Flora's Girl; he waved as the distance narrowed.

"Good-morning, Jo. Nice morning for a ride." His voice was like a caress on the cool spring air.

The sun's rays shown full on his face, illuminating its handsome ruggedness. Reluctantly, and with certain nervousness, she felt moved by the force he radiated. He would still stand out from other cowboys, she decided against her will, especially since his body had filled out some to more evenly match his broad shoulders.

*Why does he insist on calling me, Jo? It had never been, JoAnn, and certainly never, Jay! I allowed it, actually liked it, sort of something special between us.* In the deepest recesses of her heart, she knew that was the name she preferred.

"Gabe! Of all people!" Her voice feigned surprise and warmth as she called back, reining in a little, pretending nonchalance she didn't feel.

He looked her over on his approach. Roger Eastman used to look at her in the same fashion, wondering, no doubt, what Louis ever saw in her. She could have belted him. For that reason Gabe's attention now was unwelcome. Perhaps also, it was the realization of all the work and responsibility ahead of her. She wouldn't have time for sweet neighborliness, or wasn't ready for a male friend. Or, was she anticipating something that was all in her head, because she couldn't let go of those heady teen-age years.

*Lord Jesus, is that it? Is it all the "old man" of the past creating confusion to thwart your, my plans? Hold me close Father, I don't want to be cold and rude to him if I don't need to be.*

"Mind if I join you?" he asked, always the gentleman,

turning his horse to fall in beside her. The depth of his voice matched his size.

She looked away confused and began to breathe deeply. She wanted to answer him honestly, but instead was rude again. "Well, actually, yes I do mind. I had wanted to explore my land alone. Now that I am born again and own it, this place holds new meaning for me. I need to be alone to absorb its relationship to my new life."

She still didn't look at him, but kept her gaze sweeping over the land, while her mind raced with thoughts. *What is he doing here so early? His presence puzzles me as well as my own reaction to him. Is he expecting things to be like old times? Am I?*

The happy expression she had seen on his face, the look in his eyes, the brightness and excitement in his voice, scared her and she was not one to make snap judgements. *What was the meaning behind it all or was she reading something that wasn't there?* Before she quite realized, he had ignored her remark and took the lead as he had in the past, and pulled up near a grove of trees. She knew he expected her to get off her horse, but she remained seated.

"Don't you want to inspect it?" He grinned at her exasperated expression.

*How am I to outwit a person like Gabe? He seems to be able to read my mind, still!*

She had intended to examine the old swimming hole. It had been her destination, but only to appraise its usability and to remind the children of it. Well, she would not let him outsmart her. "Of course." She said it with a certain determination setting in to unmask his purpose. She even allowed him to give her a hand down and felt he had to restrain himself from gathering her in him arms. She was sure he noticed her stiffen at the prospect. *Father, things aren't going right. Is it because I'm not resting enough in you or because You and I really don't want things to be any different than they are?* W h e n they had tied their horses to the fence, which kept animals from the fresh, clear spring water, she couldn't help noticing new pieces of lumber and posts here and there, especially a brand new gate! Rusty's care had reached way beyond the house and stables. Gabe unlatched the gate, and led the way past the boulders to the bank of the old swimming hole. She rejected his offered hand of help. Unlike many at the ranch, he had always been gallant, and she had not forgotten.

At the water hole, he stood back with respect for her mood. She stood for a moment observing, listening, and drinking in the sights and sounds. Squatting down to trace her fingers in the cold clear liquid smoothness, she stated, "It looks like someone has been here recently."

"My boss's daughter comes over. She is anxious for the weather to warm up to use it. Hope you don't mind."

She could feel his eyes on her back. "No, of course not. Rusty told me about your father and stepmother. I was saddened to hear it."

Her intentions had been to spend some time here to talk to her Saviour. It had always been so cool and refreshing, such a sparkling yet contemplative spot. However, with his eyes on her, she straightened quickly and flinging the words over her shoulder, "I better get back." JoAnn headed back to where their horses waited. "I want to be there when the children wake up."

He obediently followed, and gave her a hand up into the saddle. "You've got three nice kids."

Looking down at him, she thanked him and asked, "And you?" her voice telling him she expected him to be married and have children of his own.

"None!" he grinned as he walked his gray stallion, Solomon, over the slight hill, before mounting up. "Jo, I expected you to be happy to see an old friend. But, I can see you aren't and I'm sorry about that. However, we are still neighbors and I'll be dropping by as I have been almost every day, so you might as well get rid of that chip on your shoulder."

She wanted to cry out, no, no, no! Realizing he could still read her emotions; she spoke as calmly as possible. "Whether or not I like it? Well, if you do, you will probably be put to work. By the looks of things," she motioned to the work done on the fence and gate; "you have probably had a hand in all the fixing up around here. I'm going to need all the help I can get my hands on."

Then she realized that was the wrong thing to say, for Gabe and his father could always be counted on in the past, to help where needed, so she was not surprised when he countered with seeming delight, "You can count on me."

He had given her the opening she needed to leave, why was she hesitating instead of just riding off? His next words finally cleared her thinking.

"You better get. That bell's going to clang any minute."

She had forgotten the bell, but he hadn't. It had been a disturbing surprise to see him. It bothered her that he remembered her habits, her emotions, as well as some of the workings of the ranch.

She eyed him squarely, trying to understand the meaning behind his early appearance and remembrances. "That's right. You used to say that on a clear day, you could hear it ring clear over at your house."

That was not what she had intended to say, and blushed. She had not expected to remember that and certainly not say it. But then, she had always felt relaxed and easy with Gabe. Why did it have to change now? Just because he had turned out to be so, so macho looking and still lived near, still liked to ride in the morning, did not have to signify a thing.

"He surely is a married man and is just being kind as is his nature. I must be careful not to add to the simple meaning of his actions, not to feel so threatened."

"Jo?" Gabe interrupted her thoughts. "When I heard you were coming back home, here, to stay, I thought it would be nice to be neighbors and friends again. You aren't going to deny me that, are you?"

He was all interest and inquisitiveness in one simple sentence.

"I don't know. You seem to know a lot about me and I'm sure you know that I have gone through a really rough time. Gabe, I was just getting back on my feet when the will was settled, so I don't know." Kicking her horse into action, she called, "Good-by, Gabe," allowing the soft morning breeze to carry her voice back to him, knowing she had been rude for the second time and unable to do otherwise.

Home, he had said, and indeed it was, or would be, if she had anything to do with it. But, it would be a horse farm too and her heart and soul would be poured into both to make them so. She wouldn't have much time for friendly visits with friendly neighbors!

"It's funny," she spoke aloud, as she neared the house, "all my thoughts of him had been so pleasant, so uplifting, and now, I'm afraid of him and I don't even know why. Father, is this Your doing or the devils? Help me to discern your will."

# Chapter 9

Clang! Clang!

JoAnn, sure the boys were awake, found Dana sitting up in bed having forgotten about the bell. "Out here there aren't alarms, fire whistles, or church bells reminding us of places to go and things to do. You have to find your own way. Don't you remember? The bell was Grandpop's way; right now it means breakfast will be ready in fifteen minutes. You too Samantha," JoAnn said, giving the cat a good rubbing.

In the hall she found Mitsi waiting for someone to open the door or feed her. "Come on, girl, let's go for a walk, then your food is in the kitchen."

Breakfast consisted of sizzling sausage links, crisp fried potatoes with egg, toast, and blueberry muffins. After everyone was seated, there was an expectant pause.

Rob spoke, "Mom, are we going to have our regular morning devotions?"

"Should we?"

"I can't see why we need to change just because we moved. God didn't move, but what about...?" He finished his awkward statement with a secret look toward Rusty and Marie.

His mother rescued him, looking around the table until she reached Rusty. "Do you remember how Grandpop always had table devotions at breakfast?"

"Sure do. Marie and I followed suit the day we married."

"Well, after our whole family got saved, John read about Christian families beginning their day in this positive fashion and thought we should try it."

John interrupted, "One of my Christian buddies said they had been doing it in his family since as long as he could remember. He didn't always like it but thought it was better than doing nothing."

"And what do you think now?"

"So far, so good."

"Rob? Dana?" JoAnn looked at them without censorship.

"Ditto," from Rob.

"Right," from Dana.

"Well, Rusty, from your long and warm association with Grandpop around this table, what do you think?'

"Be open to change, an' never be forgettin' you're purpose."

"Good point, old friend," JoAnn thoughtfully acknowledged his remarks as she observed the children to see how that settled with them. She noticed John was ready to speak.

"Purpose! Mom, what an excellent reminder, but I'm starving, the sun is shining, the food is getting cold, and we have work to do."

"Right you are, and I think Marie would appreciate it if we ate it before it gets colder."

"So can't we just pray this morning and work on purpose tomorrow?'

"I'm with Rob," Dana agreed

"Okay, Rob you do the honors. You know our needs and the needs of the world. You're allowed to make it short this morning."

Following breakfast, JoAnn talked Dana into meeting Lady and possibly a short ride. The boys and Rusty reluctantly headed to Donaldson to return the rented truck.

"Let's go to the corral first," JoAnn suggested.

"I like the idea of the fence between them and me!"

"Nothing wrong with that. If I hadn't grown up around them, I might feel the same way. But let me tell you something," she smiled down at her daughter who was fast catching up to her own height, "anyone who can go on a foaming, crashing ocean with a simple board and ride to shore on those fierce looking waves, won't need much time in becoming acquainted with a gentle, loving horse."

"Loving? I thought it was the other way around."

"A little of both. A horse senses your attitude for it by the way you care for, treat, feed, provide, and talk to it."

As the horses came to the fence, Dana intuitively backed away until JoAnn took Lady by the halter and asked Dana to come over and touch the horse.

"Talk to her, call her by her name, stroke her along her neck while I have her head. Some horses will bite, but not this one."

Dana reluctantly obeyed and reached out her fingertips to touch Lady.

"You talk to your horse as you approach it, and as you brush and wash it. In no time at all, you will have it eating out of your hand, literally, and you won't be able to keep from throwing your arms around it."

JoAnn smiled and taught as she opened the gate and took the reins of Lady and Flora's Girl and led them out and over to the stable. Leaving Flora's Girl tied at the entrance, she led Lady to the tack room and secured her, before leading Dana to the blankets and saddles.

"A few rules you will follow the rest of your life, Kiddo," JoAnn said while picking up a saddle and motioning for Dana to get a blanket. "Get on the left side of Lady, always the left side, as if you were standing in the back of her. Now, come forward and turn your back toward her head and watch how I put the blanket on her back, no wrinkles." she smiled Dana's way, while telling her to, pick up the saddle.

"I can't!" Dana dropped it to the ground. "For crying out loud, it's heavy!"

"I know it is, and you have to swing it up pretty high. Watch. Don't drop it with a thud. Keep control and lay it on her back." Then JoAnn reached under Lady, as Dana jumped back, to catch the girth and fasten it. "Just remember, swimming and surfing weren't easy either. And notice, my back is always to her face and I am always on her left side."

She straightened up and gathered up the reins without looking at her daughter, who was close to tears. "Now get that stepstool and put it here near this stirrup. That's it, now climb up and grab the pommel, that front part of the saddle with your left hand." JoAnn was showing as she taught. It was so easy, so natural to her. "With your right hand, hold the stirrup so you can put your left foot in it. Oops, easy girl," she spoke to Lady, who was getting jittery.

Dana was about to climb up when she suddenly let go of the reins, backed away and cried out, "I can't do this, Mom. I'm sorry, I just can't do this!"

JoAnn grabbed the reins then quickly pulled Dana to her with a hug. "I'm the one who is sorry. I expected too much." She gave her a kiss on the cheek as she brushed some hair from her eyes. "Know what, Rome wasn't built in a day, so they say."

"But it's taking forever and I haven't even gotten on her."

"Well, you may as well know now, when you come in from a ride, it takes longer till you get things put back, and brush and cool her down, and groom her properly."

"Brother! I don't think I'm interested in riding horses."

JoAnn laid her hands on Dana's shoulders. "Honey, your brothers and I went through this same routine. It gets easier and faster, I promise."

"I don't care. Right now I just want to go back in the house." She squirmed out from under her mother's hands, picked up the stool and put it where she found it. Without looking back, she left the building, trusting her mother to understand.

Someone had let Mitsi out. Dana saw her in the distance and called to her. "Come on, girl, come here," she called, patting her leg. Mitsi stopped, looked, and just sat down. "Come on, Mitsi." When Dana began walking toward her calling her name, Mitsi finally ran to Dana, who grabbed her collar and took her inside.

# Chapter 10

After lunch, JoAnn announced, "You're all on your own to do what you want. I've got to talk to Rusty, mostly business. You are welcome to stick around or unpack and work in your bedrooms, or move the television into the living room and hook up the antenna."

She didn't want to force them into a controlled situation yet, that would come soon enough. Still, she was quite happy when the boys followed Rusty and her down the wide hallway to the office and den. Dana stayed behind to help Marie in the kitchen. Samantha stayed close to her heels as if she was afraid Dana would leave the house again. Mitsi followed the troop down the hall.

The office at the end of the hall had been off limits to women; running a ranch was man's business! So of course her interest was piqued as she glanced around with great curiosity, and found that she hadn't missed anything after all. She didn't need to wonder what the boys were thinking, for they were gaping in wonder.

It was a huge, book lined, desk-monopolizing room one-man rule room. A room that suggested her grandpop, his powerful build, and his dominating personality to which she had reacted favorably, but which had turned off his sons.

Massive leather chairs, cracked and aged, guarded a black bear skin rug that seemed to growl silently as it stretched out in the center of the floor. Various trophies from hunting expeditions hung from one wall, and across one end of the large room the boys, who had never been invited into this male domain, were examining the pool table. A pool table!

A locked gun cabinet built into a wall of cabinets with drawers completed the show of male dominance. The boys were stunned into silence as they pulled their attention from the pool table to the rest of the room. It was probably much as her grandpop had left it, even with all the snooping around done by his sons and male grandchildren, following his death.

Rusty patiently awaited their reaction.

"It appears that Grandpop ruled his empire more single handedly than I realized."

"Well, not exactly," Rusty said, going to a paneled wall and opening what appeared to be a closet. From it he brought forth six wood and leather folding chairs, then proceeded to unfold a long mahogany table that remained connected to the wall at one end. In explanation, Rusty stated simply, "For when he attempted a 'board' meeting with his sons."

"You may put the table back in and a couple chairs. We're going to discuss business, not have a meeting." Then she hesitantly stepped behind the mahogany desk and assumed her rightful position as head of the ranch. *Father, I couldn't stand here if I wasn't aware that you are living in me. I'm sure Grandpop often felt the same way.*

A strange feeling came over her in the region of her chest and heart, as if there was something deep within was causing trouble. She put her hand on her chest as if trying to hold it in or to push it aside, wondering why she had never felt the strange sensation before. Not only was she crying at the drop of a hat, but now this strange thing in her chest. Was something wrong with her heart? Or, was it the Lord Jesus once again trying to grab her attention in this new-pressured life she was facing.

"Rob, you may sit if you wish, but before the rest sit down, I wonder if we could join hands and, Rusty, would you commit this ranch and us greenhorns to the Lord."

"Gladly." He paused a moment. "Well, Father, we're finally all here together an' we need your help. We need wisdom an' knowledge which we don't have of ourselves, but You be havin' all we need, that's why we're askin'. JoAnn, here, needs some help with how ta spend her money wisely. We all be needin' help on how an' where ta git horses, an' how ta get started doin' it all. You tell us ta' ask, an' we're askin'. We expect You will answer as we go along, because we come in Your son's name. Amen."

Because of the beating in her chest and throat, JoAnn sat down before she fell down, hoping the rest were busy getting situated and had not noticed the problem she was having. Then, as she pulled the chair into the desk, whatever it was, left, and she felt in charge again.

"Thank you Rusty, that was a sweet prayer. Now then, before we get into the business at hand, I don't want to seem too possessive, but I saw someone riding on our property this morning and I am wondering if this is a natural occurrence and should I be concerned about it?"

Rusty realized the question was directed at him, and answered it. "Probably Jodi Reinhart. Told her she could ride here any time she liked. Seemed ta' like the way the land breaks into open stretches, then stands of trees. Likes ta wade her horse in the creek too, an' swim in the old swimmin' hole."

John whistled, "I've got to meet her! How old is she?"

"What if I told you she is sixty, fat, an' gray," Rusty teased, watching John's face fall. "But she isn't. Fact is she's probably you're age an' pretty as a picture."

"Back to business, John. I think your face could light up a room," which made him blush. "But I am reminded about the swimming hole and don't forget to enjoy it. I'm sure you haven't forgotten where it's located. Now, Rusty, the rider was not a girl, but then perhaps that sheepherder was checking on something. Glad there is no mystery here, and I don't want to be over-protective of our property, since I don't even know where my boundary lines are."

"We can remedy that in a hurry." Rusty got up and pulled a framed survey plan from behind the gun cabinet and hung it on its two knobs where all could easily see it. It was the original surveyor's tract plan, yellow with age.

JoAnn leaned over the desk. "That's wonderful! Can you explain it for us?"

"Sure can. Gone over it enough with your grandpop. Can you find me a pencil or a ruler ta use as a pointer?"

Almost as if she was invading her Grandpop's desk, JoAnn reluctantly pulled open a long drawer and thankfully found a ruler immediately. "Here you go."

"Well, let's start with what you know, which is the house an' highway down here to the west." He continued speaking, their eyes following the ruler as he moved it along the road to the land rented as pasture. To the south, to Reinhart's land, and then east, and up to the National Forest in the north and Judd Klein's land. He cut across the top of the map with his pointer in the north before beginning an angle west, and looping back toward the highway.

"If we could ride the boundary, you'd notice a dense growth of nuisance trees an' shrubs have overgrown the posts, where insulators an' barbed wire you're great grandpap an' Pete Holland's dad, stretched on the south. Hopkins an' your grandpop, stretched it on the west. Some where's in that forest of trees on the National Park lands, there'll be some more wire an' posts with insulators."

"Rusted and broken, to be sure," JoAnn suggested, with the boys glancing at her.

"But enough here an' there, embedded in the bark of trees, so as ta know what belongs ta who."

"Where does this Klein person live?"

"Up here in the northwest, in the area of the National Forest," he pointed. "He only owns a couple hundred acres. Where his land adjoins yours an' the forest, is where he crosses over, an' I believe that's where the poor calves get hung up and separated from their moms. He ain't fit to raise animals! Seems like he don't own enough land for the herd he owns an' is fattenin' 'em on multiple use designated public land in the forest, ruining water supplies. Fish an' Game Department is worried about the land 'round Trough Creek, which water also runs onto you're land. Seems lllike his cows have broken down an' flattened out and muddied banks till it's nothin' but bare dirt right like his cows have broken down an' flattened out banks till it's nothin' but bare dirt right inta the water."

"Then why does he bother to rent grazing land from us?"

"My opinion's ta thro' off suspicion of what he's really up ta. Before your grandpop died, Klein was pesterin' him to sell off half the acreage. Then right after, he came here wantin' to know if he could buy the whole nine yards."

"Well, do I have an enemy in the trenches or is he going to be satisfied with renting?"

"For now, he's satisfied. Don't know for how long though."

"I suppose someone has tried to get him to remove his cattle from the forest land."

"Officers name's, Joel Strouse. He presides over the district. Tried to issue orders an' permits. Was told ta get off his land or he'd kill him!"

John asked, "How do you know all this, Rusty?"

"Joel drops in an' word gets 'round, an' you can see for yourself anytime you want ta go ridin' that far'."

"So he could be the rider Mom saw this morning," Rob suggested.

"Come to think about it, I didn't see any of his animals this morning."

"If you didn't go beyond the swimmin' hole, you might not. Sometimes he keeps 'em right up against the forest, other times he'll have one of his boys drive 'em right near the swimmin' hole, or some other of our fields so as we're sure ta see 'em. Seems like he was takin' advantage of two old men, who he thought had lost their marbles."

"Creepy!" Rob said.

"Sounds like we have a problem in the making." *One of many others.* "I think the next time I go riding, I'll take along a pair of binoculars."

Adjusting her position, clasping her hands together on top of the green blotter, she couldn't help looking down and noticed it was still filled with notes and figures written there by her grandpop. She steeled herself to keep from sneaking a glance at them, knowing she would begin crying.

"Well, Rusty, this is powerful information you have just laid on our door step. I'm not sure how it pertains to us, so for now, I feel that we need to put it aside and get on with the business for which we came in here. So once again, let's begin. Boys, I asked Rusty to have a bill ready for all the money he has spent and for wages, retroactive, remember, Rusty. I want to get started off on a solid footing with all past bills paid."

Rusty shifted uncomfortably in his chair. "This ain't easy, JoAnn, 'specially when you don't know how much money you're goin' ta be needin' ta git them horses you want."

She tilted her head and with a deliberate movement, took a deep breath and waved away his excuse. "Nevertheless, out with it."

"Well, near as I can calculate, thirty thousand should take care of keepin' the buildin's an' fences in shape, an' for wages."

The boy's eyes about popped out of their sockets, which expression she hoped Rusty hadn't noticed. With a warning look, to muffle any sound, the boys looked away from one another. To their knowledge, two hundred and fifty thousand was about all they had cleared in the sale of their house. However, they weren't aware of all the information JoAnn possessed

JoAnn was undaunted. "Thirty thousand to cover three years expenses, sounds wonderful good for the care of everything, but not for your wages, not for three years, too."

Again the boys looked incredulously at their mother. She was glad Rusty took a moment to look down to the floor, or he would have been embarrassed.

He looked up at her now, too. "Klein's rent and that from the Altmans who rent a couple hundred acres for corn, helped pay some of the bills, an' don't forget, I get Social Security, an' I had a house ta live in, tax free, rent free. Far as Marie an' I are concerned, we don't need nothin' for the last three years."

"That's beside the point. But, I don't want to quibble with you, so if thirty thousand satisfies you for wages and upkeep, then I'll write you a check for that as soon as we get settled and I am able to transfer my accounts from New Jersey. If you are quite certain that the money from the sheep farmer has adequately paid the bills for everything else, then we will scratch that. From now on though, when that money comes in, we'll put it in a special account, unless you already have one."

"I do, under Simpson Ranch an' my name and yours. The books are all in order too."

"No doubt about that. There won't be any trouble transferring them into my name."

JoAnn wasn't as calm and cool as she appeared. Underneath, she was paddling like the dickens, until she realized she would only have to lay out thirty thousand. Nevertheless, she had been prepared to pay whatever Rusty had presented. Still, thirty thousand would take a sizeable chunk out of her accumulated savings, sale of the house, and the small personal checking account Louis had allowed her to keep. All the insurance money and his private bank account had been bound up tightly in annuities, to insure her a stable income for the rest of her life and college for the kids. She was set for life until she moved here, and right now she could use extra money. She didn't want to touch the estate money until necessary.

"Next note of business. Where do we start? What needs to be done to get started and how do we begin?" She dropped her eyes gently on Rusty, then again, reluctantly, opened several desk drawers, before she found pencil and paper and prepared herself to take notes.

She could tell Rusty was glad to note that she wasn't afraid to admit her ignorance. "Well, first off, I'd prepare some fields for pasture, plow an' plant pasture seed an' oats, barley, rye or wheat. We need ta be gettin' planted too, or you could just go buy from feed companies, as you need it. Pasture grass of high quality is the most natural an' one of the best foods for a horse an' the least expensive for you."

"I'm glad to hear that."

"The land is already well drained, but needs ta be fertilized, an' kept free of weeds. Certain grasses, weeds an' bugs are poison for horses."

"What kind of seed fertilizers are you talking about?"

"Alfalfa an' clover, timothy an' Kentucky bluegrass are good, but you can't let it grow too high. Cattle improve the land by fertilizing the soil an' keeping the grass short enough for the horses ta eat the more nutritious young grasses."

"It's the beginning of June, Rusty. Isn't it too late to be planting?"

Rob sat forward on his seat and looked at Rusty then his mother. "We don't even have horses yet. Why can't we just wait until we see if we can find some before we go to all this trouble?"

"Because if we happen to get some horses next week or next month, what will we feed them all winter long if we don't get started ahead of the game?" John blurted out his answer with a tone that said, "dummy".

"John's right, young man, we have ta plan ahead or face financial ruin before we get started." He looked from Rob to JoAnn, "Now about the weather, Kentucky has a little longer growin' season than back east. It's late, many fields around here are already green from spring plantin', but we can still get them sowed now an' get the pasture ready for horses. We should be able ta harvest the grain in late fall, an' get two cuttin's of hay from some of the fields that appear to be nothin' but weeds.

"I don't think we should be forgettin' somethin' from the Bible. Psalms 104 tells us that it's God who causes the grass ta grow for the cattle, vegetation for man's labor, that he's the one who brings forth food from the earth. What I'm tryin' ta say is, that despite man's efforts, farmin' would be impossible if'n God didn't take care of our efforts. God isn't bound by nature; He's in control of it." Checking his pipe, he spoke without looking at anyone, "Now if you got yourself a bank full of money you don't know what ta do with . . ."

"Don't we wish," Rob chimed in again, as if he were intelligently informed about their financial condition.

JoAnn just smiled at her son and John leaned back and stretched out, crossing his long legs at the ankles, shaking his head without saying a word.

"All right then, you're goin' ta have ta rent or buy machinery, hire some men, which can be done either part-time or fix up the bunk house an' keep men here full-time, or like I said, buy as you need.

Again Rob spoke with a little heat to his words, "What do you think John and I are?" He winced when he forgot his injury and stomped his foot for emphasis.

"Rob if you aren't careful, I'm going to have to come over there and give you a hug." There was love in her voice.

Rusty smiled toward JoAnn before turning to Rob. "There will be plenty for you two to do an' not all of it pleasant."

Sighing in resignation, JoAnn stated, "If part-time men are available, we better go that route and save on the bunkhouse repairs for now. And about equipment, you mean there's nothing here that can be used, not even the old plow, tractor or harrow, nothing?" She asked courteously, not wanting him to believe that she doubted his word.

"Depends on your needs," her friend said, crossing one leg over the other knee. He put his pipe in his mouth, and was about to light it when he saw the boys watching him. Deciding against it he said, "If you are lucky enough ta get some horses, you could probably get an old plow for nothin', but gettin' the horses ta pull it would be another thing. That old gasoline tractor hasn't run for years."

A look of defeat spread over her face. When she looked at her sons and saw them intently observing her, she cinched up her spirit and suggested, "Rusty, you've been making insinuations about not getting horses ever since we arrived. Out with it! Why aren't we going to be able to get them?"

He stood then, and walked over to the bay window behind the desk, which overlooked the paddock. JoAnn swiveled in her chair to watch him.

"There's a new explodin' market for horses; just opened up here in grand scale. France, Belgium, Holland, Italy, Japan, are all importin' our horses, the meat that is, about one hundred an' twenty million pounds of it a year. They say horse meat is sweet tastin,' an' the Europeans regard it as a delicacy."

The three of them jumped to their feet and JoAnn exclaimed, "Oh, Rusty, you don't mean . . ."

"'Fraid so. That's what's goin' ta make it so hard for you ta turn this ranch back into a horse ranch, less of course you're rich or thinkin' of buildin' a band of brood mares an' raise horses yourself."

"Like steer? For meat?"

"Yep. That's exactly what I mean. Good investment, 'specially 'round here."

"Now what do you mean by that remark?"

"Well, remember I mentioned about Pierce Reinhart buyin' the Holland place?"

"Go on." She remembered, and her encounter with Gabe quickly flashed across her mind.

"It isn't a cattle ranch anymore."

"I don't understand what that has to do with us."

"He's part of a multi-million dollar export business; employs about thirty people. One of about twenty in the country, way I hear it. He buys up horses an' transports them right here ta his ranch an' slaughters them. For fifty cents a pound, they pack an' ship them off ta some foreign country where the meat sells for over seven dollars a pound."

"And Gabe is his foreman!" she exploded plopping back into her chair, finding the information Rusty had just asserted so hard to believe. Horses being killed for meat, to eat, right next door. The thought was repugnant to her. How was she to graciously handle it, and the next time she saw Gabe . . . how would she handle him!

"Yep, an' a good one too."

The office became quiet; the boys sat back down, as the tenderfoots digested this new business of dealing with the beautiful animals.

Rob impulsively declared, "The way I see it, that's a good way of getting rid of old horses. It's either that or the glue factory."

"I agree," John declared, "or make dog food out of them. What's wrong if people eat up the decrepit old nags? Frankly, I don't see why that should present a problem to our obtaining good horses?"

Rusty continued staring out the window, taking a long draw on the pipe he worked at getting lit, seeming to ignore them.

"There's more to it than that isn't there?' JoAnn asked, getting up again and joining him. "They don't take just old, injured, winded horses, but good ones, too. Is that what you've been trying to tell us?"

"It started with them, so they say, but, yep, now it's good ones too."

John stood and leaned against the desk between his mother and Rusty; the youthful tone in his voice was near despair, and it about broke his mother's heart. "Guess we're out of the horse business before we even got into it."

JoAnn turned to him and put an arm on his shoulder, and as she spoke, looked hopefully at Rusty. "The picture can't be that bleak!"

He turned and forced a smile. "You're right. Best wait an' see for yourself."

"But we're right back where we started." John exploded, hitting the desk with his fist. "We have, what, four horses now, and none of them in A-1 condition, no cattle, and sheep that belong to someone else."

"Our horses are just right for Reinhart," Rob spoke, hotly.

"Enough of that," JoAnn warned. "Our four horses will never see the inside of Reinhart's barns, and we do own twenty eight Hereford beef cattle and few sheep, for your information. Rusty when was the last time Flora's Girl had a foal?"

"Years ago."

"What do you think our chances are of getting a foal from her now, using Bill or Bob. They're names don't indicate it but, they are all a good breed of horses and well mannered." She tried not to smile outwardly as she looked at Rusty, for she could see his obvious embarrassment in discussing this part of the business with a woman.

"They are seventeen an' nineteen years old, but healthy."

Rusty, you know we need a more complete answer than that!"

Moving away from the window and her, he almost exploded, "All right, doggoned it. I've had ta keep them separated," and he would say no more on that subject. "Now about those sheep an' beef cattle. Somthin' none of you realize an' I hate to have to spell it out, but, they help keep infection down. Most folk just drivin' by don't understand that. And they make good eatin' too. John Arthur was a penny pincher, even had chickens and ducks. He was hooted an' howled at by the other ranchers, but you know it didn't faze him one bit."

"So would we be if we plowed the fields by horse power."

"Reckon so."

"But the Amish do it and they don't care. I read that horses provide a softness to the earth, whereas, tractors pack and repack the soil, causing a hard condition to develop." She was almost pleading, "And we may have to put our pride behind us too, if we want to run this ranch in the black." She glanced at the boys for their approval and found a negative attitude there instead. She found the same look when she turned to Rusty.

"Not this year; you're too far behind. You need ta get them fields cleaned up, plowed an' seeded, pronto."

Quickly resignation set in, and JoAnn moved John aside, and sat down again. "Okay, let's get to it. First order of business is to hire help and rent equipment. I think we should check out that old tractor. I don't think Grandpop would have kept it around if he thought it wouldn't run anymore."

"Let me at it," John volunteered, regaining his seat.

"You've never worked around machines, but if you want to tinker with it and see what you can do, you'll find it beyond the bunkhouse. Rusty, if you will take care of hiring help and tracking down some equipment, I'd appreciate that. Take the boys into your confidence. I want them to learn every aspect of this business."

She was making notes as she talked. "How do we go about getting horses?"

Reluctantly, he mentioned the horse auction held every Thursday in Donaldson.

"Okay, then, that gives us a couple days to settle into our rooms, become acquainted with the ranch, get in some supplies, and visit our new town. We'll make a list of our needs as we go along."

She stood, and motioned to Rusty to take her place. "Might as well get started. Come with me, Rob. I think we can take care of the evening chores. They won't need much hay since the pasture is so rich." She winked at him. "At least we won't have any mucking out to do."

"Sure," he stated gamely.

While JoAnn was slipping into bed, a blessed tiredness crept over her, assuring her of a good night's sleep; she could hardly wait to pull up the sheet. Something was bothering her as she stretched her arms and eased the muscles in her back. Was this Klein rancher and Gabe Holland going to giving her trouble?

Turning over, slipped Klein from her mind, but didn't reject Gabe.

Deal with it now, not tomorrow or next week.

Recognizing the gentle nagging of the Holy Spirit, she lay

flat on her back, crossed her legs and with her hands behind her head, said, "Okay, Father, but help me to know where to begin."

Her mind drifted back to her grandpop's funeral. Gabe had come to the viewing and service, then left. They had talked briefly; all was very solemn and formal. But he hadn't made any impression on her then, in fact she was hardly aware of him. Why? That is what she needed to find out.

"I was grieving over Grandpop and devastated about Louis. I wasn't able to think about anyone or to even remember much that was going on. Lately, I've been entertaining sweet and sometimes unruly thoughts of him like a besotted teenager. And that's where the problem lies, with me, not with him."

Gabe had been a part of her summer life since she could remember, just like her cousins. They were often here when she was and he was always here; usually even eating meals and sleeping over like a member of the family, until that summer of summers.

"So now, I have been entertaining the memory of my first kiss, my first love as if it happened yesterday. But, it's past history, over and done with, kaput! Help me, Father to really see this and mean it, to see and understand that my happiness doesn't come from outward circumstances, but from within, from You. Satan wants to ruin me, to destroy my love for You and he will probably continue to try to use Gabe or some other man, to do this. I need to be strong for my children, for myself. I need to have a clear head; so much depends on me now.

"Awake in me a pure heart, one that searches after You, not after a man. In the name of Jesus. Amen."

# Chapter 11

Dana was sitting on the back burner, as it were. JoAnn realized that there were boys and girls all over the world who had never even seen a horse let alone have an interest in them, but there were many who truly loved them. These days it wasn't only the sport of kings. Children who love animals, often love horses. She didn't mean to be conspiratorial, but after the incident with Dana, she had passed along her concern to the boys and Rusty.

The next day, Rusty called JoAnn from the hallway. "Go look at what we rigged up in the barn."

In the old barn, the men had thrown a saddle over a couple sawhorses. John was most enthusiastic. "See Mom, you can tutor her all you want while she practices tacking up."

"Whataya think, Mom?" Rob asked proudly, seeming to forget about his aches.

She clapped her hands. "Perfect. You guys are the best." Throwing an arm around them, she suggested, "Let's go get her."

"Nahuh, you go Mom," Rob protested, wriggling out from under her arm. "My wrist feels pretty good and I have things to do."

John protested too. "She doesn't need an audience, but remind her how she used to get on our bikes and ride like the wind."

"Right. Of course you're right. I will go and drag her from Marie and the kitchen."

By lunch Dana had practiced and moved unto the next step, higher up. The boys made the necessary adjustments. By noon, she had climbed the step stool, saddled and hoisted herself up and onto it often enough, that she thought she was ready to try Lady.

JoAnn helped Dana gather up the reins, but stood by Lady's head to keep her steady. Once Dana was in the saddle, JoAnn double-checked the girth, made sure her feet were positioned correctly and her knees were lightly touching Lady. "Do you remember how to get her going?"

"I think so."

"Well, go ahead, and I'll go on to the paddock and get Flora's Girl." Mitsi ran alongside JoAnn, anxious for a run. "Wow! It's so high up here." JoAnn smiled as the words came over her shoulders.

They slowly followed a broken trail weaving through a stand of trees. Pride unconsciously registered as JoAnn scanned the range, noticing her own small heard of registered Black Angus, grazing nearby. Rusty had informed her that he chose them because they belonged to a breed with a reputation for maturing fast. They were grazing on a mix of timothy hay and alfalfa pasture. He augmented their diet with leftover beer mash from a local brewery, because it is non-alcoholic and a very nutritious supplement.

"Why do we have cows? I thought you wanted to raise horses."

"Money, Dana, money, and Rusty was looking out for me and I didn't even know it. It doesn't take long to raise a fat cow and sell it. Hamburgers and steaks, Dana. We raise them for money!"

"Okay, I get it."

It was huge, challenging, making her feel as if she had been born to inherit this land. The ride required little conscious attention; the horses had been over it a thousand times. Far in the distance, hardly visible, sat a single rider. Was it Klein or one of his men, or perhaps that Joel Strouse, Rusty mentioned? It wasn't Gabe, for it wasn't his neck of the woods. She was thinking that she would have to mention it to Rusty again, when Dana mentioned a small calf among the Black Angus.

"I don't think so, Honey."

"Yeah Mom, look over there on the far edge of the herd. You'll see the color of white and some other color."

"Okay," she responded, shielding her eyes. "I see it. Let's go check it out."

The Herford calf was lying down when they reached it. The cattle had moved away from it. JoAnn jumped from her horse to check it out. It could hardly move, it was so skinny. Dana asked for help to get down to it, then was by the side of the calf in a minute.

"Mom, it looks so sweet," she cooed as she petted it, chasing flies away.

"It looks to me like we have another lost calf from Klein's herd, and if we don't get some food into it soon, Rusty will have another one to bury."

"Let me carry it, please, Mom?"

"If you think you can, swing up into the saddle and I'll lift it up." She was please that Dana was interested. As she picked it up and helped lay it in Dana's lap, she said, "It hardly weighs a thing." As she swung up onto her own horse, she cautioned, "Careful it doesn't slide off." She wasn't anxious for Dana to be riding with her attention settled on the calf, but neither was she about to discourage her interest. It seemed Dana was hardly aware she was riding a horse.

"So how's it going?"

"Okay, I guess. It was boring until we found the calf."

"Boring!" JoAnn laughed. "You have settled into the rhythm of Lady's movements nicely."

"Weren't those calves cute when they ran?"

"So are the lambs and goats, when they're young. Horses now, become more beautiful as they grow."

"You aren't mad at me, are you Mom?"

"Mad? My goodness, no. I'm just sorry I pushed you too fast. I have always allowed you to speak your mind, and I'm glad to know how you feel. You think this is boring and I think sailing and deep-sea fishing is boring. I think most water sports are boring!" She edged her horse away from the herd. Lady followed. "Just now as Lady responded to your commands, didn't it feel a little like the way the surf board moved with the movement of your legs and body?"

"It's okay I guess. I'll get used to it I suppose, but there is so much to learn."

"Think you can ride a little faster and till hold on to the calf?"

"I'll try."

"Get ready for a different feel. Ready? Pull evenly straight back, not off to the side, on the right rein and she'll turn right with mine. That's it. Good, let's go."

They slowed as they approached the barns to give the horses a chance to cool down. "Pull back slightly on the reins and call 'whoa'. The pull hurts her mouth and she'll want to do what you want quickly."

JoAnn had ridden over to the bell and gave it a pull, helped Dana to dismount, then they waited inside just a few minutes before the rest of the ranch folk arrived. "I'll teach you how to cool and groom Lady another time. Now you can see why it was important to learn to ride when you live on a ranch. All kind of difficulties may arise, and you may be the only one who can go for help, and walking will be way too slow. You may save a life, even if it is a small calf, by knowing how to ride for help."

Dana interrupted her mother and called to Rusty, "Look what we found!"

"You found a dogie, did you?" He looked to his wife, "Well, Marie, you know what ta do." Then he picked up the gangling calf from Dana, and settled it on fresh straw in the corner of a stall. "John, fetch a blanket and towel, an' Rob you'll see a funny lookin' pail with a thing that looks like a nipple near the bottom of it. JoAnn, maybe you can find a clean pail. Bring them along back. Soon's Marie gets here with warm rich milk concoction, we'll try ta git it in her."

"Then what?" JoAnn asked.

"We'll wait."

Dana watched Rusty almost force the calf's face into the bucket of calf supplement as Rob kept her on her feet. She saw it slobbering and getting it up her nose and a lot of the milk just dripped off her fur. "I'm going ta have ta get my fingers right in there and slosh in inta her mouth, till she tastes how good it is." After a few minutes, Rusty barked, "Now you don't have to bite my fingers!" He looked up at the expectant group. "We got this on' quicker than the other, and she has more gumption than the last one. Might be we can save her."

"May I try, Rusty?"

"Sure thing. I'll jest get the nipple bucket ready and I'm thinkin' she'll think it's her mama."

The boys wanted to know what he was doing and why.

"I'll hang the bucket here and she can just drink ta her hearts content when she's able."

Rob declared, "I think she's trying to stand on her own a little."

"Let me hold her awhile, Rob." As John switched places with Rob, he asked Dana, "Are you tired? Mom could take over?"

"There's not much left, John."

Rusty fixed the nipple bucket to the wall where she could reach it, then settled her in the straw with a blanket over her. She seemed too contented, but he did not voice his worry.

The boys soon lost interest, Marie and JoAnn went inside, and as soon as Rusty saw that Dana was determined to stay with her, he too returned to the work he had begun.

Dana was in her glory, and refused to leave the little calf, even during the night. Rusty told her to keep a light on, for cows don't eat well in the dark. The next morning, the calf did seem stronger and was using the nipple feeder. Later Dana was able to lead her out to the grass which she began eating.

Rusty declared, "I think we have a live one."

# Chapter 12

The next several days, following Rusty's instructions, the Cobb family, yes, even Dana sometimes when she wasn't with the calf, could be found riding fences, inspecting closely grazed fields ready to be plowed and planted, marking new fields for the sheep and prospective horses and cattle to graze in. Together they took care of and used the original four horses they already had. They were inspecting and brushing them, cleaning out their hoofs, feeding and watering them and the whole time, talking, chiding, and petting them. They were learning, learning, learning as the hours passed quickly by. A love and bond developed between the horses and humans that only a true horse person could appreciate, yes, even with Dana and Lady, and the thriving calf.

The family lingered over meals and allowed time for a trip to town, while Rusty remained glued to the office calling around for hired help and equipment.

The Reinhart ranch, like the Simpson, could not be seen from the highway, but the brilliant white fence that embroidered miles of the property was guarded by fine looking horses, for display purposes only. Obviously not cattle ranch anymore.

"Must be for his own personal use, or he's into breeding for profit," John remarked sourly, as they sped down the road past their neighbor's property.

"John!" his mother cautioned, with a side-ways frown. "Remember, little corns have big ears."

"For crying out loud Mom, get with it. I know what you're talking about," Rob remonstrated.

And I wasn't born yesterday," Dana butted in with determination. "We're living in the twentieth century, not the dark ages."

"All right, already, I stand corrected," JoAnn kindly tossed back over the seat, then gave her attention as John guided them to a grocery store.

"Same way Rusty brought us yesterday," he stated, as he directed her into Butcher's Square.

New life was being stirred into the rich historic district of Donaldson. The one aspect of moving she did not like, was searching for a dentist, doctor, and a church. However, she knew this town rather well, and had always liked it. Now, where the past intermingled with the present, historic buildings were being snatched from the wrecker's ball in an attempt to preserve a great architectural heritage. Rusty had said she would not know the town any more, and he was right; nevertheless, she was delighted with the restoration.

It was once again becoming an exciting town to visit; row houses, elaborate Victorian homes, even factories and shops had history buffs at work on them: sanding stripping, adding, removing, and rejuvenating. Main Street too, was attracting interest; cast iron fences were undergoing a marvelous metamorphosis.

The bank was open at ground level with offices above. Butcher's Square shopping area developed from within an old warehouse that used to house saddlery. There was a dry goods and craft store, a pharmacy, a small grocery, and a good 'ole southern cooking' restaurant, in the Hearthstone building. The period atmosphere was terribly appealing.

JoAnn found that the post office remained in its step-up brownstone facade, with a dentist in residence below. The library around the corner was still housed in a limestone building with European influence, and an old Victorian Inn next door to that, was still the only rest stop in town, for weary travelers. JoAnn was elated with the improvements in the old town and was sure the rebirth wasn't coming easy.

"If you boys want to look around while Dana and I begin shopping, go ahead, but be back to the store in an hour, for I'm really going to need your help with the groceries."

JoAnn and Dana each pushed a cart up and down the aisles, filling them quickly. With a final check on the note Marie had given her, she pushed her loaded cart up to a cashier's stand being vacated by two very attractive brunettes', who were stylishly dressed and sophisticated in appearance. The youngest, about John's age, picked up the car keys her mother had dropped, and turning, gave JoAnn and Dana a pleasant smile.

Suddenly she felt awkward and poor, and wished she had taken time to put on better clothes than her cheap jeans, plaid shirt, and boots. She thought of her old life just five days before, when she too had dressed fashionably or in designer slacks and shirt to do her shopping. Sure, the kids had often worn jeans or wool slacks and pants with suitable jackets, or sundresses, shorts or swimsuits. For her, Louis had insisted she dress only in the best, and seldom allowed her to wear jeans.

Hence, their wardrobes had needed to be inflated with more durable outfits. Shopping for their new rugged clothes, shoes, and boots with heels on them, had been a release valve for their pent-up anxiety. Jeans had pretty much been their attire for the past two years.

Her styles had been soft and feminine, intricate and mysterious. They had ranged in textures from hand painted silk, to satin, chiffon, and ruffled dresses or blouses of silk crepe de chine. The material sent sensuous shivers through her body when she even touched them. There were finely woven wool suits that made her feel easily graceful. She had acquired a taste for Glueck's, Blass, and Halston originals; the best and newest she had brought with her. They hung in her closet now, next to her Wranglers, Lees, and Levis. Ranching had been her own free choice, and she would not exchange her jeans for all the silk and satin in the world!

Thursday sparkled awake, but couldn't match the quickening spirits of the Cobbs and Owens, as they had devotions during and following breakfast. Rusty had suggested using a devotional guide, and Marie had tacked a world map to the wall and suggested putting up a picture of all the people for whom they prayed, not just the missionaries. It was great that they could accomplish so much in such a short amount of time.

Then, leaving Dana behind to work with the calf and Marie behind to do her housekeeping, JoAnn, Rusty, and the boys, headed for the auction barn for an early appraisal of the horses up for bid. To say that JoAnn was excited would have been a gross understatement.

After looking over the horses and making notes on their printed sheets, they entered the rectangle room and chose seats near the back.

The horse auction at Donaldson, Kentucky was not held in a walnut paneled, theatre atmosphere where the auctioneer wore a dark suit, white shirt, and designer tie. Nor did the horses walk on a plush dais where indirect lighting exemplified their characteristics. They wouldn't bring a million dollars, fifty thousand, or even ten thousand dollars.

The horses to be auctioned off at Donaldson were not thoroughbreds. Rather, they ranged from broken down old nags to good looking roan mares, and the bidding wouldn't bring more than several thousand at best, if that.

The auction house had once been a barn, and was a cheap affair. Old wood theatre seats, some splintered and broken, faced a fenced-in performance arena. A raised auctioneer's box stood commandingly in the center. It wasn't at all what JoAnn had expected or what she had learned in her reading. Although the boys weren't really knowledgeable about such things, they nevertheless raised an eyebrow at the interior and rolled their eyes. She saw a grin pass over Rusty's face as he watched them.

The early arrivals were people like them. A family of four, a young father and teen-age son, ranchers wearing the traditional cowboy outfit, ruddy-cheeked farmers in bib-over-alls and visor caps, and wily horse-traders. Then entered the few swarthy looking men in their Stetson hats and expensive boots, flashing diamond rings.

Finally, just before the auction began, Gabe, a young man who looked strangely familiar, and another man, whom she recognized as Mr. Reinhart, scattered themselves in the slim crowd.

JoAnn was glad to see that Gabe did not look around, and turned her attention to the auction. Her hopes rose after the first few horses went through. Few bidders meant lower bids, or so she thought. Rusty wouldn't inform her otherwise.

Several ponies and winded old nags went under the hammer, before a young boy led his good-looking bay into the sales ring.

"Beautiful horse, good riding, well behaved," shouted the heavy-set denim clad auctioneer. "Who will start her at two hundred and fifty dollars?"

The young man proudly put the horse through her paces as the bidding began.

JoAnn waited, hoping the bid wouldn't begin at the low price suggested. This was one horse on which she intended to bid, but she was willing to pay a decent price. The bidding not only began, but also closed at fifteen hundred, before she even became involved.

"Wow! That was fast. I didn't even have a chance to bid." she whispered to Rusty. "That was the only decent looking animal here."

"Sold to Summit," shouted the auctioneer.

The young lad, hearing the name, almost cried, for he realized that probably within thirty-six hours, his horse would be hanging from a hook in a northern slaughterhouse.

The buyer from Summit dominated the furious bidding, buying thirty-five horses. Reinhart only outbid on twenty. JoAnn backed off, and the family of four and the father and young son, never entered the bidding.

In less than an hour, over one hundred horses went under the auctioneers hammer, from Percherons and well-bred young horses, to winded old cobs, and used-up ponies. They left in disgust, tossing the catalogues into a trashcan and headed for the coffeehouse on the property.

"Point out Reinhart, Rusty."

She had guessed right. It was the same Mr. Reinhart who had helped them change the tire. His twill trousers were tucked into gorgeously designed boots and when he looked her way with those dark penetrating eyes under thick brows, she found herself unable to meet his gaze. Yet he looked like a reasonable man. Had he recognize her?

Ranch hands for Reinhart tugged and shoved the horses up the ramp and unto the bed of the trailers for the short drive through the town and the few miles beyond, to the ranch. It was a good thing they only had a few miles to travel, for the way the horses were being jammed into the trailer, would induce a lot of stress and bruises in them. It all made her heart ache for these wonderful, intelligent, and loving animals.

A young man stood out. He was louder, more brazen than the others, and probably the youngest with the Reinhart group. He seemed to be vying with the horses and other ranch hands for the attention he craved from his boss, seeking to prove his superiority, his dependability. JoAnn had seen his type a hundred times before on campus and wondered if he was the rider she and Dana had seen on her property.

When the young man thought no one was watching, he produced a stick from the side of the trailer and used it to encourage the horses to move in closer. She watched as Gabe approached the cocky, careless, loud-mouthed young man. There was animosity there; she sensed trouble brewing between them.

"Did you see Gabe Holland over yonder?" Rusty wanted to know.

Gabe was heading away from the truck with fierce determined steps. He hadn't seen them or had ignored them, she didn't know which. She had tried to maneuver their position to keep away from his field of vision, and had apparently succeeded.

She dismissed Rusty's question simply by saying, "Yes, I noticed him awhile back. The people I'm really interested in are those few out-bidding everybody. Why, I couldn't even get the auctioneer's attention to take my bid!"

"That's what I thought too, Mom," John said. "It looked like they weren't paying any attention to anyone but those two bidders."

"Almost as if they thought the rest of us wouldn't pay high prices or couldn't afford to, so they ignored us," his mother bristled. "Who was that Summit person?" she asked, remembering the bay that she had really wanted.

"Another packin' house from the Northeast," Rusty

answered, then ordered coffee, sodas, and a piece of apple pie for each.

The atmosphere in the coffeehouse was loud and smoke filled. Buyers were venting their frustrations audibly, loudly enough for anyone to hear.

"Can't afford nothin' at these prices, 'cept them old nags and they ain't good for nothin'," complained one old farmer.

"Take that first chestnut bay," ruffled another. "Prettiest horse of them all. It's a crime to see a horse like that go to the killer bidders, 'specially when there's others who could get years of pleasure from it."

JoAnn spoke quietly to Rusty, lowering one eyebrow in expression. "Sooo, there are others who are as upset as we are. Well, we aren't finished yet, are we kids?" They had a rather defeated expression on their faces, but tried to rally with their mother's question.

They might be finished; the killer buyers had high quotas and wanted to make money. They needed to buy as many horses as they could get, rarely backing off even if they occasionally noticed children's anxious faces.

When the quartet arrived back at the ranch, Dana ran from the stall where she had just secured Calfie, the name she had dubbed the animal, anxious for their report. Marie, aware of the situation, stayed just inside the screened door.

That night, her mind spent by the anger she felt, JoAnn lay awake again. Moonlight flooded the room, a gentle breeze stirred the curtains, but she saw none of it. She was determined to find a way around the auction houses, to stock her ranch with good breeding stock; she wasn't interested in raising racehorses. However, there was still a need worldwide for good saddle horses. Her head was empty of answers, only questions tumbled forth.

"Father, you tell me in James 1:5, that if I lack wisdom on

any issue, I am to ask of you, who will give liberally. Help me to think through my problem and then, in faith, find the solution. I will trust You to close some doors and open others and unveil more possibilities than I can possible think of.

"There must be people with horses to sell who don't want to use the auction houses. Help me; Father, to find them. Why do farmers take their horses to the auction instead of trying to sell them at private sales, or breeding auctions? Do they get more money at auctions? Don't they care what happens to their horses? Can't be that! Maybe it's the easiest way out, or they haven't check out the auctions personally to find out what they are like. Perhaps they aren't aware of other markets, or the market is too small, too spasmodic to bother with—endless possibilities.

"What's a gentleman like Gabe doing working in a packing house? That question may never be satisfactorily answered.

"Father, if I could find some of these horses before they reach the auction, like that bay, this morning . . . if I could find . . . horses like that . . ."

Finally, sleep overcame her weary mind.

# Chapter 13

The Cobb family woke early every day to have some individual quiet time with their Saviour. They had all missed it Thursday, but she felt sure, that as she was reading from her Bible, they were doing the same thing. She would share Proverbs 3:5 & 6 with them for encouragement. When she glanced out her window, she noticed Rusty already taking care of the animals including the calf.

A clap of thunder startled her as she left her room to head for the kitchen. There was no sign of wind, nothing to indicate an approaching storm, aside from hearing Samantha meowing. Both dog and cat were scared to death of thunder and lightning and Mitsi was outside. JoAnn sent Rob outside to call to her while she walked through the living room. The rain was falling steadily, threatening to dampen their entire day with so much to begin doing.

Mitsi should have hightailed it for home before Rob even called. As it was, he reported that she was nowhere to be seen.

Marie tried to console them. "There are plenty of buildings for her to run into. She'll be okay," while she placed on the table, fresh sweet rolls dripping with syrup, which soon made them forget about the rain.

It seemed no one could forget about the auction. "Rusty," John asked, "Why is the auction so popular with the ranchers?"

After a long draw on his pipe, only to find it not lit again, Rusty struck a match to the sole of his boot while answering, "Not sure that it is popular, as you put it." Then drawing on his pipe, for a successful light, noticing the children's eyes glued to what he was doing, he explained. "It's downright scary bein' a farmer or a rancher today. You come here expectin' ta find things as they were back when you were a young girl, JoAnn," addressing her primarily. "But it ain't so. There's nothin' traditional anymore. You want ta plow, you don't plow anymore, you till an' sow the seed all in one operation with an expensive machine. You over-seed the oats with timothy an' alfalfa as a nurse crop, you have ta have an air-conditioned tractor, a harvester costin' up ta seventy-five thousand dollars, a degree in agricultural engineerin', an' a keen knowledge of governmental policy an' state law. You study an' read an' attend conferences an' conventions. You aren't a rancher, a farmer, you're a businessman an' the bigger you get in stock an' machines, the better you look.

"So you have somethin' on the ranch that ain't producing'; you sell it: tractor, horse, what's the difference. Progress an' survival! That's the name of the game, an' progress means mechanization an' modernization."

They all seemed to slump in their seat as Rusty gave his spiel. JoAnn had indeed headed west wearing rose-colored glasses and blinders after all. The glasses she thought she had removed, but not so.

"Oh, what a perfect fool I've been. You simply affirm a dreadful misconception I have had about ranching. I was ready to plow my fields with a team of old horses if necessary and I would have made a perfect fool of myself before the other ranchers, no matter how pure my motives. But God has promised to direct my paths if I trust in Him, and I believe He is using you, Rusty, to guide me."

"Might be you're right, because I wouldn't have let you, JoAnn. I couldn't stop your grandpop, but he was too old ta care what people thought. I won't let you do anythin' ta embarrass yourself among the rest of the ranchers. I may have ta open a different door from the one you had in mind, because sometimes God has somethin' different in mind from what we imagined, then again, you may have ta do the same for me, sometime."

Her eyes filled with tears. The children turned to this man about whom they had often spoke fondly and who was now determined to take them all under his wing and protect them in a way their father never had.

John stood and reached his hand across the table to the wizened old man. Rob did likewise. "Thank you, Rusty, and thank God you are here for us," was about all they could say.

Dana and her mother went around the table to throw a loving arm around him in thankfulness. Turning to Marie to see tears in her eyes, that matched her own, JoAnn embraced her as well, and said, "You too are a treasure, Marie. You are so lucky to have such a fine man by your side, and we are so fortunate and grateful to our Heavenly Father to have both of you as our friend and co-worker." As she returned to her seat, she began to feel a lifting within.

"It's we who are the lucky ones," Marie suggested, shrinking from the applause. "You are adding spice to our old lives." Putting an arm around Dana, she continued, "Dana doesn't seem as interested in the ranch and horses as you all are, but she's a mighty fine help around here, so, why don't you and the men worry about everything else, and leave the house and meals to Dana and me?"

JoAnn could see that the remark pleased her daughter and spoke more to her than to Marie. "If that's the way she wants it, it would be a relief off my mind to know she is so well occupied."

"Now run along and finish your figuring. You've got a ranch to stock, I've got a house to run, and a rainy day is a good day to stay indoors anyway,"

JoAnn put the devotional book and prayer lists in the drawer in a cupboard, poured herself another cup of coffee, then joined the men in the living room, spilling some of it in the saucer as she sat down on the sofa.

John had asked a very sensitive question and she could see that Rusty was having difficulty responding.

"Well, you have ta think things through sideways sometimes before you understand them. For instance, in India, cows are sacred an' the people will starve ta death before eating them. We eat them with nary a thought, an' some of them are raised like pets from the time they are born, just like horses. Still, cattle become steaks on our tables.

"Then some animals get old, blind, an' hurt, same as we do, an' should be put ta sleep, like we do our pets when they are old an' awful sick." He looked the boys over as if not sure he should continue, then thinking the better of it, went on.

"But then, there's a plant in New York that slaughters hundreds of day-old ta three months old calves; too weak ta even walk ta the transport truck, because people like ta eat veal. That's down-right ugly, if'n you were ta ask me; but nobody complains about it."

JoAnn was aware of that animal program, but it was a bit tough on the boys emotions.

John spoke again. "You'll have to excuse me for being blunt, Rusty, but you're side-stepping my question."

"Straight out then, yes, you're grandpop sold his old nags at the auction, but not until there wasn't anythin' else left for them but painful arthritic old age. When they got ta be over twenty an' showed signs of age in whitened muzzles, when there developed hollows around their eyes, an' you have all seen horses with swayed backs. Well, he could have just shot them or let them die a tragic natural death with only God knowin' how much pain they were in." He was clearly defending his dead employer.

"If you haven't learned it yet, you will, horses get sick an' hurt just like you do an' they have no one ta turn ta but us."

"So the auctions have been around for some time and the exporting business too. It's just new to us," JoAnn interjected.

"That's right. Non-Muslim an' non-Jewish, even Asians have been eatin' horse meat for centuries. The Celts and Mongols, even the citizens of Venice developed a taste for it in the early Middle Ages." Rusty paused, looking at each one, cradling his cold pipe in his left hand. "Louis an' Clark ate it ta survive durin' their explorations.

"You said about it being a new business. New, nothin's new, an' by the way, you can read more about the history of horse meat in your grandpop's library," he said, with a wink of his eye and a twitch of his nose as if to say, I'm not all that smart, just read up on things. "They ain't about ta go away neither. In the last ten years, packin' plants have tripled in number in the United States."

"Then we'll have to double our efforts to find the horses worth saving before the owners sign them up with the auction houses. Certainly they must pay a percentage to the auctioneer, and we could save them that, as well as ease their conscience. Rusty, any suggestions?"

He waited for Marie and Dana to join them. "It's not easy ta find mares of good breeding who aren't in foal this time of year, in your price range."

"Louis always said I wanted everything for nothing. You're saying I have to up my sights."

"Yep! You've got ta remember that it's been a long time since I've had dealin's with our neighbors, though the Simpson name would receive good treatment on most any farm in Kentucky. An' there are still some breedin 'stock sales, tho' you'd have ta travel toward Lexington ta the nearest one an', like I said, up you'r ante.

"There's bound ta be respectable dealers who would help you find what you want, but you would have ta pay them a percentage for their information. Nothin' comes cheap now'days. Sometimes the sales places are just a place ta unload undesirables, so I would be as leery of them as with the auction houses."

Dana had a suggestion. "Why couldn't we advertise?"

All eyes were still riveted on Rusty. If he felt the pressure of it all, it was not noticeable on the surface. He seemed to really consider her question as he played with his pipe, but then Rob broke the spell.

"Way-ta-go, Dana. I noticed a bunch of magazines laying around; farmer and rancher magazines mostly. We could advertise in them and maybe the newspaper."

John suggested passing word around among ranchers by telephone and word-of- mouth.

"Don't think that would spread the word fast or far enough," JoAnn said, "but I think using all your ideas might do the trick, especially if we use the Simpson name."

"Let's get busy," John suggested, asking for some paper and pencils, then headed toward the swinging doors to get some for himself from the office.

Rusty had fidgeted while all the talk flowed like a creek after a thunderstorm, before he drawled out a command. "Hold on there."

John stopped, Rob took some magazines back to his seat, Dana quit looking through the one she had, JoAnn and Marie hadn't moved from their positions.

"Before you go getting so all-fired up, I'm not sayin' I have God's answer, but, still, I'd like to pass on my opinion."

"Oh, Rusty, I am so sorry. I am afraid in our enthusiasm, I, we got carried away. I intended from the beginning to rely on your judgement and experience and God's leading, and right from the start, I've," she looked at all the children, "we've taken someone's suggestion and run with it. Please forgive us." Her look of repentance would have convinced the hardest of men of her sincerity.

He held up his free hand. "Don't be forgettin' we prayed this mornin', so your not runnin' with somethin'. Your used to handlin' your affairs by yourself an' pretty well, looks like. You've been doin' a fine job," he said, boosting her moral, "but I think it's best if we look for a respectable dealer an' rely on his judgment. You're just a beginner. They often have scores of contacts which would be beneficial ta us an' save us runnin' around the country."

"A beginner, how right you are."

"Well, as a beginner, don't be afraid ta admit your lack of experience, an' if we find a dealer, put your trust in his judgment."

Marie, who had kept quiet with a hand on Rusty's knee, patted it now, "Seems to me an experienced friend is by far the greatest asset." A look of pure love passed between them, a look JoAnn had not given Louis nor received from him, since the early years of their marriage.

For some reason, it shook JoAnn and made that distress within tie her emotions up in knots, until the pain she had experienced the day before again tightened her chest and beat in her throat, until she felt she couldn't breathe. She was glad John diverted their attention from her as she found it necessary to grasp at her throat, and then it was gone as mysteriously as it had come.

"What harm could there be to place ads?"

Perhaps Rusty sensed how desperate the kids were to be doing something concrete. "Won't hurt a'tall. Rob, Dana, bring those magazines into the office. They'll give us an idea how ta word ours." He had gotten up and headed toward the office, but stopped and turned expectantly toward JoAnn when John again got his attention, by bringing up their financial affairs.

Still seated, almost afraid to move, JoAnn said, "Enough, John, for you not to worry."

"I don't mean to be impertinent, Mom, but enough had better be plenty from the looks of things."

"All right, everybody be seated again. You are growing up to have noticed that. So for the benefit of all, I'll lay things on the table the way Grandpop always did. We have inherited invested money from Grandpop to help run the ranch and that comes to three hundred thousand dollars. Much more than that of course was given to his sons and other grandchildren. Louis had a five hundred thousand dollar life insurance policy that was invested according to his wishes and from which I receive small monthly checks from the premium."

She leaned forward with her hands clasped between her knees. "There was about three hundred and sixty thousand in savings which Louis inherited from his parents and that has been put into a trust for you children. All of this money has been collecting interest and is of much greater worth than when originally invested."

JoAnn went on seemingly oblivious to the excitement her financial facts were generating in her offspring.

"Of course, I have no idea how much it will cost to run a place like this, and it may be years before we will begin to make any money from our horses. Our hired help starts on Monday with rented machines and grain arriving along with them. If we are lucky, it will be at least a year from now before our first foal. For the next six months, we will have to buy hay, straw, and supplemental food for the horses we have and hope to have."

Finally, unable to contain themselves any longer, the kids

jumped up. "We're rich! We're rich! We're millionaires!" they shouted, as they danced around the room.

"You guys better wait a couple years and watch the bills being paid with no money coming in but what Louis has provided through premiums, and John off to college, then see if we're rich." She didn't want to throw water on their parade; they needed to face facts.

"Think your mom's right, you young whippersnappers." Getting up, Rusty again headed for the office with the rest following him.

But the magazines were all so out of date that the boys asked to go to the library and sign some out. "What can I do?" Dana wanted to know when her mom gave the boys permission to go.

JoAnn looked out the window to find that the rain had stopped. "The trees are full of leaves, the air should be bursting with fragrance from blossoms and the fresh rain on the sweet green grass. Let's try to salvage some of this Friday by checking on Calfie and taking Samantha for a walk. Hopefully we'll see Mitsi."

Mitsi did not respond to their calls.

# Chapter 14

When the boys returned, John was more excited about the girl he met at the library than about information he obtained.

"You'll never guess who she is."

"No, I suppose not. Who?' his mother asked, only half listening as she ostensibly leafed through the pile of magazines they had brought home with them.

"The butcher's daughter!" Rob exclaimed, impressed with her in a different way than his brother.

"The butcher's daughter?" JoAnn half laughed, not catching Rob's drift.

John cuffed him as he said, "She can't help who her father is."

"There's nothing wrong in being a butcher's daughter," she remarked, still not concentrating on what they were saying, a little impatient at their banter.

"What if the butcher is named Reinhart?" Rob wanted to know.

She paused then, but her eyes remained riveted on the ad announcing a summer sale of thoroughbreds. She slowly answered Rob. "I thought we more or less settled that this morning; people have to eat and live. We each have our own taste and want it satisfied. If we aren't willing to give up eating hamburgers, then let's not be criticizing those who prefer sweet steaks."

Then she slowly turned and leveled her gaze on Rob with the lowering of her one eyebrow in warning. It was a look with which all her children were familiar. "John, what's her name?"

"Jodi. Remember, Rusty mentioned her riding on our land?"

"Yes, I do now. Nice name. Did you tell her who you are and where you live?"

"Who I am, but not where I live. Especially not that we are neighbors. Thought I shouldn't publicize that fact yet."

"Perhaps you're right," she stated, then with difficulty, turned her attention once again to the magazines. "Good choice, boys. I think we can run ads in most of these and follow up some that others have placed. Not everyone sells his horse at the auction! So we have work cut out for us for the rest of the day." A look at Dana reminded her of the missing pet. "By the way, Mitsi hasn't responded to our calls and searching, and it has been hours. If you guys want to, you may take a ride and see if you can find her."

As she continued to flip through one of the magazines, she tried not to show the disappointment she felt over not finding any ads offering just plain good horses. *Father, you know our needs. You haven't placed this desire in my heart for fun, for breeding horses for meat, or raising race horses, thoroughbreds. In that only do I seem to differ from the rest of the horse people in the Bluegrass Region. Help me, guide me, don't let me miss anything I should be seeing in these magazines.*

When she opened her eyes, she noticed an interesting article. It was about a lady who had rescued thirty-eight horses from the "killer auctions" and another one who formed an Equine Retirement Foundation which rescues, rehabilitates, then sells discarded race horses. Along into the article was information about a charitable organization that takes donations of all types of horses from breeders and owners, and then finds greener pastures for them. The money is then used for research of equine diseases.

Intrigued now, she picked up another and searching the table of contents, found an article about wild horses. Over the past eighteen years, it said, this family had provided refuge for thousands of steeds on their five thousand-acre ranch. It had developed into an adoption agency, research laboratory, and education center.

With excitement mounting, she grabbed up another and after glancing at the contents, read an article about a facility that provides college students with classes leading to a four-year degree in equitation, based on a liberal arts program, enabling students to enter a number of fields. Students can teach riding, go into management at a professional stable, and the program enhances the two-year veterinary medical technology and the four-year pre-veterinary medicine curriculum.

This was all so exciting and opened up whole new areas of thinking. But, what should she do with this information? She again leaned back against the sofa, oblivious to the sounds around her. *Father, thank You for John and Rob's choices of magazines. I'm sure You led them if for no other reason than to encourage me through the articles I just read. I love the thought of rescuing animals, making them well, then selling, but I also like the idea of teaching students, of working with the university to enhance their equine program.*

*Do continue to guide us, impress upon us the way in which you would have us go. Help us not to run ahead of you. We do have the rest of our lives to get this together, and we aren't likely to starve while we wait. Thank You Father for Your love and presence. Amen.*

The banks stayed open late on Fridays, so JoAnn took advantage of the time to transfer her accounts. She found it wasn't going to be so simple.

For a small town bank, the inner office of the bank's president was warmly decorated, richly furnished, and impressive. Mr. Ernest Strom, remembering her grandfather and beaming with the sum she wished transferred to his bank, all but threw his arms around her. His well, well, well's and yes-in-deed's lasted close to an hour.

Before she was able to get away, Mr. Strom, had tutored her into setting up several accounts to meet her needs of buying and selling horses as well as for capital expenditures and operating expenses; actually just transferring from Rusty's name to hers the one which already existed. One was put in savings to draw interest. Others would, for now, be left alone to draw interest in the certificates of deposit in New Jersey. She refused to have her children's accounts changed. His last words as he shook hands with her, were to suggest engaging a lawyer.

*I suppose I will need a lawyer.* With a grimace on her face at the extra cost, she pulled up to a drop-off postal box and sent their ads on their way. *But then, I might be fortunate enough to hire a manager eventually, with horse knowledge, connections to help find stock, who is willing and capable of being involved in the paperwork. A business man and horse man all wrapped up in one.*

When she returned home, a sinking feeling grew in her chest when she was informed by the children that Mitsi hadn't returned, and by a too smiling Rusty, that Gabe had paid another routine visit.

"Another? Routine?" She was immediately defensive,

although he had told her that Gabe visited almost every day. She silently screamed. *I need you to stay away.*

"Daily." Rusty seemed to be egging her on.

"Daily?"

"Daily."

"I see." She knew she was losing this game of words.

"No, ya don't see, JoAnn. He hasn't missed a day since your grandpop became ill, not one day." Now Rusty sounded defensive and he let the reasons sink in. "I don't see why he needs to stop now!"

"Well . . . well . . . of . . . course not." Her mind was fast tracking.

"Ya' sure?"

"Yes, of course. Why should my, our being here change things?"

"Why indeed!" he squinted at her, as if he didn't quite believe her.

"Okay, let's be up front. What's on your mind?" She folded her arms across her chest and held his eyes.

"You! You two grew up together, ya might say. There was a time when ya welcomed him with opened arms...."

"Rusty. . ." *Yes, until my parents intervened!*

"Jest you wait a minute. I sure don't expect you to do that now, but I don't expect you to welcome him like you're standin' there right now, neither..."

"Rus. . ." *You don't know everything.*

"He don't deserve that! He's the best man, friend, neighbor, I've ever had, an' he'll be the same for you and you're family, if'n you let him, as well as the best mentor you an' you're kids will ever have, you ever had, an' you know it. I needed him, this ranch needed him. Do you think I could'a done all that you see has been done 'round here, by myself? I still need him, an' so do you an' you're kids!"

She looked away, for the truth of his words was compelling.

When she turned back and was about to speak, she realized he wasn't finished. During her few seconds of silence, his emotions seemed to catch fire.

"If you want ta get mad, get mad at God. He's been pushin' me ta say this since you got here."

"I see," she raised her hand to stop him. "I mean I think I see. Thanks, I think." Then she smiled and relaxed to lay a hand on his sleeve. "I'm not mad at you or God, but you don't know everything. God does though, so I have a lot of contemplative praying to do tonight." She kissed him on the cheek. "Really, thanks, only someone who loves me would want to set me straight," she said, as she left him.

She knew Rusty was right, she was only slightly disappointed in having missed Gabe and wondered how many days she would be successful in doing so. Although she scolded herself, tried valiantly to dismiss any thoughts of him, she could not. Gabe had the same effect on her in the past. After each visit, she had felt slightly empty for months, for he had been such a trusting, easy going, good friend, and she had been tempted to correspond with him. Then slowly, she would begin to forget him as her life filled with other demands, until the next visit, then his influence would begin all over again. Just the mention of his name, the sight of him, was all it had taken. Would it be the same again, if they became friends? Would she so easily tire of him or want to forget him? What would have happened if she had corresponded, had. . .? She shook herself determinedly and declared, "But I didn't, my parents saw to that! No use crying over spilled milk."

Later that night, as she prepared for bed, she found herself standing before the open bedroom window, the fragrant exotic aroma of honeysuckle floating through it. As she watched the evening sky gradually fill with an aura of splendor, she found herself wondering where Mitsi was and how she was going to handle Gabe's daily visits with aplomb.

*I didn't know that my coming here would challenge my heart and mind so. Truly, I will need to be in the Word, prepared with the appropriate reactions, otherwise, I know one thing, I cannot, will not, allow my body to be used by a man again!*

The bitterness of the memory attacked her preoccupation like an unwelcome tenant refusing eviction, that she shivered, and twisting smartly, grabbed on her robe and headed for the bathroom door.

"I need a bath!"

But, she knew that all the baths in the world would not wash away the painful remembrances of the past. Jesus was helping her in her continuing battles; she could not deal with the devil alone.

*Shades of Hades, I've come a long way out of that cocoon in which you wrapped me, Louis, and someday, with the Lord's help, I'll be free to enjoy a real man the way a woman should.* Then she realized she was contradicting herself and that the twisting knot inside her was that great desire to be free from the very thought of Louis and to experience the other side of love.

"And I will, Louis, I will!" she decided, as she slid into the foaming water.

## Chapter 15

It was early on Sunday morning when Rob knocked on his mother's door.

"Come in."

He opened the door enough to say, "Mom, Mitsi still hasn't come back!"

Rubbing sleep from her eyes, she looked at the clock as she sat up in bed. "Do you want to go looking for her again?"

"Would you come along?"

His voice was full of stress and pain. She had been ignoring that as she tried to deal with everything else confronting her. "It's Sunday, but still early." She pushed off the covers and slid out of bed. "Sure I'll come, and maybe it would be good to invite your sister."

"Okay, I'll knock on her door, but you do the talking," he chuckled, as he closed the door behind him.

Determined to meet back within the hour, John and Dana went in one direction and JoAnn and Rob in another. When they collected back at the ranch, they had not seen the dog, but had noticed riders on the range, and their descriptions did not match the same two groups. When they had ridden toward the cowboys to ask them about the dog, the intruders had galloped off in a hurry. This was the third time JoAnn had wished for binoculars. Rusty would have to be informed.

"Now what, Mom?" Dana wanted to know. The look on the boy's faces asked the same question.

"I don't know. She isn't used to freedom and may just be enjoying herself, or . . . I really just don't know." She looked at her watch. "We might as well take care of the horses. There's nothing else to do for now and we need to get to church."

The kids reluctantly complied. "Rusty and Marie are off today. Why don't we go out to a restaurant to eat, go to church, have dinner out and relax? We'll deal with Mitsi when we get back home. What-a-ya say?"

"Wonderful, cool, way-ta-go Mom," was their varied reaction.

Rob asked the obvious question. "What church are we going to go to?"

"I don't want to start with Sunday school." Dana stated, emphatically, and her mother heard how important this was to her.

"That's fine, and I'm reminded that we have to get you two registered at school so your records can be transferred out here."

"Mom..."

"I'm coming to that, my impatient son. I know you are expecting me to have answers, and I must admit, I was thinking of starting where the Simpson's have always gone and where Marie and Rusty attend now."

"If we don't like it?" John wanted to know.

"We will shop around, just like we did after we were all saved back in Jersey."

"Sounds good to me!"

"Same here," Rob said.

Dana wanted to know, "could we drive around and find the school we'll be going to sometime before we come home?"

"Sounds good to me!" JoAnn said, mimicking John. "Better go get dressed and meet here by nine." She was so glad that Dana had Calfie to help occupy her time and mine.

The Faith Bible Church was huge, with a balcony, and at one time had a congregation of over one thousand. Now there were about five hundred in attendance. The pastor appeared to be around the same age as JoAnn. The kids observed a good sized group of young people and the bulletin listed plenty of their activities. As they were reading it and looking around, JoAnn observed their obviously satisfied looks, except for John.

The music accompaniment of the piano and organ was very professional and evangelistic in nature, which appealed to her. The singing of the old beloved hymns was robust.

The message from the pastor was interestingly presented with modulation and many illustrations to back up his points. She was glad to see her children trying to follow along in their Bibles, as did many others in the congregation. This could be her church, but she wondered what the rest were thinking.

Following the service, many came to them with warm greetings, including some young people of both sexes. "This is good," JoAnn thought, until she saw Gabe, who acknowledged her with a nod, then exited.

Once they got in the car, John, who was the driver, asked if they could drive around to look at other church locations before lunch. It didn't take much of a brain to realize Jodi Reinhart had not been in attendance at the service they had just attended.

No one answered Rob's, "Why? I like the one we were at well enough to give it another try." Dana responded positively also.

John, perhaps feeling trapped, said, "I did too, but it wouldn't hurt to look around, would it?"

They found an Independent Bible Church of smaller proportions, as well as the school campus where Dana and Rob would be attending. They were impressed with the school and willing to try the Independent church that evening. They were a car full of happy campers, until John pulled up in front of the house late that afternoon. Then they all seemed to come down from their high, when Mitsi did not run to greet them.

Rusty informed her that Gabe had dropped by and since she hadn't come directly home from church, the two of them had set out on what turned out to be a futile mission of finding Mitsi.

JoAnn asked if they had seen any riders, then explained about those they had seen earlier this morning.

"One sounds like Rocko, from Reinhart's. I remember seeing him at the auction?"

JoAnn seemed to feel that Rusty was right, but the rest were unknown, as was the whereabouts of their precious dog.

"Mom," Dana had a question. "Could we place a notice in the paper about a missing dog?"

"Yes, I think we better." She clasped her daughter's hand.

"Do you think Rusty or Marie would feel free to call over at the Reinhart's and ask them if they have seen our dog?"

JoAnn gave her hand a squeeze. "I'm sure either one would be glad to. Want me to ask, or do you want to ask Marie?"

"I'll ask Marie." Dana went right away to Marie's door.

Marie's call to the Reinhart's produced a negative response.

# Chapter 16

The waiting game had begun for the family, but certainly not an idle wait. Day hands, old and young, arrived early Monday and it felt good to have others busy at work on her farm. All were asked to keep an eye out for Mitsi.

Among them, were some experienced retired carpenters who were put to work on the stables, and outbuildings. Some, with four-wheel-drive vehicles, loaded with posts, wire, and tools, headed out to far distances to fence off some open areas.

"I wonder what Klein will think when he is fenced in near the boundary lines with just a hundred acres in which his animals can graze. Seem as if he is used to just going where he wants, like as if, occupancy is ownership?" JoAnn asked Rusty.

"Never thought of it like that. Think it's a good thing, what you're proposin', an' maybe not a day too soon."

"You said someone had planted about a thousand acres up near the forest."

"Yep. He lives down the road a piece beyond the old Hopkins place."

"What do you say, we just fence off that area too. Then down the road we won't be needing to worry about our animals wandering in there and thinking they've gone to Heaven."

"Sounds like a plan."

Other men climbed upon the old gasoline tractor John, Rob and Rusty had gotten to work. Along with the rented machines, which had been trailered in, they headed towards the fields. Next year, she hoped to enlarge the garden area Marie prized.

Beyond where JoAnn could see, some men were working to scrub prospective pastures of poison weeds and grasses, bushes, and trees that the horses might be tempted to eat, as well as filling in groundhog holes as they went along, so the horses wouldn't trip and break a leg. Frequently she heard a gun fired and hoped that a groundhog had been killed. Mitsi was not seen.

Others she knew were occupied along the natural fence lines of overgrown scrub brush, doing the same thing, as well as making sure they were thick enough to keep in any animal they wanted to protect. These workers reported at the end of the day with good news. The bushes and trees had grown so thick and strong along boundary lines, that no horse or cow could get through from one grazing field to another. No one had seen a dog. Rusty informed her that the gates would allow secure passage from one field to another. The water supplies and sheds in the far reaches needed attention, but not until she had loads of horses and cattle.

Some of the men worked closer to the house and barns. Just working with and watching them, she knew they were reliable men. Though one was Rusty's nephew, Roy Owen, whom he hoped to groom into a competent horse man, most were old friends of Rusty's, who would stay at the task till done, and then some. Rusty and the boys worked right along beside them. Marie, Dana, and JoAnn, when she wasn't outside, cooked a delicious large meal at lunchtime every day, and provided cold drinks and water all day long as needed.

Everyone literally dropped into bed at night dead tired, sunburned, and aching from the absence of their pet dog, and from overworked and unused muscles. If Gabe made his daily visit, or worked with the men, she never saw him, and was thankful for the time and space until she had to face him again. She was feeling healthier and happier than ever before.

The lavish application of paint on the barns and repaired fences, had spiffied up the place. With hedgerows trimmed, the paddocks and pastures raked, fertilized, and weeded, the fields plowed and seeded, the ranch took on a first class appearance.

Marie cooked fantastic, but simple energy meals with Dana following close on her heels. Then she shadowed Marie from the kitchen to whatever room she entered to clean. Marie answered the phone, which rang with increasing frequency, and Dana, always on the alert for Mitsi, ran with the messages. JoAnn was so happy to be released of these duties, that she heaped praise on both of them. But, she insisted on a short daily ride with Dana, until Dana felt confident enough to ride to the highway by herself, to fetch the mail, and ride into the fields or grazing lands with phone messages.

Still there were days when Gabe visited or rode her range, but she only saw him from a distance. She was too tired and preoccupied to really care. Neither had she caught sight of Mitsi nor anyone else on the land who shouldn't be there. Maybe the sight of so many people on the range intimidated the intruders. The family had begun to accept the fact that Mitsi was not coming back. Being so very busy helped them suffer the loss.

JoAnn mentioned to Marie, "Rusty never seems to tire, though he is involved in so many things at once. The first weeks in June, he was on the phone, or in the fields, the corral and back again and never complained. There was never a grievous moment as he worked with our ineptness. Now, here he is directing like an orchestra leader."

"That's my man. He's in his element."

Rusty was greeted warmly by delivery men and was still Johnny-on-the-spot at the end of the day, when he sat down with the family to schedule the next day's work, or to guide JoAnn in recording expenses.

"Ain't gonna be around forever, you know," he warned her, when she protested that he was doing too much. "You have ta learn to run this ranch by yourself."

She looked up at him with love in her eyes and threw her arms around him. "Thank you, thank you, for being Johnny on the Spot, and for reminding me of your frailty. I expect so much from you, but, I am learning and feeling every inch a farmer, not a rancher." Nevertheless, a delicious shudder passed over her as she thought of the ranch and it's re-awakening. All was in readiness for the horses. She had begun!

Her barns were empty, but her soul was full. *My winters won't last forever. Spring days will come when foals will be friskily playing. Heavy hoofed mares ready to drop a foal, will receive special attention, and stallions will be stomping and whinnying ready to serve as a result of the spring and summer advertisements. Thank God, the barns and lofts will be full of oats, hay, and straw.*

Or, was she just a dreamer? There had been no quick response to her letters. She had not shared her back-up plan with the family, those other ideas about which she had read. Frequently she had mulled over the magazines, about ready to take the dive and begin any one of the programs, but hesitated. She didn't know what she was waiting for.

About six days after Mitsi had disappeared, JoAnn stepped inside the door on the side porch, when a 4-wheel drive vehicle drove around to the side of the ranch house, stopping at Rusty's house. The lettering on the side told her it was the Forest Ranger, Joel Strouse. She waited, wondering if Rusty would call for her to meet Joel. Disappointed when he didn't, she went about her business of helping in supper preparations. After about twenty minutes, she almost ran into the boys in the hallway as they headed for the kitchen.

"Good timing," John remarked.

"Very good," she laughed. "I'll be right there." She wanted to see if the ranger was still with Rusty. He was not, and Rusty stood with his back to the ranch house, holding something. Still he didn't come in until called for supper. Something was up!

Surprisingly, Marie was the one who called Rusty to task. "Seemed like Joel was here on a mission. What's up?"

Rusty removed his unlit pipe and put it into his shirt pocket before going to the sink to wash his hands. He spoke rather softly over his shoulder to the gang ready to hang on every word. "He's been ta Kleins'!"

"He's been there before and nothing any good ever comes of his visits." She handed her husband a towel. "You might as well tell us what he wanted."

When Rusty turned, he could hardly look at the kids. "He saw the notice in the paper about your dog." He cleared his throat as he watched JoAnn move to stand beside Dana.

"He's not certain now, but, before he saw the notice, he thought he saw Misti tied up there. After readin' the notice, he went back an' asked and looked 'round for her. Klein told him, she got loose an' ran away. But in his searchin', he found a dog collar." Rusty's throat filled up and he had to stop.

"Mom?" The kids seemed to ask in one voice as they drew closer together.

"Well, Rusty?" Marie asked, as impatient as the rest.

Clearing his throat again before he could answer, he said, "It's hers."

Dana began crying and sat down with her head on her arms on the table. "Oh, Mitsi, poor Mitsi."

The rest coughed and wiped at their eyes.

John asked with chocked voice, "Could it be she is running free somewhere?"

Rusty shook his head. "She would have come back by now if'n she was able, don't you think?"

John just nodded his head and walked into the living room.

"I don't think I want anything to eat just now," JoAnn said as she followed John.

Later, after the family had walked or rode off their anguish, and the sun had set, Marie gathered them together and set a light meal in front of them. They literally fell early into their beds that night and slept late the next morning. Dana spent some time with the calf, who would soon be returned to pasture, but, when inside the house, she kept Samantha close beside her.

Crafty warm sweet days of June stole into the atmosphere and life took on a more natural pace; only a few part-timers lingered to finish up with Roy Owen, Rusty's nephew.

The bumblebees was busy during the day, the fireflies sparkled in the darkness at night. Moths swarmed around the outside lights at night also, and robins protected their young from the many predators sniffing around during the day. Beautiful and flashy red cardinals filled the air with their own unique sound. Hard working ranchers consumed strawberries, full of juice and sweetness, and the summer solstice subtly came and passed before another Sunday arrived, almost unaware.

JoAnn was only slightly disappointed when the kids decided to give the Independent Baptist Church a month's trial, which meant Sunday school, prayer meeting and other activities. The Cobb family's life suddenly became much busier.

*At least, if we go to this church, I will be free of Gabe on Sundays and that is a definite plus as far as I am concerned.*

JoAnn rose earlier than usual, and after her time with the Lord, happily pulled on her jeans and shirt, then the boots so obviously broken in, brushed her growing but still short hair quickly into its loose free style, rubbed in skin toner, before running to the tack room.

She needed to have some time to herself to absorb this new life, to cope with the new person she was becoming. She made a mental note to give the children this same free space this week. She had been a seaside lady of leisure: swimming, deep sea fishing, crabbing, as well as an ideal hostess for her husband's cocktail parties, his volunteer organizer for art shows, concert parties, and a myriad number of other functions.

From St.Laurette to Wrangler in a few short weeks, took a little getting used to; this too she must not forget when it came to her children. It was the constant tug of war on her inner resources that made her tense, and the constant bantering about the butcher living next door and Gabe working for him. It appeared she was taking it all in stride. They didn't know how many times in a day she communed with her Lord over every little pressure, joy, and hope.

She was happy to find herself capable of any task so far, many of which took her from the familiar safe environment to which she was accustomed. But then, God rarely allows us to stay in those safe environs for any length of time. She was learning a lot and making some stupid mistakes, but the ranch was beginning to resemble the way it had looked in its heyday; it had cost her a lot, emotionally.

It was a rare, cool, wet morning, following a full night of light rain, that she encountered Gabe again. The air about her hung heavy with humidity and dusted with the fresh aroma of pollen. The birds filled the air with a bright symphony of song. Her hat made her head hot!

Seeing him in the distance, she immediately turned Flora's Girl around and headed back, disappointed in such a short ride. "Oh, Father guard my tongue, control my thoughts."

As she heard him galloping, closing the distance between them, she pulled up. She had not discouraged him, after all, from having some private time with her. He had never married, according to the jesting she had heard among the men.

*Why do I feel it necessary to know the answer to his marital status? So I'll know how to act, whether or not to steer clear of him, don't think about him, turn him against me? What?*

As he approached now, she looked down to find her suntanned scratched hands, clutching the reins, and she refused to look at him, but cried desperately, *Gabe, please stay out of my life!*

"You have been a long time in resuming your morning ride," he breathed as evenly, as unperturbed, as if he believed she had not seen him and simply turned toward home.

She looked up, stretching her neck with a long sigh, "We have been terribly busy."

"Yes, I know. I've been here watching the progress with great interest."

She couldn't look at him, but stared past him, realizing his eyes were searching her face. "No doubt helping as well."

"Of course. Do you mind?"

"Of course not. I believe I told you I would need all the help I could get." *Or did I just tell myself that?* When she urged her horse on, his kept pace, when she slowed, so did he. A sneaky smile threatened to ruin her reserve.

She had experienced short-lived magical crushes on the other cowboys in those years of growing up and visiting the ranch. It had been so difficult to separate the man from his horse and hat. Their courage, versatility, companionship, dignity and strength, were all rolled into one glamorous fantasy, cowboy!

Gabe had stood apart. Her face flushed at the remembrance. He had turned from being a friend to a first love and, no thanks to her parents, back to a friend again, before she had enrolled in college. Although that had been so many, many years ago, he must remain just a friend, a distant friend, an almost forgotten friend, whether or not he was married. *Isn't that right, Father?* She didn't sense an answer immediately and before she knew it, asked straight out, "Gabe, why the dickens aren't you at home in bed with your wife?"

He roared with laughter, as if something finally dawned on him, which made her horse nervous.

"Now see what you've done," she spoke angrily, controlling and moving her horse ahead on the path where she could see the fence between her land and the Reinhart's. She would wait for another opportunity she decided.

The old path, so well-trodden in years past, was still as easily negotiated. She reined in and turned in the saddle to look at him. "So that's one fence we didn't get fixed."

"Why should it? It's used too often. In fact, I use it every day. You'd have to find some other way for those of us who desire to ride the Simpson land to get in." He was still grinning at her.

*Every day!* That unnerved her as before, "Okay, that's it! Stop that stupid grinning and answer my question. Why don't you ride with your wife?"

He was trying to hold his face in a grave expression, but apparently found it difficult. "I don't have a wife, yet, and I like to ride with pretty women my own age."

The years wanted to fall away as if they never were, but that knot inside twisted a bit from fear, and feeling it, she just exclaimed, "Oh, you!" She nudged Flora's Girl forward into a gallop, away from the fence, the path, the memories, but not away from Gabe.

She hadn't expected nor intended such easy dialogue with him. She wanted to stand aloof, to be hard against men as she had back in Jersey. Until that first thought of Gabe back in May, she had remained hard and cold. Would this place and its memories, this place and its stimulating appeal, this place and Gabe, allow her to remain hard and cold?

"And he's not married!" she inwardly groaned out the words.

Solomon, Gabe's magnificent horse, easily kept pace with Flora's Girl, until they came to the creek which flowed through the Simpson property. In her hesitancy of turning or continuing on, Gabe reached over and grabbed her reins and stopped her horse, as well as stopping his own.

"Jo, what are you running from? You can't be afraid of me!"

The eyes that pierced her own were the same clear, kind eyes of the past. Against all her determinations, she felt something exquisite and tender lure and hold her. It told her that he meant her not harm, no anxiety, just sincere friendship, just as in the past, and against her will, she found herself responding to them, just as in the past. Sooner or later she would need a male friend who would be just that and nothing else, a manager of sorts. What was it she had thought, a businessman, a horseman, a manager, all wrapped up in one man. *Could that man be Gabe? God is that what you are trying to tell me?*

With a feeling of, I can't win, she shrugged and tilted her head toward him. "I'm sorry, Gabe. I was taken back when you said you aren't married . . ."

"Yet," he mocked her. "Yet, I said."

"Yet. Yes, you did say that." Her attempt to gloss over the word as if she did not get his meaning, didn't work. She could see a smile develop on his lips when he realized she understood it. "Anyway, I found it strange that I didn't know, since everyone seems to want me to know all about you." That was only part of the truth, but he didn't need to know that, yet.

"I just assumed you did. Rusty knows, of course."

"I didn't ask. Your personal life is none of my business." *Why do I have to cut him so?*

"I don't mind if it is," he said, unperturbed at the sound in her voice, trying to hold her eyes again, but she quickly glanced away, for she did see hurt there, and it did something to her heart.

But I do, she wanted to scream, however, in order not to offend him again, she simply asked, "All right then, I have to know something. How can a man like you work for a man like Reinhart?" It had always been so easy to speak her mind with him, something she had missed with Louis.

Gabe pretended not to have noticed her torment, her confusion, and the distressing sound in her voice; nor to interpret it. "He's a fine man, Jo. His business is his, not mine. I do my job and he does his."

"I see, but his business has a lousy reputation, 'Killer Buyer', really! It's interfering with mine and the lives of simple farmers and young children, and it makes my blood boil."

"You are unfairly casting him and me as a villain. That's not like you."

"Gabe, you don't know me anymore, twenty-two years is a long interval."

"I know you better than you think I do, but let's not go there. Let's stick to the issue at hand. We aren't the ones who make the horses lame, or starve them and let them be sick instead of calling a vet. We haven't filled them with drugs or caused abscesses or injuries. Reinhart is a legitimate businessman, but along with the others, gets blamed for all that's wrong with the horse industry."

"I don't believe you," she almost stuttered with anger, seeming to ignore his explanation as legitimate. "You who always loved animals, especially horses, and who rides one of the most beautiful horses I've ever seen, can actually lead a horse to the slaughter." She really shuddered, just thinking about it. "I think I might be actually sick talking about it."

She took back the reins and moved her horse away, holding her stomach.

Gabe patiently waited. "What else is troubling you?"

"I almost hate you for working in that kind of business. How you've changed in the intervening years!"

"Sooo," he laughed, "you do have feelings for me." Then calmly he replied, "If you can believe evil of me, you too have changed and not for the better." He didn't wait for her reaction but could see she needed something more. "His home used to be mine, if you haven't forgotten. A home I loved more than just about anything, where I had hoped to . . . well, let's not go there either. Anyway, I want to stay as close to it as I can. He offered me a job, and I took it. Shall we head back?" he asked, as if to close that topic of conversation once and for all.

"You go where you want. I'm going home."

He wasn't discouraged by her attitude and rode part of the way with her. At the parting of their paths, he spoke her name softly, tenderly, "Jo. I have to believe you really haven't changed, that you are still dealing with the past and allowing it to color the present. I can wait. We both believe and pray to the same God you know, and he answers my prayers too. But, I have to tell you, you're just as beautiful as when you were a young girl. I have found I could not forget you."

Caught off guard again, she met his eyes briefly, "Thank you Gabe, that's the nicest thing a real man has said to me in a very long time. However, if we are going to be friends, you will have to learn to keep thoughts like that to yourself, or you will not be welcomed here. Now I must go."

She left him watching her gallop into the wind, away from him, his eyes and the feelings she saw there, away from this voice full of hope, love and concern, away from this man who insisted on making her think about him and the future. Had she deflated his ego? She doubted it.

*I don't really know him anymore; I may have just made him more eager to challenge me.* She was left to wonder from where that thought had come. Was it his mentioning twice in one hour something about "us" past and future? He certainly isn't afraid to speak his mind even if his ideas are one-sided. *They are one-sided, aren't they, JoAnn?*

# Chapter 17

JoAnn figured there had been plenty of time for people to respond to their ads, therefore, a small group began gathering each day when Dana would arrive with the mail. They just as quickly returned to their various duties, disappointed.

Praying for courage, she decided to attend the auction again, alone, and carefully selected her darkest plaid shirt to go with her jeans; she did not want to stand out.

As the horses were quickly bid through, something formulated in her mind. She did not bid; had not intended to without someone to guide her. Therefore, following the auction, she walked over to the trucks and trailers where horses were being loaded, and attempted to strike up a conversation with anyone who would talk with her. Horsemen never tire of looking at horseflesh and there were several men at each area.

"That's a fine looking horse," she stated, matter-of-factly, pretending more knowledge than she possessed.

"Not for long though," came the sad reply.

"Well, he brought a good price."

"He did that all right."

"Are you from around here?" she asked, wondering if her ad had reached into his area.

"Henderson."

Yes, he should have seen it. She edged him on. "I have a couple old mares. Can't decide whether to bring them here or sell them myself."

"You'll pay a whoppin' percent to sell them here. If you aren't in a hurry, ah, forget it," he said, stopping abruptly in mid-sentence and beginning to walk away.

But she wouldn't let him, "Thanks for the advice." She fell into step behind him. "I saw where someone is advertising for horses and thought about giving them a call. In fact their address is right here in Donaldson, Simpson, I think was the name of the ranch."

"Know the name," he paused, turning to her. "Saw the ad too."

"But you still sold at the auction?" she asked, watching his expression carefully.

"Yep."

"Any particular reason?"

"Yep."

When she saw he was not going to elaborate, she prodded. "I'm new at this business and I'd like to maybe sell my old stock and buy new. But those bids run too high for the horse. I was thinking of answering the ad."

He scrutinized her then, and asked, "You new around here?"

She could honestly answer, "Yes.

"Thought so," he said, matter-of-factly, as he turned again to walk away.

Somehow she knew it wasn't her clothes or accent that gave her away. Not to be deterred, she approached several other sellers and went through the same routine, all the while noticing the handsome, reckless young man, whom she had seen with Gabe before, now loading horses unto a trailer. Their answers were the same as the first man. Something strange was going on; the sellers seemed to be intimidated.

With this thought troubling her, seeing that Gabe was nowhere around, she approached the good-looking young man whose typical ranch clothes seemed uncomfortably molded to his lithe body. After a few words of greeting, she asked him if he liked his job.

"Sure. What'sittoya?"

It was hard to answer him civilly after that sassy remark. "Just wondered. I hate to think of some of these beautiful animals heading for steaks on some Frenchman's dinner plate, when there are people around who need good horses for work and pleasure."

"Who are you? From some cruelty to animals club?" he asked, with hatred flashing from his green eyes.

"No, no club, just an interested by-stander."

He stopped then and really looked at her. "Look, it's a job. Those horses are gonna' die anyhow, so we sign an early death warrant for them. Whose to care?"

As if to underline his brazenness, he procured a stick from the trailer and used it unnecessarily to hurry the horses along. This caused her blood to boil. There was one thing she knew about horses; they bruise easily and don't travel well when herded together in a trailer. Pretending ignorance, she asked, "For whom do you work?"

"What'sittoya' lady?"

What an expression! "Your boss might be interested in that stick. He just paid a thousand dollars for that old horse."he had dismissed her, she walked around to the side of the trailer to find "Reinhart and Company" printed in gold leaf. Of course Gabe came to her mind and his reasoning for working for Reinhart. She saw that not all the horses they slaughtered were old, decrepit, full of drugs, or lame. Her ire was up as she thought her earlier conversation with Gabe. *You try to sweet talk me and fill me with reasonable excuses as to why you work there. Well, you won't catch me off guard again!*

Rusty's reaction to her report was the same as her initial feeling. "Someone's intimidatin' the ranchers, and it don't take two guesses to figure out who it is!"

"Shades of the Wild West!" Rob boomed.

"Living on a ranch is proving to be very interesting," John volunteered.

"I love you guys," their mom said, giving them each a hug. "You are constantly rewarding me with your upbeat attitude and all I do is ask you to work, work, work."

"We love you too, Mom," they both stated.

Rob asked. "But are you going to hug us forever?"

"I hope so!"

Once JoAnn decided on a course, she wasn't likely to turn back. "I refuse to be intimidated and waste my money trying to out-bid the syndicate. We're going to find those horses before they reach the auction if we have to scour the countryside to do it!"

"Way to go, Mom!" John encouraged her. "You're on a crusade to "save the horses". Yahoo!"

"Hold on there now. You're competin' against a multi-million dollar monopoly. If you've got any plans, they better be good ones."

"You know horses well enough to bid just to the point of not going too high, but high enough to make the killer bidders raise their ante."

"What are you drivin' at?"

"John, Rob, you, and I will sit where the auctioneer must see us and stand if necessary to get his attention. Then we'll place bids, even on horses in which we aren't interested, just to make the price go higher. We'll give those killer buyers a run for their money and maybe, just maybe, we'll be lucky enough to have them back off and get a good horse for ourselves."

"That's risky, unethical, and unchristian," Rusty reminded and warned her. "You could lose the shirt off you're back an' up the ire of the ranchers. Can't afford bad friends in the horse business."

"What if we bid on only the very best ones, the ones in which we would be truly interested." She shifted position, curling a leg up under her on the old sofa. "Maybe when Reinhart and Summit and some of the others see that a family is interested in some of them, they will back off. I guess it sounds a bit crazy, now that it's laid out, but we have to begin someplace, or that corral will never be full and all the work and money invested so far will have been for nothing." She got up and went to the window overlooking the corral. "I believe God has allowed me to see this for some reason." Then turning again to Rusty and seeing a doubtful expression of his face. "At least I think He did . . ."

"Mom," John said, going to her and laying an arm across her shoulders, for he was taller then she, "If you're thinking of buying and reselling just to save them, how do you know there is a market. We don't want to get stuck with a bunch of horses we really don't want ourselves."

"I heard others talking."

"We could always sell them back to the auction or just take them right over to Reinhart and sell them to him!" Rob expounded with importunity.

"Rob, my dear child, you do keep me smiling."

"How about a riding academy," he kept on, "from what I see in town and around here, there are city slickers just like us, who don't own a farm or a horse."

She snapped her fingers. "That reminds me, I read some very interesting articles about groups of horse lovers who are saving unwanted or unhealthy horses. They give them tender, loving care, and then sell them reasonably to people who really want, and have land for horses. "If push comes to shove, we have other options. We could buy from them if they really have good horseflesh. And Rob," she went to him to lay her hand on his back, "there is a liberal arts college whose people are working with a rancher to develop a riding, teaching, training school. They pay half the expenses and provide half the horses, and most of the teachers. So," giving him a pat, "you aren't so far out in your thinking, Dear Boy."

"But first things first," she cautioned. "How about we wait until next Wednesday and see what the mail brings in. Then Thursday, we'll go to the auction and try out our strategy, and if that proves worthless or risky, we'll get in that station wagon and wear off the rubber, traveling back roads and highways and knocking on doors, if necessary, until we get some fine bred horses." Heading for the kitchen, she asked, "Coffee anyone?"

Marie almost bumped into JoAnn in her hurry through the dining room. "I think there's been an accident on the highway. I've been hearing sirens and can see a red glow along the lane."

Dana burst in from the front porch. "A car's coming up the lane!"

There was a scramble for the front porch. John and Rob went down the steps and out to the car as it stopped. A couple of men dressed in typical cowboy attire, jumped from their car. "Could we use your phone to call a vet?" one on them asked. "There's been an accident down there in front of your place."

"You bet," John answered, leading the way up to the house. He showed one of the cowboys the kitchen, and pointed to the phone hanging on the wall. JoAnn followed him, intent on listening to the conversation.

Outside, the other man was trying to answer questions

thrown at him. "An elderly gentleman was heading home pulling a horse trailer. Seems like his horse is worth a powerful amount of money. Any which ways," he went on, hiking at his suspenders, "seems like he might have dozed off and swayed a right amount to get back on the road. The trailer went one way and he went thataway." A smile passed from one young face to another, when the man used both hands to demonstrate the action he was describing. "Horse and trailer's now in the ditch right off your lane. Horse's making an awful noise."

JoAnn had walked to the doorway and heard that last part. A pain seemed to shoot through her. She glanced at the man on the phone who seemed to have a nervous twitch in his shoulders as he talked to the vet.

Rusty had stood impatiently by, but now told the boys to git on down there, that he'd follow soon as he grabbed his medical kit. John diverted to the kitchen for the car keys before joining them, and then decided to wait for Rusty.

JoAnn and the caller now joined those who remained. He tipped his hat, "Thanks ma-am. It'll be a space before the vet gets here." Nodding to his friend, "Guess we might go see if'n we can help." He spoke his thanks again as he climbed into the car to turn it around and head out.

JoAnn looked at Dana and Marie. "What are we, chicken soup?" They looked at one another for a second before Dana made the motion with her hands of let's do something. JoAnn finally spoke the one word, which sent them scurrying to the paddock. "Well?"

In no time at all they had trotted to the end of the lane to behold the catastrophe.

# Chapter 18

The tow truck had set the splashy truck upright, but the trailer was still in an awkward position on its side. The horse was making an awful sound, and no one could reach him, for the trailer door was wedged and could not be budged. No one seemed concerned at this point with the horse.

JoAnn motioned for Dana and Marie to stay there while she dismounted and gave Marie the reins. "I have to go to the horse and talk to it." She walked around the front of the truck to reach the front of the trailer. She thought the poor horse looked beseechingly at her. Usually light horses such as thoroughbreds, are highly strung and the slightest touch sends them up in the air. But this horse, except for its cry of distress and perhaps because of the stress of the accident, hardly moved, or couldn't.

JoAnn spoke softly to the distressed horse while reaching her hand in to scratch its muzzle. It quieted some, just as the owner hollered at her to get away from the horse. She noticed Gabe and Pierce Reinhart, drive up. Just then another tow truck arrived from Donaldson. With attention diverted, she moved back to the animal and continued talking and touching it.

A State Policeman had arrived to direct traffic. Some people stopped with an offer to help. Louis would never have become involved in such a situation, but most men couldn't resist.

She pitied the animal so. The minute the trailer was set upright, and the men had gone back to try to open the door, she sneaked back, never stopping her flow of comforting, soothing words. Her touch seemed to stabilize it a bit. "Rusty will help the minute he can get to you and you'll like him. He's so kind and gentle. The vet will too when he gets here. They're working on the door. There it's open. They'll make me go soon, but I'll keep talking low so others can't hear, you'll be all right." She watched the owner and Rusty as they entered the trailer.

"Watch him now," the owner, Skye Lakewood cautioned. "He's a thoroughbred and flighty and feisty." Skye Lakewood, still wearing his cowboy hat, was tall and heavily built, but well dressed in characteristic cowboy attire. When he spoke his voice seemed to say, 'pay attention'.

"Well, he's takin' it easy right now." Rusty voiced. "He must be hurtin' real bad."

"Back him out and let's find out," Skye demanded.

"Whoa there, Mr. Lakewood," Rusty barked. "Don't mean ta be tellin' ya your business, but if he's hurt real bad, maybe we could get the truck ta tow the trailer into a stall in one of our barns. Wouldn't want him ta go runnin' off crazy like, an fall down right here in the middle of the road, if he's lame."

"I've worked around horses all my life," declared the gentleman rancher, who was more finely dressed than Rusty.

"Is that a fact! So have I," Rusty countered. "But he's yours, an' if he's worth all the money you say, you better be thinkin' twice how you're goin' ta handle him."

Tipping his hat back to scratch his head, he reconsidered. "Let's see if the tow can do it then."

JoAnn was back at the horse. "Good for you Rusty. See, I told you, you'd like Rusty."

A parade of horses, cars, trucks and vans, including the vet's, that had just arrived, followed the tow truck up the lane. JoAnn rode close to the trailer, talking, before suddenly galloping ahead. She knew to which stall they would put the horse and she wanted to be inside and as close to it as possible.

Night had descended, hours had passed, traffic along the highway moved on now that the drama was over. Rusty almost snapped to John and Rob to get the lights on in the stable and auxiliary ones ready. Other men jumped into the fray and subdued the animal. After introducing Stu Farley, the vet, to Skye Lakewood, the owner of the horse, Rusty stood back, along with the boys, Gabe, Pierce, and other neighbors, to let the real players do their work of examining it.

JoAnn hurried and opened the window to the stall she thought Rusty might use, before running back outside to stand and watch. What she had seen and heard when the horse was backed out and walked into the stall, was pitifully frightening. *Do horses scream?*

Though obviously injured, he had bucked, twisted, reared, and seemed to cry with pain. Or, being a thoroughbred, was he just bursting with uncontrolled energy. Had the accident affected his mental attitude as well? JoAnn was in a fit herself to find out the answers, as she talked to him through the window she had opened.

Stu talked as he examined the horse. "There is some swelling in this left hind leg and it feels pretty hot." He looked up at Skye Lakewood. "He'll have to be cooled off to get that down, then some heat treatments will restore circulation, but, what's this," he asked of no one in particular.

Skye and he both looked at the lacerated skin on his knee. Skye suggested, "He broke the divider bar. Looks like it ripped into his knee."

"He's been banged up and stressed. I can get him fixed up but I can't promise he'll ever race again."

Skye stepped back and away from him. "I knew you were going to say what I've been thinking, and he's no good to me lame. No matter how much he was worth, he's not worth a hill of beans now." He looked around and spotting Rusty among the chatting group, took him aside and did some straight talking.

JoAnn had seen and heard it all, and unnoticed, ran inside, intent of learning what Skye had to say to Rusty. Noticing Gabe and Pierce, she mouthed a thank you. She had been so thankful for all the men who had stopped to help in the emergency. She went to her sons. "What a terrible shame. Such a beautiful chestnut."

John looked past her and pointed, "Think Rusty wants you."

"Come with me." She went over to the two men and waited for one of them to direct their conversation her way. With a hand on her shoulder, Rusty explained the situation.

"Buy him! We couldn't possibly afford . . ."

Hang on there," he admonished. "'scuse us Skye." He walked down the alley, motioning the boys to follow.

JoAnn caught Marie and Dana's eye, and motioned for them to follow her.

"I'll make it simple an' quick. He's an old man, been cartin' this three-hundred-an'-fifty-thousand dollar horse all over the country tryin' ta sell him. No one would give him his price. Now that he probably will never run again, he's had it an' will let you have him, here an' now, as is, for five thousand dollars!"

"Wow!" Rob began with quick shush from his mom.

"I feel the same way," John spoke quietly. "Can he do that?"

"Of course. He can do what he wants. But, we cannot

take advantage of the man. He is obviously beside himself. Tomorrow, he'll feel differently."

"And if he doesn't?"

Rusty spoke up. "That horse would be a peck of trouble, that's what. I don't think you're wantin' ta go there, JoAnn, even if he offered him ta you for one dollar.'

"But just think of the great start it would give us."

"Man, what a chance!" Rob voiced his youthful thinking, as usual.

"That horse's manners aren't the best, but then he ain't castrated either." He chewed on his pipe stem a minute, while the family and Marie watched him. "We don't know about his breeding potential or his age. He may have a handsome pedigree, but if he can't get along with our horses, we couldn't keep him."

"In other words, right now, all we know is that he's a race horse worth money. Sounds risky, except, that, he likes me!" She wondered what their reaction would be to that statement, and waited to hear it and for them to calm down. "Dana and Marie know that I've been beside that horse from almost the beginning, talking and petting it, even outside the window. I believe I kept him calm down at the highway, and he calmed down in the stall the minute he heard me." She watched their reaction. "Believe me or not, I know what I know!"

Marie spoke up, "I watched and listened, Dana too, and she's right. Crazy to say, I know, but it's true, isn't it Dana?"

"I thought she was crazy to go to that trailer. But he did quiet down with her there and up here too."

"It wouldn't hurt to talk to him, would it?" John wanted to know.

"All," looking each in the eye, "come with me."

He wasn't reasonable, but he was old, probably older than Rusty, and he already had had one heart attack. After looking over the group, he told them, "Skys The Limit is for sale for five thousand dollars." He let that sink in. "Vet bills, trailer and all, for what it's worth." Again he waited. "No contingencies."

"What?" the children asked.

"I watched your discussion. I read lips; my wife can't hear. I've learned a lot from her."

JoAnn declared, "Mr. Lakewood, excuse me for saying so, but, you are in no condition to be making a business deal tonight. Why don't you stay over with us for a couple days, and see how Skys The Limit does. Maybe . . ."

"Nope. I'm dealing now and if you are accepting, the deal's done and I will still stay over a day or so, thank you."

Mr. Lakewood had all the papers necessary to climax the deal, for he had expected to sell Skys' The Limit long before this. First, they waited for Stu Farley to finish stitching Skys' The Limit's knee and check the strain, which Rusty knew would need continual care and anti-inflammatory drugs and rest. How to accomplish that would be a problem.

The joint capsule had been exposed. The tendons showed through a ripped layer of fascia. It must have been a sad sight. Putting his gear away, Stu said, "I'm happy to have the horse stabled and behind bars, as it were. I sewed him up with everything nicely in place, covered up the knee, and gave him a tetanus shot. Rusty, Ma'am, if you have a stable bandage, I'll put it on, or you may, if you can get near him."

Gabe and Pierce were still standing nearby. All were acquainted. All seemed to sense that something momentous had transpired, but what? Stu looked at Mr. Lakewood, and with a snap of his leather satchel, said, "I swabbed out every inch of his wound and puffed in some iodoform powder before I tacked down the loose ends of fascia. I think I did a pretty nifty job of needlework, if I do say so myself.

Think it will heal without a I think it will heal without leaving a scar."

Without waiting to find out, as always Gabe was right there reaching out his hand, "Rusty, JoAnn, you are going to need help with that horse. Pierce and I will run over any time of the day or night. Just give the house a call. Okay."

"Will do, thanks," Rusty said, as they shook hands. "Now while I get that bandage, you boys take all the people 'round here up ta the house for some coffee an' ice tea. Then I'll meet you in the office." He had a curious smile on his face, that said, "Somethin's up."

"Thanks, both of you," JoAnn said, shaking hands.

Gabe reintroduced Pierce to JoAnn before she jokingly suggested, "Mr. Reinhart, if you are as good with food as you are with tires, maybe right now you and Gabe could give Marie a hand in the kitchen, so she doesn't get trampled to death."

"Pierce, did you bring your apron?" Gabe asked, keeping step with JoAnn.

"Thought, I'd wear yours!" Pierce laughed.

"Mr. Farley," JoAnn, spoke to the vet as he reached the porch. Reaching forth her hand, "I haven't met you yet. I'm JoAnn Cobb, John Simpson's granddaughter. Would you join Mr. Lakewood, Rusty, and my family in the office, please? Boys, go ahead and take them in." Then turning to the many people scattered around the porch, kitchen and lawn, she spoke her sincere thanks on behalf of Mr. Lakewood and Skys' The Limit, "You might have to help yourself, but there'll be plenty of drinks and cookies in the kitchen."

Mr. Lakewood stayed three nights. He was amazed when JoAnn was the only one Sky would allow to touch him. She had changed the compresses and cooled and applied heat treatments to his leg, even slept in the next stall to him the first two nights. She was there when the vet checked him and she was the one to clean his stall, brush, and feed him.

Skye Lakewood, had no intention of selling the family a pig in a poke, even for a lousy five thousand dollars, so he said, as he pocketed JoAnn's check and closed the deal. He looked at JoAnn with the greatest admiration, and was a most satisfied man with new friends, when he finally drove down the lane. Skys' The Limit would never race again, but was with a family who fell in love with him, as much as Sky would let them. He had a clean, dry bed, food and water, and quiet. He began the long road of healing.

As soon as the car was started, Rusty declared to no one in particular, "Now we're in for it!"

"Please, no more, Rusty. We will have to deal with him best we can. He responds to me, so I'll care for him. I think, that eventually he will quiet down for you all too. Let's be patient, talk quietly and frequently, and Mr. Lakewood said he likes carrots and apples, soooo, let's see who can get him eating out of his hand first."

She looked around at the three of them for their reaction. Maybe Rusty was thinking that she was running with her idea but the only thing he said, was, "Don't forget ta be prayin' mighty hard about all this."

"Rusty, my brow is becoming furrowed from praying." She picked up her empty coffee cup and headed for the kitchen, but not before she heard him say, "Then, you're not trustin' enough."

She twisted around and spoke with a little ire in her voice. "Well, maybe, but neither does He expect us to sit here on a rocking chair and wait for Him to drop the answer into our lap. Sometimes He expects us to put feet to our prayers." She started to turn again for the kitchen but stopped. "We're going to have horses, I know that is what He wants. We're not planting those fields with seed for human consumption!"

"Now hold on there. Seems like that's becomin' a special phrase of mine." He winked at her. "Glad I don't have ta be remindin' you all about God's hand in all this, but the question comes, is this how He would want it done?"

"Okay, Dear Friend, maybe I haven't been as open to His way as I should be, so determined am I to have horses. I have heard," pointing her finger to the three teenagers, "you guys have heard too, so. . ."

The next day, when John returned from an errand in town, he informed his mom about an unplanned visit to the library. "I drove by and sat for a while outside that big old grey building, until I gathered up the courage to go in and ask Jodi for a date. You should have seen her," he said, as he pranced about the room. "She was dressed in a tan skirt of some kind and had on a grass green shirt; man did it look good with her hair. I watched her from behind the stacks and waited until she was alone before gathering up enough courage to talk to her. If she turned me down, I didn't want the whole town to know it."

"Well?" JoAnn asked, impatiently.

"She said I had to meet her parents, then, we could use a couple of their horses and go for a ride. I couldn't help myself, I almost danced down that long marble corridor!"

"In other words, she said, yes."

"Yes! Yes, of course she said, yes," he shouted, giving her a hug.

"You don't know whether or not she is a Christian, do you? My next question, when do I meet her? I trust your judgement, but think that I should meet her the same as she feels her parents should meet you."

Caught up short, "No I don't, but I've been thinking about it and I'll find out right away. I know better than to get seriously interested in someone who isn't saved."

"It sounded like you had thrown caution to the wind."

"No way, man. I know which side my bread is buttered on, and since you trust me, perhaps we should wait awhile to let her know we are neighbors."

JoAnn watched with satisfaction as he fairly danced to their station wagon that evening right after dinner. Oh, how she would have to talk to God about John and Jodi. A horse is one thing to control, but a son, that's a horse of a different color, and he didn't even know if she was born again!

She had dropped Rob and Dana off at church for a youth activity and John would pick them up later, so now she was alone for the first time since arriving at the ranch, and it didn't sit well with her. Wandering about the house, straightening up here and there, settling down to read, switching on the television, nothing took away the miserable feeling deep inside.

*Don't tell me, I'm beginning to need a friend,* she mused, slapping shut the book in her hands and turning off the television. *I can always find something to do in the office, or outside.* But she didn't and couldn't and retired early to her bedroom where she succeeding in reading herself to sleep.

# Chapter 19

Before noon on the first day of July, when Sky's The Limit had been in the paddock for a few days, Dana cantered up the lane waving the mail. She handed the two envelopes with embossed return addresses to her mother without taking time to dismount. As she had gained more confidence and strength and could saddle-up by herself, she was allowed more freedom, and JoAnn happily noticed that she was actually beginning to enjoy riding.

"Ring the bell, Dana," she spoke up to her. "The Lord has blessed us with positive responses and they sound quite interesting."

Josh Miller and Tim Evans, were still employed and working under Roy Owens' leadership. Rusty was confident that they knew their business and with a little prodding occasionally, would work conscientiously. Rusty and Marie joined the Cobbs as they crowded into the station wagon and headed out the dirt road. They planned to reach the Cloverdale Ranch before noon, which was one of the two responses they had received in the mail.

John drove, Rusty navigated without his pipe; the first

time they had seen him without it. About forty-five minutes on, they turned into a rural route, which led them past dark railed pastures and groves with mares and foals nibbling on the lush pasture. On impulse, JoAnn directed John to turn into the lane between a fenced driveway of the Sedgewick Farms.

They hadn't traveled but a hundred feet before coming to a small stone gate house from which emerged a cowboy, who indicated for them to stop.

"Howdy folks. Lost?" he drawled out, scanning them as he spoke through the opened car windows.

JoAnn, who was seated in the middle in the back seat, leaned across Dana to answer. "We're here to inquire about buying horses. Could you direct us to the building where we might talk to the owner or manager."

The old timer stooped down and looked everyone over before he answered, "Don't reckon we have horses to sell to you."

Incensed, she demanded, "Why not to us? What do you know about us?'

"Well, now, don't go and get all heated up, Madam. I only meant that we sell and buy only through a syndicate, and I don't recollect ever seeing you here before." He turned to spit a long stream of tobacco juice, which made JoAnn grimace, before he continued. "Can I be of further help?"

"No, guess not, thanks anyway," she said, leaning heavily back against the seat.

John however, asked the old cowboy for directions to the Cloverdale Ranch, before he began to turn the car around. "Thanks," he called, as the cowboy put his hand out to stop him again.

"Jest thought of something. Wouldn't hurt none for you to look around. It's a might nice place."

After checking her watch, JoAnn decided they had about a

half-hour to spare since the Cloverdale Ranch was just down the road.

"Why not, John stated. I've always wanted to see inside a thoroughbred ranch."

"Please," Dana begged.

"All right, you win."

"Good," the cowboy said, pushing up his hat from his forehead with his thumb. "Just follow the fence as it bears right around the curve, till you come to a long white building, with green doors. Should be someone there can show you around. Give me your name, so as I can call ahead."

For some reason, she called out, "Simpson Ranch."

"Simpson! From Donaldson?"

Yes, Sir!" was John's proud reply.

"You're more than welcome here," he said, with a wave forward of his hand.

Rusty remarked, "Wouldn't be a bad idea to use you're grandpop's name from now on."

"I think you're right," she agreed, looking around, secretly pleased that they had all taken the extra time needed to look so spiffy. The new dress outfits of jeans and cotton shirts, yet unwashed, the boots and hats kept for clean up only, gave a sharp edge to their appearance, and hopeful dickering. Marie was wearing a denim jumper with an embroidered blouse and JoAnn knew why Dana wore her jumper. Rusty, of course was dressed as they were.

Pete Weaver, the manager, a middle-aged, tightly built cowboy, upon learning that the guests weren't just a bunch of tourists, was in an expansive mood as he led them in an inspection of the meticulous mahogany paneled stables to show off some of their champion occupants.

A powerfully built stallion stood in isolation at the far end of the aisle. Except for the blaze marking the length of his face and white socks on his strong back legs, he was a masterpiece of reddish-brown velvet.

Dana, beginning to see the beauty of ranching, pointed him out. They stood about twenty-five feet from him, still he excited them as they did him. Showing his teeth, laying back his ears, he warned them to keep their distance, even as JoAnn would have approached him. The manager and Rusty called to stop her.

"Can't afford to contaminate the others," he warned.

"Whew! What I'd give to ride a horse like that," John said, drawing in his breath. It seemed he was forgetting about Skys' The Limit.

Rob whistled softly, but stayed true to his colors, when he remarked, "He's a beauty, but no better than Sky."

"He's a beauty for sure, young fella'. Too bad we may have to get rid of him," the manager remarked sadly.

"You mean he's for sale?" John asked, excitedly, looking from Rusty to his mother.

"Could be, Son, but he's just come sick with a viral disease which we haven't isolated yet. We haven't decided what his end will be."

"Oh, no, Mom," Dana cried out.

"Back to the slaughter house!" Rob remarked, disgustedly.

Mr. Beaver noticed the look of dismay and caught the meaning through Rob's statement. "Not so fast there, young man," he scowled at Rob. "Brawn Beauty, might contaminate the rest of our thoroughbreds and that could run into a loss of millions of dollars, but you didn't hear me mention anything about a slaughter house."

"I apologize, Sir."

JoAnn broke in before Rob could say anything else. "It's just that we have inherited Grandpop Simpson's ranch, and we are having a hard time finding horses to stock it." JoAnn explained.

The man looked at all the women, and then focusing in on JoAnn said, "You must be John's granddaughter. He never came here that he didn't speak of you."

"Yes, I am. Thank you for the special thought." Then unable to hold back the question that propelled itself to the surface, she asked, "Sir, do you really think you might sell him?"

"He may not be any good to you, Madam. He is twelve years old and he might just up and die on you."

"But if we could look him over and then were willing to take that chance." She turned to Rusty.

"What can you tell me about his symptoms?"

"Like I said, he's only been incubated a few hours," the man said, indicating for the rest to stay while he led Rusty and JoAnn to a stall where they put on masks, gown, and gloves.

Since Brawn Beauty became more excited by their movements, JoAnn waited nearby, listening.

"Any fever, nasal discharge, cough, sensitive lymph nodes," Rusty wanted to know, waiting for the manager to take the reins and quiet the horse.

"No cough yet. Lymph nodes seem okay." He patted the horse on his neck to keep him quiet as Rusty felt the horse's legs and feet and noticed some swelling and heat.

"For a sick horse, he's patient an' quiet now, I'll say that for him. Maybe he was just testin' us or is depressed an' doesn't want ta move." He moved to the horse's head to see if he had been chewing on the front of the stall where he was standing, and to check his mouth, his eyes and nose. They weren't running and his coat was "blooming". "Any fever, diarrhea, loss of appetite?"

"All just developing."

"He's a real mystery."

Observing, listening, made JoAnn realize she was in over her head, but she also remembered a time when Rusty and her grandpop had cured a horse that had developed cold-like symptoms and on which the vet had given up. She had slowly moved closer to the horse and looked at Rusty before she asked again about buying him.

"Well, now, Madam," Pete Weaver, demurred, "the syndicate owns him and they would have to make that decision, and have the option of acquiring the shares, first. I could show you the stud book and papers . . ."

"Oh, no, thank you. I would want him just because he is beautiful and deserves a chance to live. I am not interested in racing horses but I want this horse. So you call the members, or whatever it is you do, and I will talk to my leader, the Lord Jesus Christ, and we'll see if they both give us the go ahead.

Walking back to the stall to remove their protective clothing, JoAnn stated, "We couldn't take him back with us today anyway," JoAnn having removed the protective clothing, was searching her purse for the note pad she had placed there. Then writing her name and address and her grandpop's name in parenthesis, she handed it to him, shook his hand, and asked him to get in touch as soon as possible. "Sorry I don't have a card."

"I'll be in touch, maybe tomorrow," he said looking at the note, then nodding briefly to them as they joyfully headed toward the car.

They broke into a chorus of happy shouts and war-whoops, once back inside the car and past the gatehouse,

"Do you think you can save him, Rusty?"

"Well, he could have anything from influenza ta rhinopneumonitis, possibly even encephalitis or any number of internal parasites. I wouldn't want ta touch some of them with a ten foot pole."

"Whatever rhinopneumonitis is or even encephalitis, although I have heard the last one before. But why?"

"It is an upper respiratory infection passed along by

horses' coughing or handlers not washing their hands. Seems simple, but it can be fatal."

"Ouch."

"Wow!" Dana exclaimed. "Mom, you said horses get sick just like we do and he looked so healthy."

"Now hold your horses, so ta speak." The sound in his voice had a warning in it, which made them all listen intently. "You're here at a first rate establishment which means the vet takes good care of every horse an' would have them up to date on vaccinations. But his symptoms stymie me an' I have a feelin' they have the vet up a wall too."

"So it could be a fatal disease or it could just be a troublesome one with which they wouldn't want to be bothered."

"That's what I think all right. Happens all too often an' the horse is put down. I think God led us here today ta see this animal an' wouldn't be a bit surprised that you get a call. A few more days will tell an' a few more days could be too late for the horse, but good for us. Of course, if it's God's will for us to get him, He'll help me. Another thing, they can't take the chance of contaminatin' the other horses."

JoAnn suggested, "We have all the room in the world to protect him and keep him away from our horses until he is well."

John looked over at him, "You mean, the disease by that time could have proven to be encephalitis, which is bad for the horse, but good for us, because we wouldn't have thrown away our money?"

"That's it!"

"But a few days could also mean it's just a simple, time consuming troublesome infection with which they don't have the time and space to deal." JoAnn considered aloud.

"Think positive, you guys. Don't forget we have the Lord on our side," Rob suggested.

"That's right, Brother," Dana chimed in.

"Well, Rusty?" JoAnn asked, reaching forward, laying a hand on his shoulder.

"Well, why are you in such an all-fired hurry. We gotta' pray, then see."

Things got quiet; this old cowboy was mentoring them again. What a job he had on his hands! Before they arrived at Cloverdale, he spoke again. "Now don't be forgettin' the trouble we'r havin' with Skys' The Limit. Thoroughbreds an' good grades take more care an' cost more ta feed. Brawn Beauty will stand alone, probably shouldn't mix him with others. If he is always testy, he could be a pain in the neck, just like Sky was, is."

Rusty's words of caution seemed to go in one ear and out the other. She had ignored the suggestions about bloodlines, and performance statistics from Mr. Beaver. What a fool! It's a wonder Rusty hadn't berated her for it.

He was just the most beautiful horse, and the most powerful looking horse she had ever seen, even comparing him to Sky and Gabe's Solomon. She might have to end up putting him to sleep, but she certainly hoped not. *Father, don't let this deal go through unless he will live. I have played the fool in this transaction, running ahead again. Forgive me and trip me when I do that.*

Still thinking to herself about him, she decided he would have every chance in this world to recover. *One thing sure, you will never see the inside of a slaughterhouse as long as you would be with us.* Then, *Wait till Gabe sees him; I hope he's a little jealous.*

She turned her attention to Rusty again, who was lecturing the children. "Never buy an animal without doin' a lot of checkin' an' lookin', certainly not ta let the past experience be you're rule of thumb. Buyin' a horse ain't a beauty contest."

He turned to look over his shoulder directly into JoAnn eyes. "What price did you decide on for Brawn Beauty if you do get a chance ta buy him?"

"I remember what you said about establishing a price range. I certainly don't expect another bargain like we got for Sky."

"You're not forgettin' about a sales contract, trial period an' other contingencies? Are you goin' ta give them a down payment an' the rest after a two-week trial, or jest pay outright? What about an insurance contract against death, debilitatin' injuries before the contract is signed or you remove the horse from their property?"

"Actually, I didn't set a price in my head because I don't know what it should be. I trust your guidance on purchases. But, I was wondering, after what you said about Brawn Beauty, that if I could reduce the price with cash on the barrel head without a trial period, considering his condition, if it might not be wise to go that way. I mean, coming from a reputable stable and all . . ."

He didn't answer her but pointed instead. "We're comin' up on the other ranch now, so just keep in mind what we talked about an' don't go runnin' ahead of yourself."

# Chapter 20

At the Cloverdale Ranch, Rusty explained through example, why they would or would not want this or that horse.

"This mare's got good limbs, head is well formed, prominent withers, won't be hard ta keep a saddle on her. Any horse should fit into a rectangle, except for his head an' neck, an' look at her eyes, kind they are an' well proportioned."

"What's that mean?" Rob wanted to know.

"Means she's probably reliable, with a good temper, not nappy. Now look at that one," pointing to a brown and white mare. "Her eyes are little, squinty, probably a horse I couldn't trust an' you've got ta be able ta trust your horse."

Rusty worked with them as if the owner was not there; this he had to do. "Hop up there, Son," looking at John. "Put her through her paces, I want ta watch her legs, see if she favors one or the other, an' then take her for a good ride an' gallop. Listen for a whistle in her breathing."

On and on he taught them, showed them what to look for. About the only thing he didn't do was test for worms and parasites, but he did ask to see the latest vet report.

There was no doubt that the horses from these ranches had

been lovingly and patiently trained. They came to the small group with friendly whickering sounds.

Finally, between the two ranches from which the Cobs had received letters, the family was satisfied with a total of four mares with good blood and conformation, which could be used for riding and breeding. One was a registered mare which hadn't dropped a foal in three years. One had produced a beauty last spring. If they were successful in obtaining Brawn Beauty, he could breed with Flora's Girl and the seemingly barren new mare, as well as with the beautiful chestnut mare from the Cloverdale Ranch. They were in business!

JoAnn pocketed her checkbook and other papers, then shook hands in confirmation and thanked the ranchers for their patience in allowing Rusty to teach them how to choose horses. Both ranches had been well run with a reputation of excellence. She was very pleased when they offered to deliver the horses for a nominal fee. Finally, as they were leaving, she asked to have her name and interest in buying good stock, passed around.

Bubbling over with their good fortune, they could hardly settle down long enough to bow their head in a prayer of thanksgiving to the One who had brought this all about. They knew deep in their hearts that these two ranchers, who were the only ones to answer their ads, had not been a stroke of luck, and they wanted to thank their Sovereign God. As the sextet headed home, they were singing songs of praise to the King of Kings, the creator of horses. But, as they neared the ranch, the wise voice of wisdom persisted in arousing their cautious instincts.

"What will you do with Brawn Beauty if God opens the way for you ta buy him?"

JoAnn knew the question was directed to her. "Well, I had planned on breeding to establish stock in the cheapest way, but also with a controlled, careful, and rational program. I have to confess I am saying something I have only read about, which books also warned that chance has much to do with the final product."

"And what is your end plan for these horses?"

"Sell them for profit through advertisement or through auctions, and I don't mean the kind at Donaldson. Also, I really like the idea of getting a college program started. We have lots of room and the right kind of buildings, which we won't be using for years down the road.

"The only thing is, I hadn't considered such high class bloodlines as Brawn Beauty and Sky's The Limit have, nor those good breed mares from Cloverdale, to enter into the picture. And, you know what, as I compare the horses we have seen today, I realize Bill and Bob are pretty decent looking."

"That they are, but if'n you get that stallion, you'r doublin' your problems."

"So you said, I really was listening."

"But not hearin'!"

"Okay, you're right, Rusty. I'll hear now. So teach, but let's stop at a nice restaurant and eat and learn at the same time."

The group adjusted themselves around a corner booth and placed their orders before Rusty spoke, primarily to JoAnn. "You'll need a strong six foot high fence an' it may need ta be double fenced, wherever other stallions will be pastured. Brawn Beauty'll go crazy when he first gets his freedom on a strange place with strange trainers. Should you get him, you better have the Sedgewick people send someone ta turn him out when the time comes. You need ta check up on local zoning laws an' restrictions, an' third, how will you use him? Begin you're own syndicate an' sell stud fee, shares?"

"You say that as if you have a bad taste in your mouth about it. We didn't have this discussion when we bought Sky!" she said, a bit testily. "I should have asked about his breeding history, so, I guess I'm not thinking of originating my own syndicate." She almost scoffed at the redundancy of their conversation.

Marie, sensing the overloaded circuits, spoke up. "Aren't we counting our chickens before they're hatched?'

"That's right, Mom," Rob said. "We may get Brawn Beauty and he may just die on us, so. . ."

"So, all I know is that I want to raise horses, good horses, and had never thought of thoroughbreds. Our horses won't have to be worth millions of dollars or have distinct bloodlines. We'll match selectively, improving the stock; a touch of Brawn Beauty and Skys' blood will better any breed, and I didn't plan on outside mares coming to our stables either. If my mares won't foal and my stallions can't perform, then they'll have to be retrained to make good riding horses for us or someone else." She spoke with more resignation than determination.

"Let's eat," John spoke up, seeing the waitress coming with an overloaded tray of food.

Rusty seemed satisfied in that he had gotten her to think more openly than before, even though he had parted a few hairs in doing so. "I think you'll get what you want, JoAnn. We'll manage our program ta bring your dreams ta reality, even if those dreams have ta be a bit rearranged. That's a promise." He reached across the table ta lay a big, rough, but friendly hand on hers.

"Thanks Rusty," she spoke meekly, "you are a true and valued friend."

# Chapter 21

Summer had shifted into high gear, with hazy, shimmering, heated days. Flat yellow masses crowned the yarrow, and the honey-filled purple thistles were alive with black and yellow bumblebees. Gray young starlings and large cowbirds followed their adopted mothers; baby robins peeped endlessly to be fed.

Storms spread across the fields of wheat, corn, hay, and oats in sweeping deluges, sometimes destructively, but always nurturing. Their own small herd of beef cattle grazed on unneeded pastureland, and the neighbor's sheep continued to nibble land that had been unused for years.

These days a person could nibble his way along a trail gathering handfuls of raspberries or pinching off a spearmint leaf full of mint flavor to chew on. By the middle of September it would show-off it's pretty pink blossoms. During the coming weeks, one could count on a bounty of blackberries and wild cherries as each ripened in the sunshine and heat of the July days.

Every day as JoAnn worked with Sky, she thought of Brawn Beauty. She and Sky had clearly bonded and he was healing and responding to exercise beautifully. Howbeit, he was still feisty around others. Now Solomon was a different story. He shied from Gabe, but whickered at the big horse as he trotted to the fence in welcome. Solomon and Sky had bonded too!

JoAnn felt God wanted her to have Brawn Beauty, and sure enough, by paying cash without limitations, she had gotten him for a song. His health chart and records accompanied her contract registration certificate and receipt, and from it, she and Rusty learned everything about him, from his normal respiration rate, worming program and inoculations, to breeding history and pedigree.

It was time for booster shots to ward off normal viral diseases, and Brawn Beauty received them pronto from Stu, the vet, whom Rusty had been using for years on a regular basis. Stu also tested the feces for the presence of parasites. Like with Sky, for ten days Brawn Beauty did nothing but rest. Well, if you could have visitors every daylight hour, and someone checking for diarrhea, swelling in the legs, food consumption monitored, or checking his eyes and nose for discharge, and of course, keeping a watch with a thermometer for high fever, and on and on, and still call that rest, well. . .

Even Gabe, and Roy who was now the acclaimed head equestrian, and the other workers couldn't stay away from him. But Gabe, who resolutely visited every day, was not jealous, just impressed "with all one thousand pounds of him", as he put it.

JoAnn found him one day getting a feces sample. "Really, Gabe, you don't have to do this."

He quickly tried to stand between his product and her, seemingly to protect her.

"And you don't need to protect me. I know what has to be done, has to be done, by someone."

Clearly embarrassed, he walked away from Brawn Beauty to the tack room and back again. She knew that when he heard the horse whinny, he would know she was in the stall with Brawn Beauty.

He watched the horse nuzzle her as he returned. "You're not afraid of the big brute are you?"

"Sometimes I am a little nervous. Today he's gentler; tomorrow, who knows. We patiently take one day at a time and hope for the best." She checked his eyes and nostrils as she spoke. "I hope your sample will be negative."

"It looked right, a good omen he doesn't have worms." He slowly approached the animal as he talked, ready to pat him on the hip, but Brawn Beauty began gamboling about. "Easy boy, easy." Gabe spoke as he continued to move toward JoAnn, not touching the horse.

Without warning, Brawn Beauty lunged toward them, "Whoa!" Gabe yelled, pushing JoAnn away as he grappled for the halter. "Get out Jo! Whoa!" he yelled.

"Mom, look out," came Dana's voice. She had just reached the stall and cried out upon seeing the horse's reaction.

Just as suddenly as he lunged, he stopped and whinnied, as if to say, that was a fun game.

Gabe still held the halter as he looked at the animal and patted his neck. "Don't do that again," he said in a firm voice. "There's a couple kids around here we don't want hurt. Understand!"

Brawn Beauty turned his head and whinnied as he looked at JoAnn. A little shaken, but not undaunted, she started to step back into the stall.

"Mom, don't! Just because you had such good luck with Sky, doesn't mean you will with every horse." Dana called, trying to stop her.

"I honestly think he understands what Gabe said. You do, don't you, boy." she stated as she patted him, before stepping back out into the aisle.

Gabe, picked up the sample he had dropped before he

followed her and noticed a little tremble. "You okay?" he asked, attempting to put his arm around her shoulder.

She twisted away from it, but did lay her right arm across Dana's back. *Something is wrong with my left arm!* "It's the first time I've had a train try to run over me, but yes, I'm okay now." But she wasn't; that beating of her heart in her chest and throat was there again, hurting and making her want to rub her arm. *That's new, I never had it traveled down my left arm before.* She looked at Gabe but didn't let go of Dana, who didn't mind her mom touching her. She couldn't be totally ignorant to him. "Thanks for being there."

"Anytime," he grinned, unaware of her problem, as they walked into the sunshine. "The way the fog enveloped the earth this morning, I didn't think the sun would be as industrious as to sting. It's going to be a corker of a day."

Feeling better again, she looked at Dana, "Well, before this July day winds up too tightly, Dana, Rob, and I are off to tour their new school facilities and become acquainted with the band and choral directors. We're a little excited."

"I can hardly wait," Dana smiled at Gabe. "That's what I came to tell you. Rob is ready. I'll go get him and meet you at the car," and she ran off.

When JoAnn and Gabe reached Solomon, she waited for Gabe to take hold of the reins before approaching his magnificent head to give his nose a pat. "If you want, I could drop off that sample at the vet's."

"Jo . . ."

"Gabe, I know what horse manure looks and smells like," she laughed then. It actually felt good to unwind a little with him. "If it would make you feel better, I'll put it in a container."

"It would," he grinned again, handing it to her, and starting to say something else, thought the better of it. "Guess I better get back to work."

"And the kids are waiting." She gave Solomon a pat on the rump as Gabe rode away. "Thanks again."

"Anytime," he said, laughing aloud this time.

She watched him ride off for a good piece, before turning to the car. *It is nice to have such a strong man around as a friend. He never pressed her for personal information, never referred again to how she looked or to their past relationship. Perhaps, I could be more civil with him, could greet him more enthusiastically and be more optimistic about our future relationship. After all, since we are neighbors and I intend to live here untill I die, and we will be seeing one another, I had better learn to relax around him.* Deep in her heart she knew there was more to it than that.

She had persevered in the attention given to Brawn Beauty's incubation period, and nothing developed that Rusty and the vet couldn't handle; JoAnn felt they were home free.

"We still need ta watch him, he could become reinfected," Rusty warned.

"Don't say that!" JoAnn cried.

"Think positive," Rob, reminded them again.

JoAnn wondered aloud about that. "Positive is a good thought and if you think about it, with all this attention, he has become less agitated and testy, just as Sky has. At least he hasn't lunged at anyone again."

"I think he's ready for a little ride, don't you Rusty?" John stated, with a gleam in his eye.

"And you are the one ta do it?"

"I'd like to think so."

"JoAnn?"

"You had thought the Sedgewick people should turn him out."

"Changed my mind. I never worked with hot-blooded racehorses, but this horse is extremely well mannered and greets us with friendly whickers of welcome. I think John could give it a try."

They all watched as John approached with the blanket and saddle. Brawn Beauty seemed to wait patiently, just pawing at the ground a little, as if anxious to run. At first they thought the stallion would fast-start, his powerful muscles were quivering to get going. His dark eyes watched everything and his beautifully sculpted head turned as John put one foot in the stirrup and swung his weight up and into the saddle. Brawn Beauty was ready when John gave him the get-go.

What a sight, as John walked him through the gate, then allowed him to run into a gallop down the road and back.

"He's perfect. Man, I love this horse!" he exclaimed, as he dismounted. "He'll do anything you ask him to," he said, taking the reins and leading him back to his private paddock.

"Well, that's enough for today. Let's watch him an' see how he reacts ta that little run," Rusty suggested. "Skys The Limit is about ready for a ride, too."

JoAnn pointed a finger to herself. "I am the one to do that, when he's really healed."

Reluctantly they all agreed and went about finishing up required duties.

# Chapter 22

The Simpson name, the rumor that JoAnn would buy good horses for eventual resale to keep them from the auction block, as well as her fair price, brought responses. Inspections were made of various establishments' stock, from the yearlings, to the broodmares. It seemed that the managers wanted to show off a bit before bringing out the animal that they knew she was seeking.

These trips consumed valuable time, but established her name with the ranchers; it was time well spent. She was able to purchase several mares: palominos, a black and a brown chestnut, and a roan.

By the middle of August, JoAnn was feeling swamped with the workload and more concerned than she wanted to admit regarding that rapid, frightening heartbeat she felt in her throat, arm, and the pressure in her chest. Still she did nothing about it nor told anyone, except that quite by accident, she found that if she touched the artery on either side of her neck, she could bring the beating back to normal. Too frequently she had to use this technique. One time, however, she apparently pressed either too hard or too long on the same spot, and almost fainted, so she was more careful now and not so worried.

She kept in contact with Mr. Lakewood, always bringing him up-to-date on the physical and emotional condition of Skys' The Limit. Every horse before it was purchased, had been carefully examined, put through its traces, and passed the twelve-point list they had compiled. Each registration certificate, pedigree, and owner/seller was checked. Rusty was the lead man; Stu was the one who actually made the decision on the health of the animal.

The boys, Rusty, and JoAnn hovered over the signing of the written contracts, the record of transfer, especially for the breeder's certificate for the mares in foal. They were instructed to file the transfer on them immediately, so that, after the foals were born, she could register them. Every name had to coincide. Rusty and the reputable owners were very helpful.

Although they were pasturing the animals and the ranch had more than sufficient acreage available in which to adequately separate and isolate the horses, they still needed to supplement the natural nutrients and minerals they received from the grasses. The family of six, which included Marie and Rusty, enjoyed the job of making sure each horse was ridden and grained regularly. These rides afforded Dana a chance to keep a check on her Hereford, and their small staff of three, took every opportunity to ride also.

Adequate clean water was a necessity, with the ground surrounding the trough well drained. Cleaning out old bathtubs twice daily was becoming a pain in the neck, but the men worked for her grandpop and would work for her till she had firm footing.

Roy and his men saw that salt blocks were put in the bottom of the protected hay bunks, for few pastures adequately supply all the minerals a horse needs. Three sided deep access shelters were built on the highest point in each pasture to give the horses shelter from the wind, rain, and eventual snow. These were large enough to work as storage sheds as well.

JoAnn found herself spending more time in the office than she desired. Yet the workload continued to be unbearably demanding and the pressures intimidating. The children had assumed more of the burden than teenagers should have, but they would soon be off to school and involved in their own activities.

Already she or John took them to school twice a week for band practice. They hadn't spent much time practicing their instruments during the summer, and it was good to hear the trumpet and clarinet sounds wafting over the paddocks. That would leave her with two men short, for the children had worked like men. Marie now worked alone. Should she consider help for her? Should she hire a manager? Could she afford it? Could she afford not to? The books, the books, the books!

So tired, she had curtailed her infrequent morning rides in favor of that extra hour's rest. She missed them and refused to entertain the notion that she missed her occasional ride with Gabe.

One thing certain, she knew they could not afford to miss church, prayer meeting, and their own quiet time with the Lord. Through the Bible they found guidance for nearly every situation they encountered. Through wise teachers and pastors, God provided help in their understanding of His book of instructions.

One particular Sunday, Rev. Miller reminded the congregation that the Christian life is like a sporting event. "That's why, five different times in Ephesians, the apostle Paul referred to one's spiritual life as a "race". This race takes preparation, determination, diligence, and it requires completing the race. To help you in your race, Ephesians lays out God's plan. We have God's patience, His grace, but we have to accept the responsibility for change . . ."

*Well, taking on the ranch was a lot like running a race. I had no idea the stamina, determination, and diligence it would require. I am determined to complete this race with the help of Almighty God! Thank you Father, that I have already taken the initial steps of responsibility by accepting Jesus as my Saviour and agreeing with you, for you to take over the leadership of my life. Being your child, your daughter, has not been an easy concept to understand, but you have changed my life, my behavior, my thinking, and you will strengthen me to finish the race through your grace.*

*Right now, I feel like I am in a race against time, trying to get John ready for college, looking for a good used vehicle for him, transporting Rob and Dana back and forth to band practice, and school hasn't even started. Oh, how I thank you for them, for the help they have been to me, for their steadfastness under all this pressure. Continue to lead and direct their lives and protect them against the wiles of the devil.*

*Thank you for this congregation, for the young people, the pastor and their positive influence and the depths of their maturity.*

Dana nudged her and whispered, "Mom, is something wrong?"

"No, Honey, just a private talk with God." JoAnn took her hand for just a minute as she smiled a thanks to her daughter. You simply don't hold on to a teenager's hand for long for fear of embarrassing them, the last thing on earth this mother would want to do.

# Chapter 23

JoAnn occasionally attended the auctions to keep a check on them and noted only a slight drop in the number of horses up for bid. She still remained aloof from the other bidders, but made a mental record of the disappointed buyers. She wasn't ready yet to buttonhole them or invite them to look over her stock.

Gabe was there of course, but she was able to avoid an encounter with him. Their two businesses did not jibe.

At the end of a very busy, frustrating day, she picked at the stuffed pork chop, parsley potatoes, and green beans au gratin. The Waldorf salad, her favorite, was the only food she couldn't resist.

The kids, too, were so tired at the end of the day; they literally fell into bed following dinner. John complained of never having time to see Jodi, and Dana, that no one had time to be with her. Rusty never complained, but JoAnn realized he was too old for the heavy workload he had assumed.

The kids were right; the only time she had a relaxed moment to talk with them was to or from band practice. There were still sixty seconds in a minute, which meant they still had as much time as always, it was just that those sixty seconds were too jammed full of activities. John had informed her that Jodi seemed to have a typical liberal attitude about being born again and JoAnn had never had the time to talk with him about her again. Time had become a diminishing convenience.

Stocking the ranch had become a 'cause' with them, as Rob had mentioned, and would send them all to an early grave, unless they hired someone to help them, and soon. Persons with less fortitude would have quit by now and searched out a less onerous mission. She had read that pressure turns coal into beautiful diamonds; she would have to talk to God about that. She wasn't thinking of becoming a diamond.

Some days later as she sat in the scroll back Duxbury armchair at the head of the dining room table, she asked Rusty, "Remember awhile back I mentioned hiring someone to take over here as manager? Have you given it any thought?"

He knew that until she began selling horses, she was already laying out a lot of money, but he realized more than she did, that she needed help and he knew just the man.

"Yes, I have."

"Anyone come to mind to fit the bill?"

"Yes, an' I've been prayin' about it too. The name God has given me was an' still is, Gabe Holland!"

It seemed as if he had been waiting to say that ever since the first day in June when she had arrived there, as if he, God, and Gabe had a conspiracy going.

"But Gabe . . ." She knew she couldn't wrangle with him about this, but she didn't dare consider him; could she even pray about him? Still, how could she argue against Rusty and God, without revealing more of her personal life than she wanted him to know, and without taking hold of the reins she had given over to God's hands. God knew, so what was she to do?

Rusty stopped her run away thoughts. "I don't know what

you're thinkin', but I happen ta know that he's unhappy over there an' would jump at the chance ta work on the other end of the horse business."

Did he know about those morning rides? "Do you know something I should? Have you already talked with him about this?" she stalled.

"Yes and no. The way I've been hearin' it, is, there's a conflict of interest over there by the name of Rocko. He's a young go-getter, usurpin' authority an' violating Reinhart's practices."

"And," John interjected, "pushing his weight around, the way Jodi talks."

"I believe I've seen the man," JoAnn stated, not happy with the mental picture she could recall of him.

"He's a bad egg, I can tell you," Rusty remarked, sourly. "He'll ruin Reinhart if someone don't stop him."

"And you think he's the reason Gabe would leave, not because . . ., well, never mind."

He grinned as if he knew her thoughts, but said as carefully as he could, "Sure of it. God has a way of workin' our circumstances ta His an' our benefit. His dad taught him everything a body needs ta know about ranchin', an' horses an' beef cattle. That's why Reinhart kept him on as manager."

She had been praying about it too, but Gabe's name, no one's name, ever came to her mind. Possibly because it was an insincere cry for help, or she was too blind, too much against Gabe.

Reluctantly, against her better wishes she murmured, "Since you have already talked to him, contact him for me, Rusty, and arrange an interview if you find he really is interested."

"What's that?"

"You heard me."

She could at least do that for God and Rusty, although

Gabe would be the last man she would want as manager even though he was probably the best man. Knowing God, Gabe is just the man she needs in more ways than one! Could she take the chance of him living closer than next door? That too would have to be up to God!

"Nope," he declined, between puffs of his pipe.

"What do you mean, nope?" she asked, astonished at his attitude. She happened to glance around at the children and Marie and saw a glint of amusement in her eyes, and something she didn't understand in John's.

"Too formal, that's all."

With a raised eyebrow, she suggested more carefully, "Call him then and ask him to drop by, that you have a business proposition to offer him that he won't be able to resist."

*That's it! Get it over with. Resist? He will not resist. I know Gabe will not refuse an invitation to visit me, the ranch, or anyone connected with it or me. Resist? He would not resist! He will jump at the chance. I feel trapped, but that feeling inside of me is not tightening nor causing me dismay.*

"Nope!"

"Rusty, what is it with you?"

"I'll do the askin' all right, but you do the talkin'."

"All right, already," and the kids burst out laughing and she couldn't help joining in when Marie did. Was God forcing her hand? Suddenly she found the thought slightly pleasant. Perhaps Louis's hold over her was diminishing for there was only one area of ranching that literally turned her stomach. It was handled so unnaturally to her, so much like he had handled her. She didn't like to hear the rutting squeal of the stallion as he mounted the mare. Those were the days she stayed as far away from the breeding barn as possible.

"Well, let him come! What harm could there possibly be? Rusty, why did you think of Gabe in the first place?"

"Because you, Roy, the help, and I can't always go out ta

care for the horses, be here for the phone, the deliveries, go lookin' for new stock, keep abreast of the care of the property, an' what else I can't even think of.

"You're spreadin' out over many acres with the beef cattle, sheep, and horses. Too many for just us. You're ancestors built well an' we have completed all the preparations needed for now, so you're ranch is in good shape."

He hesitated, before went on. "But you're just startin'. The worst is yet ta come an' I . . . you . . . we, won't be able to handle it." It seemed like he was having such a hard time finding the right words to say. "You need ta hire a manager you can trust implicitly, someone who won't cheat you."

"How could he cheat me?" she asked, taking a drink of Marie's delicious ice tea, giving her a look that said, "this is great". She didn't want to believe it but had to, life was unfair in areas other than love.

"Well, let's say you send him out ta buy some horses. He comes back sayin' he spent two thousand on one an' seventeen on another, when actually. . ."

She interrupted, catching the drift. "When actually he might have spent three-quarters that and pocketed the rest."

"Couldn't have said it better myself," he declared, rising slowly and heading for the kitchen. "But that means, he cheated you on the kind of horse flesh he bought you, too. Because if'n he'd cheat you one way he's do it with some help on ta' other end an' the papers he'd hand you wouldn't be worth a hill of beans."

He went on into the kitchen, knowing he'd said enough.

Maybe she did need someone right away, someone close, ready to begin very soon. One who wouldn't have to have fill out an application, submit a resume, and waste her time and energy with advertising, and interviewing. That would certainly just put more wear and tear on Rusty, the kids, and on her.

*Oh, my but I do need to talk to you!* She cried out to her silent partner.

Later from her bedroom window, she saw Marie and Rusty walking hand in hand toward their cottage, and envied them.

The light from the solid brass Stiffle lamp on her dresser, played softly on the aged wood and hand-worked lace coverings made by her great-grandmother. It relaxed her; opened the door to ancestral hospitality without rigidity, with warmth and graciousness. She was glad she had decided to keep the antique furniture.

She half reclined in bed, playing with her iced-tea, slowly circling the edge of the glass with her finger. A beguiling picture of cider, mint leaves and lemons, tea and sugar, of swirling skirts and tapping toes, of soft lights, violin and banjo music filling the air, sometime before cantankerous October drifted in, perhaps after the harvest. Sitting down the empty glass and turning over, she still thought about it as she drifted off to sleep, seeing cars parading up the lane lined with luminaries for an evening's entertainment.

# Chapter 24

Late the next afternoon, the Cobb family headed for the old swimming hole, a sorry substitute for the ocean. Still, they had enjoyed it as frequently as possible, even if just a dip to cool off.

Along the trail, the smell of hickory nuts filled the air. Boneset, well remembered by her great-grandmother, for its medicinal qualities, and gathered and dried on attic rafters to be ready for the first cold or fever, was spreading its tall gray mist against the fencerow.

Chicory's purple blue flowers lined the path, awaiting some ancient person of remembrance to dig its roots and grind them for coffee or to eat its leaves in a salad. The purple coneflower was beginning to wither drawing its last breath before dropping its petals to help carpet the earth's floor.

It was sweltering hot and the family was in need of refreshment and relaxation. John reined in upon seeing Jodi's horse, Blazing Glory, tethered to a branch of a tree. It was a masterpiece, a shiny coat of brown velvet with a white star on her forehead and two matched white socks on her slender front legs. Her dark mane and tail were as matched as the rest of her body. She was the most beautiful mare JoAnn had ever seen.

*Her father picks good horseflesh for his own needs.*

"What's she doing here?" Rob was indignant or jealous, and questioned while he dismounted from Dalemont, one of their new purchases.

"Not so loud," John hushed him, as he tied up Dale's Choice from the Cloverdale Farms to another branch, "She'll hear you." He turned to help Dana who, at times, was still a little insecure with Lady.

"So who cares," Rob answered, following John's example, as did his mom.

"That's enough boys, there's enough heat in this day."

John ignored his mother's remarks and said, as he headed down the bank and around the boulders. "I care, that's who!"

JoAnn was getting concerned about John's relationship with Jodi. He hadn't been able to get a definite answer from her about her relationship with Christ. In that respect, JoAnn was actually relieved that he hadn't had much time to spend with Jodi and would soon be off to college.

Jodi had not heard their approach and apparently was not used to company at the old swimming hole, for when she saw four people suddenly appear from behind a boulder, she started to scream in fright, then recognizing John, called questioningly, "John?"

"Hi." he called out, beginning to remove his shirt. "Mind if we join you?"

JoAnn and Dana immediately recognized Jodi as the girl they had seen at the grocery store. She believed Jodi had remembered the chance meeting also. She was as beautiful as her horse, with her long dark hair twisted into a knot on top her head and held in place with a large barrette.

John jumped in with the others following, and surfaced

near her. Immediately she questioned, "How did you find this place? Do you know the Simpsons?"

John couldn't hold back the information he had been dying to tell her. "I not only know the Simpson's; I live here. We own this ranch. This is my brother Rob, my sister Dana, and my Mom, JoAnn Cobb. And this trespasser, ladies and gentleman, is Jodi!"

He proceeded to pretend to dunk her, but she out maneuvered him as she tried to say, "Hello everyone. You own this ranch?" as if she couldn't believe it.

As the rest joined them, John said, "Remember, I told you we had just moved here. Well, John Arthur Simpson was my maternal great-grandfather. I'm his namesake."

"Why didn't you tell me you lived right next door?" she asked, pursing her lips in playful anger.

"I like to keep women in the dark," he teased, as he dived into the water and swam to the shore to follow Rob's example of diving off an overhanging ledge. When he surfaced again, Jodi was sitting on a spread-out towel on the bank.

JoAnn, treading water, was observing everyone, especially watching John surveying Jodi, whose bathing suit was as conservative as Dana's. She was beautifully tanned and JoAnn noticed John hesitate, as sure as she was a mother, she knew that there were awakened stirrings going on in his young body and that he wanted to be beside her.

How proud she was of him when he swam instead to Rob, calling, You're it with tag's back allowed, except for Mom."

Suddenly Jodi was back in the water playing tag with them, Rob seeming to enjoy her as much as John, and Dana was aglow at having another girl in the group.

JoAnn relaxed in this pleasant company, the first she felt really relaxed, but it wasn't nearly long enough for any of them. She realized as never before how hard she had been pushing them, and that, with school approaching, they needed the rest of the summer for themselves, if possible.

That evening, shortly after dinner, she watched as Gabe Holland drove his jeep up to Rusty's cabin door. His neat body sported a cream-colored embroidered western shirt of fine woven cotton that looked smooth against his skin. His dark blue denims smoothly molded his thighs and made him look like some Hollywood star.

From her open window, his voice wafted her way. "Let's go look at that horse out in the open."

"Come on then." She could hear the smile and pride in Rusty's voice, as she left her room to join them.

Brawn Beauty and Sky didn't get along, therefore, Sky grazed in his own paddock by the old barn, but where he could whinny and find some needed satisfaction seeing other horses. In the soft glow of the setting sun, Brawn Beauty looked up and sniffed with care at Gabe. Then he took a few steps away, turned and pretended to lunge, then just as quickly turned back and stood with all four feet placed as though he just wanted Gabe to look at his conformation. He held his head high, his ears alert, and with his velvet coat gleaming with a rainbow of colors in the slanted rays of the late day sun, he looked his name, Brawn Beauty. He whinnied as Gabe spoke his name.

"You are beautiful and you remembered my warning." JoAnn heard him explain, as she stepped from the porch and headed toward them.

Without turning around, Gabe seemed to know she was there. "Did you see him show off?"

"Yes, I did." Still he didn't turn to look at her, but continued to lean on the fence beside Rusty, who did turn and couldn't hide his admiration.

She felt beautiful and was hoping Gabe could see the extra

pains she had taken with her face and hair. Maturity had not only settled gorgeously upon her, but had softened and refined the rough edges. He didn't even turn toward her and notice, or pretended to be only interested in horseflesh. Perhaps he was simply obeying her wishes to keep his comments to himself.

*Okay, let's keep it all business. Good for you JoAnn! This is how you wanted it and now you have it!* Pulling herself together and leaning on the fence beside Rusty, she asked Gabe, "Well, don't you think he's looking really well now?"

"You are a lucky woman." Still, he did not look at her.

"You can say that again, but you know that with God, there is no such thing as luck, and with Him and Rusty, I can't go wrong." She laid a hand on Rusty's shoulder. "But enough talk, let's get a horse saddled for Marie and go for a ride. I understand you would like to ride him, so if you think you're man enough, go for it."

She knew he wouldn't refuse the challenge. Did she dare tell him John had already ridden him? Naah!

"Watch me."

Brawn Beauty's ears pinned and he showed his teeth while shaking his head for good measure. Gabe waited, talking softly, while slowly stretching forth his hand. Finally, the ears relaxed and he shook his head and whinnied, as horse and rider met; he blew warm breath into the palm of Gabe's hand. JoAnn and Rusty gloatingly looked on, before they all went after their saddles, he had the magic!

The setting sun made the grass appear golden before them, and the streaked yellow and red sky blazed above, reflected on the pristine elegance of the newly painted fence marching off into the horizon.

JoAnn recounted their latest efforts of refurbishing, which were obvious to anyone familiar with the ranch. Still, he praised their efforts as if he had not seen it all before nor had anything to do with it. Two pretenders!

"The men have been talking about some riders way up in the wooded areas beyond where we have been working. Gabe, do you know anyone around here who rides a pinto?"

"Yes, one of our hands rides a pinto. Rocko, by name. Can't imagine what he's doing on your land."

"Rocko. He drives one of your horse trailers?"

"Most of the time."

"I've met him, and can't say the meeting was a pleasure." She waved her hand as if to dismiss that subject. "They also report hearing roosters crowing, a lot of roosters."

"I've heard someone around here holds cock fights, which are illegal in the state of Kentucky. I have my suspicions about who it might be, but nothing certain."

"I see. Well then, guess I'll have to keep my eyes and ears opened, too."

As they rode along Gabe asked, "So you really are making this into a horse farm?"

"That's right, and we have a good start, don't we Rusty? We have made some excellent purchases and have some really good stock. But then, you know all this since you visit every day." She looked at both men, as they reined up. Gabe seemed to want to lock eyes with her, which made it hard to talk with him. "What we need is someone to manage the ranch. Someone who knows and loves horses and how to buy, breed, and care for them; someone who is accepted by the other ranches, who can hire help, and handle those he hires."

As she spoke, she realized that Gabe fit the bill to a tee, and she could feel her nerves tingle clear to her toes.

"She's asking a lot, isn't she Marie? Like give me the world and put a fence around it. You women are all the same."

JoAnn saw he was teasingly smiling. "I'm prepared to give a lot." she told him robustly. If she wasn't careful, that smile of his would be her undoing.

"For instance?"

Her answer could trap her and reveal to Rusty and Marie other conversations with Gabe. To hide her lack of innocence, she turned her horse toward home to be in front of them for at least a minute so they couldn't see her face. They followed suit, and Gabe was beside her in a flash, grinning at her lack of self-control.

Determined, she continued. "For instance, he would live in the house on the second floor, until the manager's apartment, at the end of the bunkhouse is finished. I don't know what he is making, but I would give him five percent more than he is making now and more as the ranch prospers. He would take a hand in the day-to-day operations, help make decisions, and have authority the same as Rusty, and to draw checks from the various bank accounts. He would have to be someone whom we could trust explicitly."

"You are asking for the moon too, not only the world! Where do you expect to find this miracle worker?"

"I expect God will tell me since He already knows who it is. By the way, have you see John over at Reinserts?"

"No, should I?"

"Well, he's had a few dates with Jodi. I thought you might have run into him."

"There's a young dude over there who thinks Jodi is his girl and has been giving her a hard time since this other guy has shown up, and he turns out to be John!" Gabe was really surprised. "John had better watch out. Rocko takes what he wants, whether it's my job, the boss's daughter, horses, whatever, and he thinks Jodi belongs to him."

"Well, that's up to Jodi to set things straight, then."

"I wouldn't expect Rocko to take it lying down."

"He's a trouble maker, then?"

"You could say that."

She felt a little uneasy with this information, and felt John could take care of himself, but she would make it a matter of prayer. Now she needed to turn her attention back to the matters at hand. She didn't like it that Rusty was so quiet and holding back, although he did seem to be satisfied with the way things were going.

"The ranch is turning out to be too much for Rusty, Roy, and the boys and me to handle. I had no idea there was so much paperwork and administrative responsibilities, not to mention the day-to-day work of meeting the horse's needs."

She looked from Rusty to Gabe who blurted out, "I'd like a try at putting a fence around your world and lasso the moon too, if that's part of the job description."

She pulled up sharply her mind in a whirl, her eyes misty, and a crazy sensation around her heart, causing the others to do likewise. "You would?" she asked, feeling curiously weak, her face and neck flushing.

"I believe you heard me correctly. I would."

She immediately screamed silently. *Help me Father, Rusty, or Marie. I'm in over my head.* She had expected a positive response but not before she could even ask the question. Rusty has been at it again!" She saw to be the truth when she looked at him and urged her horse on.

John and Rob were leaning on the fence, each with a bottle of soda in hand, when they reached Brawn Beauty's paddock. A look of pleasure spread over Gabe's face when he saw them, as if he recognized a challenge, to teach the boys and run the Simpson Ranch at the same time.

With greetings over, Rusty, Marie, and the boys took care of the horses, while Gabe and JoAnn headed toward the house to finish some business.

"I need someone right now." Would that stop this cowboy who was intent on becoming a part of her life whether she wanted him to or not? She might have to answer that question sooner than she thought.

He grinned. He was not only extremely good-looking,

even in his over forty years, but that smile was so disarming. It almost demanded one from her and she was trying so hard not to give it, when he said, "I am available right now!"

She shook her head in dismay and did indeed grin. "You are impossible!" she said, glancing up at him in the most relaxed manner he had seen.

"Am I?" His voice, so full of emotion, was gradually melting her frosty demeanor.

"You are! Don't you even need to think about it?"

"Not anymore. I have been thinking and praying about it since you returned. Don't you think that's long enough?" He grinned at her as she stopped in mid-step. He took hold of her elbow, and began walking again. "I tendered my resignation two weeks ago. I was looking and praying for the work that God had for me, and you were praying and looking for me."

Offensively, she answered, "I wasn't looking for you. Rusty and God may have been, but not me. I was looking for a manager!" He was so confident, just the kind of man she needed, rather, the ranch needed.

Turning red again, she stopped at his jeep; she wouldn't ask him in after all. It wasn't safe.

"Well, look, do I get the job or don't I?" He asked, leaning against the jeep, pushing his hat from his forehead with his thumb as the last rays of the sun disappeared over the far hill.   With her hands half way in her pockets, she scratched the dirt with the toe of her boot before looking up to answer. "If you think you can handle all the jobs I mentioned, then yes, the job is yours." The look she gave him was one of respect, hope, and challenge all wrapped up in one.

A smile played at the corner of his mouth, and she saw in his eyes that he was having a desperate struggle to keep from laughing or something, and if they both stood there long enough, they might do or say something that needed to wait. Consequently, she quickly stepped back, "I'll talk with you again." Saying, "good-night," she began walking toward the house.

He started the jeep and when he came abreast of her, he leaned out the window and said, "By the way, you look smashing," then quickly rolled it up again and sped away.

# Chapter 25

Jodi stopped at the Cobb's on her way to the library the next morning to hand deliver an invitation to a party her parents were holding the upcoming weekend.

"Mother would have sent you one much earlier, but, of course, she didn't know you had moved right next door. She apologizes for the lateness and hopes that you will, nevertheless accept. She is quite anxious to become acquainted with you. The whole family of course, is invited. Rusty and Marie already have received invitations and sent back their reply. May I tell Mother that you will be there?"

JoAnn was amused at the way Jodi tried not to look around, for John she assumed, as she told her, "You may, and thank you. I had been anxious to meet you and now of course, your parents. I believe you have a brother, Christopher?"

"Chris, please, he doesn't like Christopher."

JoAnn had never seen the inside of her neighbor's house, even when Gabe lived there. The outside had been intimidating enough. Its fresh coat of gleaming white paint was enhanced by newly planted nursery stock of hothouse beauty. Perhaps at this party, she would meet people she would want to invite to the one formulating in the back of her mind for October.

"Whew!" she spoke sideways to her children. "It's like leaving Lincoln's log cabin and entering the White House!"

The interior was classically beautiful, screaming wealth, but still warm and inviting. The dining room and front parlor were through pocket doors on either side of the large entrance hall where the Reinhart's received their guests. JoAnn was not prone to envy nor staring, but the huge crystal chandelier hanging from the dining room ceiling sparkled like diamonds, and the illuminated French Provincial credenza displayed ostentatiously, a magnificent collection of lead crystal.

John was searching for Jodi among the crowd. However, when JoAnn noticed Jodi standing with her parents in the receiving line, John remained at her side.

JoAnn briefly reflected on Mrs. Reinhart's stunningly designed ankle length white organdy dress. She recalled the moment in the grocery store when she had seen Jodi and her mother, and had felt self-conscious. Not this time. On this occasion she was in her element.

Her own hair had grown long enough and was curly enough to blow dry into a soft bouffant style, and her real emerald and diamond necklace and earrings, augmented her dress, which was subtly simple but tastefully appropriate light mint green crepe de chine.

The children, likewise, stood out in New York originals, not new certainly, but more than equal to the occasion. She happily noticed that no one in the crowd was dressed finer than they were, and for once was thankful that her past social life allowed her to feel comfortable in any occasion.

Jodi introduced them, when they reached the Reinharts in the receiving line. "Mrs. Cobb, my parents, Mr. and Mrs. Pierce Reinhart."

"Please," Mrs. Reinhart said, "call us Cynthia and Pierce. You know Jodi, and this is our son, Chris."

"Thank you, Cynthia, and you too, Pierce. Thanks again for your help with the U-Haul and the trailer accident." As she shook hands, she introduced herself and the children. "My name is JoAnn and this is Rob and Dana, and of course, John. Thank you for including us in your guest list. I have been impatient to meet you, Cynthia."

JoAnn was impressed by their open friendliness and when Gabe threaded his way towards them, Pierce mentioned, "I'm losing the best foreman a rancher ever had."

Should she pretend innocence? Not knowing what Gabe had told them about his new job and Pierce's face telling her nothing, she rushed in, before Gabe reached them. "I don't know what arrangements Gabe has made with you, but, I have hired that best foreman."

Again, if Pierce was surprised or upset, he handled it with poise. "Well, you're getting the finest there is," then he reached out his hand to congratulate her.

"Indeed," Cynthia said. "Our loss is your gain, but at least he's not going very far away."

She felt it necessary to divert this line of thought. "I am sure you are aware of the long standing close ties between the Holland's and the Simpson's. Gabe's father was an old and valued friend to my Grandfather."

"I see, but your name is Cobb," Cynthia stated.

"JoAnn Simpson Cobb."

"That does ring a bell."

"John has probably told you that we moved here from New Jersey. What he failed to mention, perhaps, is that the Simpson Ranch now belongs to me. John Arthur Simpson, was my beloved grandfather. But I expect Jodi has already told you that."

"Yes, quite recently, in fact," Cynthia remarked, smiling a

dismissal as more guests arrived. JoAnn saw she had already turned her attention to her next guest in the line.

As Gabe reached them, he offered to escort the children and JoAnn to the buffet table, where lavishly displayed finger food reminded her that she hadn't had a classy evening out since moving to the ranch, and, she hadn't missed it.

John did not stray far from Jodi, and when she turned to look for Jodi and saw Rocko shadowing her also, she understood why. Rocko, all spruced up and hatless, now appeared to be about thirty years old, too old for the sixteen year old girl, but if anything, more handsome. However, that cocky attitude still existed, and John was intimidated by his apparent domination of the girl.

JoAnn looked at her miserable son, then at Jodi, whose expression seemed to be pleading with him. "John," she whispered, "the receiving line is over, go over there and rescue that poor girl before Rocko gets to her; for your sake, as well as for hers."

That was all the encouragement he needed. She didn't see him again until she went to him to tell him that they would go home with Rusty, and he could have the car to come home when he was ready.

Chris Reinhart, who seemed to be slightly younger than Rob, nevertheless, to her great joy, took both Dana and Rob in tow and escaped outdoors, where a jukebox, drinks, and food, more in line with their age and taste, awaited them.

Gabe looked spectacular in off-white slacks and light blue tie-less shirt, with an intricate design embroidered in a color matching his slacks and jacket. He monopolized JoAnn by keeping her dancing or eating.

*This I have missed, and being held in a man's arms, I must admit, particularly this man's arms.*

She knew she would need men in her life; men with whom she would work and help her run the ranch. She had thought about Gabe, to be sure, but had not expected him to be single and so available.

She had gotten used to doing things herself. As long as Rusty was at the ranch, she thought she would be able to handle that also. So much for book knowledge! He had helped the situation by having a dear wife who took such a great load from her shoulders. Now Gabe seemed destined to do the same, which was both comforting and a dangerous situation.

Rusty and Marie danced by; others nodded and smiled. A few were familiar to her, but all knew Gabe. John and Jodi soon joined the other young people, and Gabe purposely guided their dancing toward the French doors, which led to a terrace and garden.

She understood why he pulled her arm through his and really held on, because he knew she would try to retrieve it, which she did. He led her away from the house. The full moon danced along the path in front of them as the music from the stringed instruments intoxicatingly floated around them.

"How can you leave this place?" she asked, attempting to remove her arm again, while he placed his other hand on it and held it just tightly enough. "It is truly beautiful." Her voice was warmer, kinder than she had ever allowed it to be. The nearness to him sent warm shivers circling her body, disturbing her peace.

"I left it when my step-mother inherited it and sold it without my knowledge." There was no bitterness in his statement. "Anyway, home is where the heart is and my heart is not in this house." Almost in emphasis of meaning, he gave her arm as extra squeeze. She had caught the meaning intended, the third time. Why was she counting?

The extra pressure allowed her to ignore his remark, somehow feeling that it would open a dangerous subject. She, being a woman and knowing him rather well, realized that his feelings still lingered in the rooms of his childhood. "Rusty mentioned that she sold it shortly after your father died."

He kept his eyes straight ahead, searching out the winding path, as he answered, "Quickly too. She was in such a hurry to return to the city, and I couldn't raise the cash fast enough to buy it. I think that is exactly the way she wanted. Dad left almost everything to her, never expecting to die so young. I believe he intended to change his will, but that's all water over the dam. Now she's dead too, and the money was spent on her few years of lavish living or given to charities, so there wasn't much left for me."

He stopped and turned her to him, holding her ever so lightly at the shoulders. "I brought you out here to ask you something."

Suddenly, she was afraid of his question, and tried to move from him, but he refused to let her go. "Hey, what do you think I'm going to ask? You don't have to stand there so rigidly."

She drew a deep breath, "I'm sorry, I don't know..." *what a fool I am, wanting and not wanting all at the same time.*

"All right then, relax, Jo. I was just going to ask if I could begin work Monday."

Such obvious relief flooded over her, she forgot herself and briefly relaxed against him. When she felt his arms gently, like with unbelief, wrap around her, she stiffened, pulled away, and turned toward the house. A person could only take so much moonlight madness, but oh, how wonderful it had felt to be so near to him. He must never know that or hadn't she stepped away fast enough? Good grief, what was she getting herself into, or, better yet, what was God getting her into?

She was walking faster than a lady should who was wearing heels, and he was trying to keep a hand on her elbow to assist her. "Let's make it Tuesday, then you'll be there to go to the auction with me on Thursday."

There, the decision had been cemented and it didn't hurt at all!

He stopped her. "I don't want you going to places like that."

"Gabe, wait a minute," she turned to him again, "I thank you for your interest and your desire to protect me, but I don't need a protector, just a manager."

"Well, we'll see about that later on, but right now, if I am to be your manager, I should be the one going to the auctions, if anyone goes."

Ashamed at being defensive and confused at being ashamed, she laid her hand on his arm and implored, "Gabe, this isn't the time or place to be discussing business. What do you say about waiting until you are actually working for me to discuss your duties. Let's mingle."

As she looked up at him, the bit of light from the terrace and the moon showed her something she hadn't been able to see under cover of the trees. He hadn't meant to discuss business at all. There was so much love in his eyes, that she knew his motives had been purely romantic. It was a good thing she had thwarted his attempt at romance, for he would have read something in her eyes as well. Quickly, she stepped up on the terrace with the French doors just a few feet away, because if he had tried to kiss her, she would have allowed him and probably returned it.

"Gabe," she let out a deep breath, "we'll talk later, right now," she touched her throat, "I'd enjoy getting to know the rest of my neighbors and it's time I check on the children."

She left him standing there. She had hired a man who was in love with her, or, who cherished a childhood image of his love. *Oh, Father what are You getting me into, because I'm afraid I'm falling in love with him also.*

Stepping back down from the terrace, and heading toward the sound of loud music, she found the children enjoying themselves, and as she re-entered the house from the patio, she encountered Cynthia on her way out to check on the young people also. Thank God for the diversion.

"Everything under control out there?"

"Seems to be. You have a lovely home, Cynthia. In all the years I've visited Grandpop, I was never invited inside this house, although Gabe and I were good friends."

"We love it and you are welcome any time." Then looking into the dining room, she said, "Come with me, there's someone you should meet."

She was the perfect hostess, keeping people talking, dancing, eating, and drinking, without a nervous flutter. She led JoAnn up to a man who smelled and looked like he had already had too much to drink, but was accepting another.

"This is Judd Klein. Judd, I'd like you to meet JoAnn Cobb," then she was gone to speak with someone else.

The thought of Mitsi flashed before her and she almost shivered as she stepped away from him. "Mr. Klein, I believe you are the sheep rancher who is renting land from the Simpson Ranch." When Rusty had told her who was renting land, she had not recognized the name, and now putting name and face together, the man was still a stranger to her.

He was a big man, with expansive features set off by white hair and a mustache. His voice and breath matched his size.

"And who might you be again, you pretty little thing?" He asked, leaning much too close to her.

Again, she stepped back. "I'm Simpson's grand-daughter. I own the ranch now." He didn't seem to be grasping what she was saying.

"What, oh, Simpson." Getting up close to her face once more, so she had to draw back again, he asked, Not going to chase me off the land I want to buy now, are you, you pretty little thing?"

"No, Sir," she tried to reassure him. "I'm glad to have the sheep and cattle."

"Well, that's good to bear, I mean to hear, and I am still ready to buy any time you want to sell." He spoke with a slur, taking another long drink. "If there's another thin' I can do to help you," he burped, "jess you let me know. We're neighbors, don't forget. 'Cuse me," he said, and was about to go off in search of another drink, when JoAnn stopped him, by firmly grabbing at his arm.

Her voice was controlled, but just loud enough so he could clearly hear her words. "Mr. Klein, I just want you to know that I believe you killed my children's pet dog. If anything else is ever missing on my ranch, I will come directly and immediately to you!" She turned away from him so abruptly, she almost bumped into Rusty and Marie who, thankfully were looking for her. She had not watched to see what his reaction had been, or had he been too drunk to even understand what she had said. "When you are ready to go home, could three of us bum a ride with you? Actually, I guess if you will, we should switch vehicles with John."

With their consent, although flustered at her audacity in confronting Klein, she then tried to mingle, to dance, and chat. In so doing, she found people whom she learned had known her grandpop, and a couple who had attended his Friday night classes. She recognized some names, but no one seemed to remember her.

Gabe danced and socialized and although he didn't approach her the rest of the evening, she felt him watching her. He disturbed her placidity, making her cheeks flush, her eyes bright, and she had tried so hard to be unresponsive to any man. But then Gabe could never be just any man, and he was so near, so unattached, so handsome, so much like the Gabe she remembered.

Finally, beginning to feel uncomfortably out of place as

the atmosphere of the occasion settled upon her, she felt she no longer belonged in this kind of society. Noticing Rusty and Marie sitting against the wall, probably ready to leave but not wanting to hurry her away from the festivities, she decided to ask them if they were ready to say their farewells and call it a night.

Deciding to allow Rob to come home with John, she had collected a reluctant daughter, and was about to leave the patio area, when she noticed a movement in the darkness beyond. When she walked into the shadows herself, she caught Dana's arm and made her wait until she could see who it was. Rocko! He was too old to fit in with Jodi's crowd but that didn't keep him from hovering near them.

With a quick glance toward the patio, she sent out a silent prayer for God's protection on the young people, and headed for the car, where Rusty and Marie waited.

# Chapter 26

Gabe arrived, lock, stock, and barrel on Tuesday, immediately following breakfast. He came in pretentiously, wearing shining armor, riding his charger, Solomon, so to speak; John drove his jeep, and Rusty followed in his pick-up.

It was evident they had been planning behind her back while she had been busy in the office. She wanted to work hand in hand with her new manager, and since God had sent him, with His help, she intended to do just that; not holding hands, but working with him. He was the best around, she was sure of that, and to work with him meant she had to keep pace with him, or at least pretend to.

Before he arrived, she had her plans and perspectives were well thought out and written down. June, July, and most of August, had passed quickly, but not so fast that she had not had time to get an excellent grasp of the situation. She had talked to enough ranchers, examined their horses, studied her men at work, and in fact, worked side by side with them when possible.

JoAnn had ridden with Roy, Josh, or Tim, assisting them in their daily rounds, learning their trade. She had led horses in and out of fields and stables, up and down ramps to and from the horse trailers, watered, fed, groomed them, and mucked out their stalls. She changed bandages, cooled hot legs, cleaned feet and teeth, checked eyes, ears, and on, and on.

When she first arrived at the ranch and reality began to settle in, JoAnn had moments of indecision when she was afraid that ranching had been just one of those childhood dreams. She wondered if even Rusty expected her to falter and rent out the land once the hard work began. Possibly he had expected her to sell the ranch, after all. He and others through the years had underestimated her, all but her grandpop.

There was a great deal of magic connected with owning a ranch and stocking it with beautiful horses, but she found that her liking of horses had turned to a love of them. There was something about them with which nothing could possibly compare. She was sure her kids saw that in her if no one else did.

It was more than their size, their beauty, and the fact that one end bites and the other end kicks. She knew horses to be courageous, versatile, dependable, and fascinating, as well as intelligent in their ability to reciprocate human communication. They could round up and cut cattle and run at almost unbelievable speed from a standing start. They could walk a path through the woods or high step and jump fences.

Their strength, sure-footedness, and dignity were obvious. There was, and probably always would be, a bit of mystery, a reverence connected with them, and she found herself searching for the same courage and loyalty in humans. Somehow, she had to communicate her profound purpose to those who would enter her office with Gabe.

JoAnn sat aside an empty coffee cup. She was ready for Gabe, even though the thought of his arrival, his soon to be constant nearness, created havoc with her emotions. "I must not show it, I must not! I have to overcome them. Without control, I will reap a whirlwind. It happened before, it must not happen again, it must not!"

God had been the receptor of her time and energy, her mind and emotions too. She thought of Proverbs again and determined to trust in the Lord with all her heart and not to lean on her own understanding, to acknowledge Him and let Him direct her paths, come what may. Otherwise she would not, could not face Gabe.

Was she ready for him? She wanted her walk and voice to convince him she was, therefore, she was dressed in jeans and cotton shirt, just like any other day. She noticed he was dressed for work too. They shook hands on the surround porch at the side of the house, where she told him he could take care of his belongings later, and then led him through the hall to the office. Rusty, Roy, John, and Rob, all dressed as if this were just another day, followed. She included Roy because he had arrived on the scene first and had already assumed his role of head equestrian, and that job would remain his. He had the gentle hands and voice to train and control the animals, even Skys' The Limit, Brawn Beauty, and the well-bred mare, Golden Girl.

She breathed a prayer with every step and had the office ready with enough seats for *everyone*. *If Rusty thought her fascination with the ranch and horses' was just a passing fancy,* her presentation impressed him, and she relaxed and finished with:

"I'm a newcomer at this business to be sure, and have been unbelievably favored by God's goodness. Still I, we, the children and I have a lot to learn. I will trust your judgement, Gabe, as I have Roy's and Rusty's."

"Then, you won't mind me saying that for now, that you should forget the idea of a riding academy and boarding horses."

"Why?"

"It would confuse the issue. You have some good stock, according to these papers and some good blood in a couple mares. You have been successful in breeding a couple of mares with Bill and Bob already, and Sky and Brawn Beauty are well and ready to serve now, not just to your own mares, but outside, if you choose. You have enough on your hands. I'm sure Roy agrees with me." At which point she saw Roy's headshake, yes. "A fee of a several hundred dollars or much more, is something to consider. You need to begin getting a return on your investment."

"I know they are my ace in the hole, however, using them just for stud services repels me right now. Roy has already talked to some ranchers. You two will have to get together, perhaps then we'll talk more on that subject."

"Whew, how time flies when you're having fun," John commented, glancing at his watch.

She smiled at his obvious satisfaction of the morning's business. "You enjoyed this?"

"Sure, why not?"

Gabe stood when JoAnn did, but stopped her from moving from her desk, by saying, "One more thing."

She looked up at him, a little exasperated, but with a 'go on look' in her expression.

"Those well-bred horses should be kept for breeding to build up your stock the cheapest way possible, even though they cost more to keep and require more care. They usually have to be stabled during a severe winter; you aren't in New Jersey and we get some nasty weather here."

John piped up, "Rusty already told us all that."

Jo arched that eyebrow of hers, but Rusty helped out by standing and saying, "JoAnn is the first ta admit that God has blessed her in her purchases."

"Lucky too . . . well, you know what I mean," Rob put in, standing next to his brother.

Rusty put a hand on his shoulder, "There was something about Brawn Beauty that didn't matter a pinch of snuff, but brought down the price, that wasn't luck."

"I know better than to trust in lady luck. It was God and our common sense."

JoAnn handed more papers to Gabe. "I think you will be pleased as you check our records against the horses. God has been really good to this struggling ranch family, giving us wisdom and knowledge beyond ourselves."

He took them and said, "One more thing, I need to know whether this is to be a breeding farm, a resale of good horses, or are we to be on a campaign to "save horses from slaughter" farm?"

"Well put," JoAnn said with embarrassment. "I readily admit to that being our primary goal when we first arrived here and heard about the slaughter house next door. I admit to our ignorance of them prior to our coming."

She had sat back down with her hands folded on top the desk. "I'm afraid that as a result of my glorified image of a ranch, I had us all thinking more of one like Clairborne Farm, than this one, the Simpson Ranch.

"I won't go into details about our experiences at the auction, which led us to place and look for ads. I can't say we stumbled upon ads, because that leaves the Lord out of our dealings again. When the Lord led us to horses that had a speck in their eye, so to speak, and may very well have ended up as meat, we bought them."

She adjusted her chair. "It turns out that with Rusty and Roy's know-how, these horses are as sound as the ground they stand on."

"Now."

Everyone seemed to shift position, waiting her answer. "Now, yes, well, I guess you have boxed us into a corner and we will have to make a decision, all of us. Anyone want to speak up?"

John spoke up. "I think we have accomplished our goal of rescuing some horses that weren't just useless. Who's to say we can't save thoroughbreds? Others are saving race horses and wild horses, so we have saved a few really good horses and I say if we find more, to save them too."

"I'll work with these horses anytime," Roy said.

Rusty just sat with his leg crossed at the knees, his cold pipe cradled in his hand. She noticed more and more that he rarely lit it, and thought it had something to do with the boys.

"Well Gabe, you will be the boss of everyone here. What do you say?"

"I know you have an opinion," Rusty too egged him on.

Gabe gave an amusing look JoAnn's way, as if to say, do you realize what you just said, then looked at Rusty, none too happy to be put on the spot. "My opinion, for what it's worth, is, keep checking out ads, question carefully those who call by phone, and only buy what you can't live without, and don't waste your time at the auction. I'm willing to use my Solomon in your program."

Everyone sat up straighter. "I never expected such an offer. At what price Gabe?"

"I choose the mare and get the first foal."

Rusty and Roy winked when she looked at them. The boys had no reaction.

"Done, for this time, but what about later?"

Exuding confidence, he stated, "By then, there won't be a problem."

His direct look and the sound in his voice told her more than she wanted to know. The fourth time. The flush she felt on her face spread to the rest of her body so that she had to squeeze her arms against her sides to control the erupting emotion. Everyone in the room understood his statement, except for the boys, and she wasn't sure about them.

*Father, you aren't holding me close enough, or I am not walking close enough to you, for something is going awry.*

Gabe wasn't finished. "Those two new stallions are well now and could be resold for a powerful amount of money. I haven't read their pedigree but, with our two, you don't need them and you could get some return on your money, or keep them and sell Bill and Bob for pleasure riding."

A look of dismay and a slight sucking in of breath gave him his answer for now, so he moved on. "As a start-up, you have your work cut out for you with the harvesting, new pastures to get ready, a breeding program to initiate when the next breeding phase comes in March, and a new manager..."

JoAnn stood again; she would not reveal her knowledge of what was considered the good, better, and best breeding periods. She thought they stood a chance of success if they didn't wait. She would say something to Rusty.

"I don't know about the rest of you, but I think Gabe is right. John heads for Tennessee tomorrow, with Rob and Dana to school the day after and band practice and football games. Yes, we have enough right now."

"Mom, I was wondering if I could get in here at the campus and take some of my science and biology courses I will need later..."

"No, John, I want you to keep with your original plans and you just reminded me that we have to finish packing the car God gave us." Then turning to look at everyone, "are we in agreement with Gabe for now?"

"Yes, okay, right," were the answers she heard.

It was so difficult, but she moved around the desk to stand before Gabe, who measured at least four inches above her. "I appreciate your input and interest in our welfare. That's part of your job too. It will be good to have you with us." She had to extract the hand she held out to him before he grasped it with both of his.

"Welcome aboard," Rusty grinned, shaking his hand too, as did the rest in procession. When John reached out his hand, Gabe not only shook it firmly, but also temporarily threw his arm around the boy's shoulders and followed the rest down the hall toward the swinging door and lunch.

She really had to pull herself together to lead them to the dining room, but was glad to miss the inspection Rusty had planned after lunch. Dana was promised several hours of her time and it was important that she keeps that promise, and John wasn't completely packed and ready for school.

More importantly for herself, she simply could not be in Gabe's presence any longer. She was convinced that he took the job because of her; Rocko had nothing to do with it.

# Chapter 27

Pre-occupied with John heading for school in the morning, the unusual warmth of the night, and the noise from the ceiling fan made it difficult to get to sleep. JoAnn slipped on a cotton top and Bermuda shorts, before stepping out unto the side porch, which sheltered the office and several bedrooms. She could look over the corrals with a sheltered view and had hoped to catch a breath of cooler air than came in her window, as she had on other nights; but it was humid everywhere.

September began the swan song for so many things: lifeguards, bathing suits and swimming holes, outdoor band concerts, family reunions and parades, spectator shoes and anything pure white for the women. Parents gaze after children leaving for school or college wondering where the time had gone.

The days were growing imperceptibly shorter, but heat still beat at the land. Still, there is something about the air, the soon to be harvested fields, the brightness of the moon, that says, summer isn't over yet enjoy the warmth.

Although it was a very warm evening, insects and nocturnal animals' singing rose in melody around her.

She was about to return to her room when she caught a movement by the corral. By the time she realized it was Gabe throwing something away, it was too late to turn back. As they approached one another, he returned a pouch of tobacco to his pocket.

"You not only get up early, but stay up late." His voice was kind, as he looked at her in the dim light of the night.

She heard the sound wafting musically, surrounding her, and successfully shook it away. "It is so hot tonight, even the horses are restless." Pointing to his pocket she asked, "When did you take up that filthy habit?" She leaned against the fence, fanning her face with one hand.

"Years ago, but before you express your opinion, I'm trying to quit."

"Good. It is so disgusting to watch men spit that juice all over the place, laden with germs, to say nothing of the possibility of cancer of the mouth."

"I said I'm trying to quit, already!"

"Good, because it doesn't set a good example for the boys."

"That's one reason for giving it up."

"One?"

"I'll tell you the other sometime down the road."

*There he goes again, the fifth time. He's got me married to him and I'm afraid the day will come when I will want to do just that!* The realization was a happy resignation.

He turned to lean on the fence. "I met Rocko in town today. He puzzles me."

Too flippantly, she remarked, "they can advertise for horses the same as we do."

He couldn't see her well because the moon only shed half its silvery glow of a week ago, but he could hear the nonsense in her statement. "I wasn't thinking about his job. You don't understand the situation, nor know men like Rocko. Do you think I would have left over there if Rocko were just a simple man? He is young, complicated, dangerous, and he troubles me."

As he rested one foot on a rail he said, "What would you do if you were about to go bankrupt because someone was taking your business away from you?"

"I would just go into another business and if that didn't work, get a job, like everyone one else."

"Spoken like a woman."

"What's that supposed to mean?" she asked, testily, her back to the rails. "Hold on Jo, don't get riled up. Let me put it another way. I think we're heading for trouble with the syndicate." He shifted position to more easily look at her. "They have a quota to meet and they don't want to fill it with just any old cob, not all the time. I wasn't going to mention this, but sometimes they buy a good stallion just for stud use on their own mares. Frankly, they don't worry about the right time for breeding. They don't think about the mare. Just so she can produce."

"You mean they have breeding farms just for the meat."

"That's right. These men have millions of dollars invested and they won't lose it without a fight. We're not talking about the corner grocery going out of business because a supermarket opened up across the street."

She was quiet a long time, then pushed from the fence and started walking. "I'm not quitting, Gabe. I've invested too much of my family's time and energy to give up. I mean to turn this place into a prosperous horse ranch and if I can save some beautiful, useful horses from the slaughterhouse, at the same time, I hope to do it. However, I'm not naive enough to think I am making such a difference. If I have gotten the ranchers and farmers to think about where their horses are ending up, then I am happy." She turned to him, "are you still with me?"

The proximity of their bodies was too close for comfort.

Gabe casually threw an arm across her shoulders and said, "All the way, Jo, all the way. Let's get something to drink."

She wanted to remain in the comfort of that arm but forced herself to maneuver out from under it. "Would you like to see how your apartment is progressing?"

"Why? Trying to get me out of the house already?" He teased.

"No, if you don't want to see it, just say so." She must not let him get the upper hand.

"Hey, simmer down Jo, the night is hot enough, just lead the way."

She was being defensive toward any emotion that might develop, but he was doing such a good job of breaking down those defenses and she was beginning to enjoy every broken down fence.

His apartment was located at the southern end of the long bunkhouse. It was quite private with its own porch and entrance. It contained a small kitchen with an eat-in area, a bedroom, and an office-living room. The roof had been renewed and insulated and the walls and floor insulated, painted, and ready for a rug. Some of the furniture was in usable condition, and she planned to replace others with unneeded furniture from the house.

"Afraid I'll get lost in here, Jo."

"Not after it's all furnished," she said, heading back toward the open door. She turned to switch off the light at the same moment as he, and found herself in his arms.

He kissed her gently, then touched her face as if in wonder.

At the first touch of his lips upon hers, she stiffened in surprise. Then his hands on her face, in gentle tenderness made her realize she had nothing to fear from this man. However, she made to move from him, and immediately, she sensed his relaxed hold.

"Jo, I love you. I knew it would be wonderful to hold you

again, but I didn't know how delightful." His voice so warm and soft, his hands not letting her go beyond arm length. "I have loved you while I waited twenty-five years to hold you again, never knowing if God would give me the chance. I did not intend to press my attentions this early. The situation just presented itself so perfectly, I couldn't help myself."

"Gabe, please," she protested, remembering the look of love in his eyes at Reinhart's party. "We were just kids experimenting with what we thought was love."

"So you do remember!" She heard the hope in his words.

When she tried to get away, he refused, but she did stiffen her arms and pushed back at least that far. "Of course, I remember. You were my first love." She must not, must not, give him more ground, and this time she did move from him and out into the night.

"That's all it is Gabe or will be, just a sweet memory. Please try to remember that." She wished she believed what she was saying for her heart hammered in her throat. Would he notice the uncertainty in her voice?

"Jo," his own husky voice trembled as he walked beside her. "You are more than just a pleasant memory, and your response to that kiss told me that you know it. You ruined me for anyone else, and I never minded, not until I heard you were no longer married, and saw you again. You have grown into a beautiful woman, lovelier than I could ever have imagined. I have prayed for you and about you ever since I came to know the Lord, and, I do not believe He wants me to follow your advice, not for one minute."

She didn't dare stop but she did respond. "You bringing God into this isn't going to change things. Remember what I said about keeping words like that to yourself? Well, it still goes. Anyway, don't we have enough problems with those thoroughbreds, Judd Klein, and whoever else is riding on our property and keeping an eye on us, without us adding more?"

In an attempt to change the subject, he asked, "About that ice tea?"

"I'll pass tonight, after all. I think I'll just say good-night here." She did not condemn him, nor offer any hope. "Gabe, we got carried away, just now, that's all. Please forget what happened, for it won't happen again."

"Wanna bet," rang in her ears as she turned sharply, and with a hurried step ahead of him, made it to the porch and through the door, where fortunately for her, being the gentleman he is, he hesitated.

She was in her own room before she heard the hall door being bolted shut. Crossing to the bedroom window, she stood for the longest time, deep in troubled thought, wrestling with her emotions.

*Oh, I am going to have to be strong, very strong, for a man in love is a fearful thing. He isn't anything like Louis, never was, but can I ever fully trust another man to be a man?*

She was no dummy, but educated and worldly-wise. She knew all men were not alike; each one deserved a separate analysis. Did that include Gabe? She knew she would have to have that question answered in her mind sooner or later, before she had to deal with it in her heart.

But, oh, right now, she felt like a teenager in love. She wouldn't sleep well tonight, and it wouldn't be because of the fan and the hot night. Gabe would love to know that she was finally aware that she had held herself apart from men for too long because of Louis, especially from one man, no matter what she had told him. Her parents wouldn't stop her this time!

# Chapter 28

The whole gang saw John off to school right after breakfast. Marie made sure there was a large box of goodies to take with him, sitting on the front seat of his car. JoAnn had tears in her eyes and realized this was just the beginning of good-byes. Tomorrow would not be any easier for Rob and Dana. She remembered it was never easy to adjust to a new school. They would survive.

JoAnn couldn't help but to be often with him, since Gabe was invited to eat his meals with the family the same as Rusty, until his apartment was finished. Other times she saw him with a clip board, or pointing to some far direction to a ranch hand, then he might be exercising an animal or feeding or grooming one. He kept tools in his jeep and along with the other workers, was making sure buildings, sheds, feed boxes, and water sources were winterized for the horses' comfort.

At times, she found herself standing unobserved at the office window, staring at the sweep of his neck and his broad shoulders, feeling more of the stubbornness and fierceness regarding him, ebb away.

Unwillingly, the magic of his kiss was as if it happened

a few minutes ago, such a sweet memory. These days, every thought of him, filled her with unutterable contentment.

Other times, she felt him watching her and knew he was protective of her and her interest as no man, other than Rusty would have been. Already, she had felt relief from the many pressures as the men handled everything so capably, or shielded her from some activity to which she was very sensitive.

The weather of Kentucky had never been more helpful or beneficial to the fledgling, would-be rancher. The horses cooled beneath the leaf quilted blue sky; a colorful leaf here and there, loosened by a breeze, kicked off by a bird, drifted earthward, unafraid to blend with the earth that nourished it.

Forecasted showers, sent at the Lord's direction, delayed activities, only briefly at times, and at others, for whole days. At times, the rain dropped gently, blessing the earth, while other times it beat a soft tattoo on the leaves of the tulip and oak trees surrounding the house, refreshing the flowers at their base, bouncing like tiny silver beads on the stone sidewalk.

Still there were times when it clawed at the windows like a cat's scratching, and washed deep gullies in the dirt road, along the creek, and laid deep pools around hedgerows and fences.

These were welcoming, refreshing pauses in their routine, a time for a relaxed breath, a quick catnap or an extra snack and cup of coffee, readily provided by Marie.

JoAnn found the economics of getting the kids ready for school and financially caring for the ranch, required careful accounting. Costs were spiraling; her bank account was going down, down, down. Still, she availed herself of every opportunity to be out doors to breathe deeply of the earthy smells: soil, plant matter, manure, horseflesh, as well as to ride Sky or Brawn Beauty. It was all a far cry from the salt laden ocean air, which Dana only mentioned when she received a letter from her friends, the twins.

September was JoAnn's favorite month of the year and this month was writing its signature in warm, green-plush days, soon to change. Gabe and she were often unavoidably alone together, though he or Rusty with Tim, or Josh did most of the traveling looking over potential horses. He was always the perfect gentleman.

If she and Gabe should touch, she quickly jerked away, and although he grinned with teasing pleasure, she pretended cold indifference. If he knew how much pleasure she derived from each touch, he would have been uncontrollable. Every time, that knot unraveled a bit more. One day. . .

The Simpson stock grew as Rusty, Tim, or Gabe, discovered and were able to bid on the right horse and purchase it at the auction. The losses to the corporations at the sales barn, made the syndicates settle for lesser hacks, or go farther afield to complete their quotas. What had appeared, before JoAnn's influence, as the easy way out for the farmers and ranchers, now seemed cruel and inhumane.

JoAnn was amiable she encountered Cynthia at various business establishments throughout the town. Rob and Dana traveled the same school bus with Jodi and Chris; from whom they also received the sincerest cordiality and friendship.

JoAnn had been careful in her use of terminology when speaking about the bidders, and had never unfairly maligned them or cast them as villains. If hate was generated or unjust criticism circulated, it had not begun with her. She literally breathed a sigh of relief, when after each encounter with a Reinhart, no feelings of animosity were displayed.

Gabe, in the meantime told her he was seeing a horse of a different color. Roy and Josh reported seeing a large man on a palomino or another rider, in the north range, almost every day. The one description fit Rocko and his pinto, and reminded JoAnn of the lone rider she had seen that first day, which, now seemed so long ago. The other, no one could place.

When he was seen several days in a row, Gabe and JoAnn rode out to see for themselves, but Rocko or the other rider, would be gone or would never show. Then for days thereafter, Gabe was too occupied to rise to the challenge. Finally, one day at lunch, he announced that he had seen Rocko riding the fence line between Reinhart's land and theirs. "He couldn't keep his eyes off our horses!"

"So we better keep on our toes," Rusty suggested.

Observing Rusty that day, JoAnn was alarmed. Relieved of so much of the pressure and responsibilities he had carried for so many years, age seemed to be catching up with him. Although he couldn't spend as many hours in the saddle, and his eyes and ears didn't always respond to his demands, his mind was as sharp as attack.

The sky was suddenly grayer, the sun not so bright, the grass more brittle and brown, and a new knot developed in her heart, as she rode over her land, the same land he loved so much.

She thought of her grandpop and how he must have felt, as age slowed him down and kept him from even attempting to do many things he had always loved doing. *I wonder if he didn't die from a broken heart as well as old age.* Her emotions crumbled with the thought, as she threw her hands to her face and cried at the reality of it all.

The dinner bell clanged in the near distance, always a welcome sound around mealtime. Dana had loved her job as bell-ringer, and would return to the kitchen immediately, to help Marie with the last minute fuss over the meals. Now Marie worked alone, with some help from JoAnn, except at dinnertime, when after school, Dana pitched in too. She had begun to listen more intently to the conversation around the table, becoming more interested and actually intrigued with the workings of the farm.

John had made it home for his first weekend visit, in time for a Friday night meal of stuffed pork chops, scalloped potatoes, fresh string beans, cantaloupe and cottage cheese salad, and peach cobbler, for dessert. Jodi's name was injected into the conversation. Gabe picked up on it.

"Has Rocko taken over Reinhart enterprises yet, John?"

"Jodi has mention him in her letters. It seems all he really wants is the prestige and money he would get if he could get to Jodi."

JoAnn always the brooding mother, asked, "Does she see this, John, or are you just so interested in her yourself, that you don't care for the competition?"

"Yeah," Rob said, still harboring a bit of jealousy. JoAnn was glad he had started school and was meeting new people his age.

Dana giggled, "You'd think you were in love with her, John."

"Well, maybe I am, Squirt. What do you think of that?"

JoAnn returned to the business of eating. Where had she been? What was happening right under her nose that she hadn't seen? John and Jodi held hands, sat close together when they weren't riding. But in love?

John had promised her that he had talked to Jodi about her need to accept Christ as her Saviour. Still she resisted, but John persisted in dating her, although he hadn't seen her since going to college. They were all praying for both of them, but especially for Jodi.

She needed to find out if John thought himself in love with Jodi, if Rocko had ever threatened him, and would he be able to handle himself if he did. Rocko did not seem the type to take losing Jodi lying down. Did Reinhart still approve of John?

"John," her voice was full of concern, "do Pierce and Cynthia realize how much Jodi is beginning to mean to you?"

"How would I know?" he answered, impatient at the turn of questioning into his private life. "They're around, same as you."

"Okay, don't get huffy," glancing from him to Gabe. Why had he brought up the subject in the first place? Boy, did she have some talking to do with John this weekend. Jodi and Rocko were the Reinhart's problem, not hers. Perhaps she should speak directly with them at the shindig which was still in its very early planning stage, and all in her mind. This might just be the time to mention it and change the subject.

"What a super idea!" "It sounds like a lot of work." "You have really thought this thing through, etc." were some of the remarks she gratefully received.

"None of that, JoAnn," Marie scolded her, when she heard some of the plans. "If we women can't put on the proper trimmins' for a hoe-down, when the whole ranch has just gone through a fixing-up, then we should throw in the towel."

"The trimmings aren't what worries me. It's the food."

"And the food doesn't worry me. My women friends owe me." Marie retorted.

"Oh Marie, you are simply wonderful," JoAnn cried, throwing her arms around her housekeeper and friend.

"It's the three of us then, right?" Dana inquired, wanting to get the record straight.

"The three of us, dear, with a little help the last day."

Days later, Rusty and Marie followed up the written invitations by visiting some of their ranch neighbors and personally inviting them to the party. They received a favorable reception. The barn dance was on!

# Chapter 29

JoAnn lounged amidst the exotic perfumed beads of rich emollients, which kept her sun tanned face, arms, and the exposed V-neck of her cotton blouses, soft and smooth.

Then, smoothing penetrating oil over her skin, she thought of her guests who would soon be arriving, and Gabe sneaked into her mind. Dana's knock was a reminder to hurry. Rescued from what might have been a perilous introspection, she carelessly splashed on cologne and while the curling iron heated up, used the blow dryer on her hair.

When the first car moved over the road, she was slipping on a simple but perfectly set deep blue sapphire ring. Her pale blue long-sleeved blouse, tucked into a full gathered blue print skirt, was enhanced by a beige leather vest, which was edged in beads. Several slight necklace strands of gold jewelry lay softly on her sun-darkened skin, matching those wrapped around her wrist.

She stepped out onto the front porch, followed by her family, all sporting appropriate clothing for the occasion, as the first driver was directed to a parking place. Other cars were within sight like a parade up the old road, just as she had imagined in that hazy dreamy state a month or so ago.

There were old friends of Rusty's, Marie's, Gabe's, of JoAnn's grandparents and family, church friends, as well as a few relatives, who were more than eager to see the old place. She was glad to see Ernest Strom the banker, Drew Lingle her lawyer, Stu Farley the vet, and Joel Strouse the forest ranger, along with their wives and children. Judd Klein had been invited against her better wishes, for she had not told anyone what she had said to him at Cynthia's party. He was single and his rent money still came in handy. There were a few acquaintances of the children from church and school, and of course, the Reinhart's, and ranch hands with their families, rounded out the guest list. She hoped they were expectant as they rode up the lane, which was lit on both sides by luminaries in the form of old kerosene lanterns, each sitting in a little pile of sand for safety.

JoAnn wanted it to be a magical night of square dancing, singing, blue grass, and gospel music, with plenty of wonderful food.

The renovations to the newer barn, in preparation to filling it with the fall harvest and purchased winter food supply, were completed. From it came sounds of toe-tapping, hand-clapping folk music: guitars, banjos, fiddles and other instruments, blending in perfect harmony, welcoming the guests.

Filtered floodlights, lampposts, and paper lanterns lit the way from the parking area to the music, to tubs of ice cold drinks, and the food. Wow, the food! Marie and her women friends, with Dana and JoAnn's help of course, had lavishly cooked, prepared, and displayed it to the most discriminating Epicurean's delight.

Blue denim jacketed young men and women prepared cider, tea and soft drinks, and served fried chicken, ribs, roast pork, baked white and sweet potatoes, as well as corn on the cob and a variety of other vegetables, salads and wonderful desserts.

There was a bonfire with plenty of hot dogs, buns, and marshmallows and Graham Crackers, nearby. JoAnn noticed the young people eventually had gravitated around it. She was so pleased to hear southern gospel music being played by some of the young people from their church, and sung by most in the group.

People had been encouraged to bring their instruments and there was music floating around the ranch. As it lifted aloft, she hoped her Heavenly Father was pleased.

The evening was fantastic; not a cloud in the sky, allowed the moon and stars to add to the splendor of the party. The air had just a hint of late September crispness in it, with a gentle, light breeze.

It truly was an exciting, intoxicating night for the Cobb family and their friends and neighbors, as they paired off with first one, then another, to the dance calls. The ladies full skirts billowed out as they went swirling, bowing, and laughing as the square dancing went on and on.

Time and time again, JoAnn found herself with Gabe's arm around her waist, as they promenaded and moved through interesting patterns with the caller's voice ringing out: "swing her high, swing her low, don't step on that pretty little toe."

A satisfied grin spread across Gabe's face and his eyes tried to tell her something, something loving and beautiful, which she tried not to see, nor to feel.

"Do-si-do and promenade," ended the dance. While they waited for the round dance to be called, Judd Klein moved in, and motioned to Gabe that he would like to take his place.

He was a powerful affecting looking man, in his late forties. There was something about the way his eyes darted from her, then over the crowd that unsettled her. For some reason, his boisterous, good-humor, rubbed her the wrong way. She couldn't help thinking that he fit the description of a horse and rider who trespassed on her property. It was something terribly artificial about him, something counterfeit and unnerving, which reminded her of Louis and Roger, and just the thoughts raised goose bumps on her arms and neck.

He lived alone, she had discovered, but entertained single women and men frequently. Therefore, the extra pressure around her waist, the closer hold, repelled her, as his meaning was quite clear. She avoided his eyes and was so relieved when Drew Lingle cut in.

Judd had yet to visit the ranch; seemingly satisfied with the arrangements Rusty had made with him prior to her arrival. If Drew had not cut in, Judd's "pretty little thing" would have given her reason to scream. He wasn't drunk this time. She had expected and was prepared for a confrontation, then noticed him leaving immediately after the dance. Had he come to show her he held no hard feelings, or was it all a show, a cover-up, and she would yet see or hear his retort.

With one child or another in tow, she visited, ate, or drank with everyone for at least a few minutes. Some remarked having seen her at Reinhart's party but did not know who she was. Now and then a confidential whisper represented an offer to help in any way he or she could, to which she responded with a hand shake or a hug and "thank you".

Pierce and Cynthia were equally at ease and responsive to the music and conviviality, and made honest, pleasant remarks about what she was doing with the "old Simpson place". At one point, while clapping their hands in time to the music, Cynthia pointed out Jodi and John.

"They make a nice couple," she spoke quietly. "We have come to like John very much."

"Thank you," JoAnn said, "I couldn't be more delighted with Jodi than if she were my daughter."

"Thank you. It makes their relationship rather convenient living next door to one another."

"Doesn't it" JoAnn said, but other words went through her mind; too convenient, and wondered if Cynthia didn't think the same thing.

The musicians sang and played the last, "Don't Fence Me In", then took a refreshment break, at which time a few guests departed.

When John and Jodi, walking hand in hand, left the barn and headed for the paddock, JoAnn assumed rightly that John had prearranged the two horses already saddled. Jodi, wearing denim culottes, a long-sleeved western shirt with a blue scarf tied around her neck and beautiful alligator boots, looked lovely as she swung easily into the saddle.

She grew increasingly uneasy about their relationship and yet rather envied their freedom to take off from the party and go for a ride down the lane. The moonlight, the distant music and laughter would play with their emotions. She breathed a prayer for them.

Later, during an idle moment, she glimpsed they had returned and noticed a special glow, a secret smile spread across their face when they looked at each other. Her attention was quickly diverted when John stopped suddenly and ran back to his horse. She unobtrusively separated herself from the hoedown and followed Jodi to the corral gate.

"John thought he heard something among the horses."

Because of the barn dance, all the horses had been stabled, or driven into Eden, the corrals or paddocks nearest the ranch, so that each hired hand and his family could be free to attend the party.

"They're quiet now, but I know I heard a horse galloping away, I'm sure of it," he reported, when he returned and had tied his horse to a post.

He looked at Jodi. "Did you tell her?"

"No. I wanted to wait for you." She took his hand in hers.

*Oh, dear*, JoAnn thought. *What now?*

"I think you need to tell someone right away, and Mom is the perfect one."

She looked at JoAnn with pride and honesty. "I asked Jesus into my heart a few minutes ago." She blurted it out as if, if she didn't, she would explode.

"*Thank you, Father.*" JoAnn said, as she gave Jodi a hug. "We have all been praying that the Holy Spirit would open your heart and mind to understand your need for a personal relationship with the one who died on the cross for you and reach out to Him. He has been waiting . . . we have all been waiting," she said with a little laugh as she hugged Jodi again. Then she turned to her beaming son and gave him a hug while whispering in his ear. "Now you become a teacher to open her mind to His wonderful power and love."

# Chapter 30

It was after midnight when the last guest departed and Rusty and Marie shooed off to bed. It was well after one o'clock before the excess food was refrigerated or made airtight and placed on the counter or put away in a cupboard and the most necessary clean up finished; the rest could wait. Dana and Rob had been in bed an hour when Gabe and JoAnn closed the barn doors and switched off the last light.

Quiet reigned, except for the chorus of insects enjoying their own nightlife. In the near distance, a campfire was still burning brightly. As John added more wood, embers still tried to celebrate the party by whirling, sparkling into the darkness of the night.

He insisted on keeping watch after having heard that rider among the horses. He was afraid, of what, he wasn't sure, but something was bugging him; or perhaps, he just couldn't settle down after an emotion packed evening.

JoAnn too, was reluctant to call it a night. The spontaneous urgings, which had been gradually building, would be difficult to restrain. She was afraid the time had come to deal with the question she had put off, with which she struggled and tried to evade.

She recalled how nimble Gabe had been as he swung her around, circling left, and then right. How easily he had lifted her off the ground. Her blood had raced scorching through her, and not just from the music itself, but because of his face so close to hers, laughing, drawing her to him. It was love she saw there, so frank, so vigorous, so beautiful, that she tried to steel herself to keep from being drawn into it, and could not.

His arm around her waist had been so sure and firm, the rhythm, a part of their combined movements. At the end of each dance with him, his arm remained firmly, possessively on her back. She couldn't, didn't want to move from it until it was absolutely necessary. She had allowed it, that's what had surprised and amazed her. But then, when God's timing has arrived, there is not much His child can do, but follow His leading.

"Well, guess I should get to bed. What a day! What a night!" she exclaimed, hugging her arms as they stood outside the barn. Her first mistake following the party had been working with Gabe in closing up, instead of excusing herself and going to bed.

"Yes, I told John, I would relieve him since he has to drive back to school tomorrow. So . . . I guess . . . I should head for the fire."

She heard a sound in his voice that stimulated her auditory nerves, a sound that signaled a warning that he had reached the end of waiting. Now, right this minute, might be her only chance to put off the inevitable. Her heart raced strangely, not the kind that she had been experiencing.

Still they stood, like two youths on a first date.

That was her second mistake.

The moon moved in and out of slight clouds, at times bathing them in its silver light.

"God gave us a beautiful night and I hope it was pleasing

to Him." She looked up to the sky, her body pulsing, her mind whirling with wonder at what was happening to her.

"Cold?" he asked, his hands in his pockets.

"No, just a habit," she answered, still rubbing her arms. "I thought things went well. Plenty of food, fun, and music. People were very gracious."

If Gabe would have looked down at her, he would have seen how bright her eyes were. She felt as if the glow that was spreading over her body had to be visible, and she knew it was only partly because of the successful party.

Her third mistake was to allow Gabe to take her hand and lead her down the dirt road in a pretense of gathering up the lanterns.

"At least I can pretend to be earning my pay," he said, as they walked along, turning down the wicks and blowing out the flames. "We'll blow them out as we walk down and pick them up on the way back when they've cooled." He wasn't looking at lanterns, his eyes were glued on her, and he couldn't help but see the smile of contentment and the look in her eyes when she raised them from the road to look at him.

Her fourth mistake, and one from which there was no turning back, was to allow him to release her hand and put his arm around her, drawing her close to his side, just till they reached the next and last lantern.

Neither spoke. She was familiar with the stirrings within her, but he would have to be the one to make the next move, and she wondered how long before he would. He turned the wick down and when he stood up and looked at her, he uttered her name with all the love and affection of his aching, longing heart. It was almost a whisper, but the love behind it ran through her blood like wine. She said nothing, not even his name, for the rising flood of her own emotions choked sound from her voice.

She had fought him for four months and could not, did not

want to fight him anymore. When he turned her to him, her arms just naturally encircled his neck as he drew her to him in unbelievable wonder.

She felt the triumph in his kiss. The years of waiting seemed to flow through him like a tidal wave. She responded with equal determination.

What she was feeling was not new to her. She had experienced it once, ever so slightly, delicately, with Gabe, eons ago, and thought the promise was there with Louis. However, it had become a weak expression of love, soon after their marriage. Then, unknowingly, she became only an object for his sexual perverted expression, a puppet, a toy, until . . .

She never expected to trust a man again; never intended to let any eligible man become more than an acquaintance. Now here she was full of love for this man whom she had known almost all her life. Never again would she let him get away from her.

But then again, neither could she allow herself to totally abandon her principles. God, after all, was watching. Gabe must have been realizing the same thing, for he suddenly cupped her face in his wondrous hands and pressed his lips to hers as if they were very precious.

Then he pressed her to his chest with one hand on her head, the other on her back with her arms encircling his beloved body. Together, wordlessly, they calmed their emotion packed body and mind.

Finally, "Jo, I love you, love you, have loved you, these many years. Now I can only pray God will finally give you to me."

"Oh, Gabe, if only I would have been truly born again that night, instead of pretending, I might have realized the true intent of your feelings. My parents kept us apart by not allowing me to visit. Then my whole life changed when I went to college and met Louis."

She shuddered at the thought.

Gabe just held her closer. "Believe it or not, I knew your parents were behind you not visiting anymore. I don't know what they held against me, but it's over, Jo."

She leaned away from him, resting her hands on his arms. "I'm sorry, but I'm not sure it is."

He groaned and tried to pull her to him again, but she resisted. "I thought, just now, that you were feeling the rapture of love I was."

His voice was so full of anguish, and it hurt Jo so much to hear it that she allowed him to hold her close again. "Oh, Gabe, I love you with my heart, but I'm not sure of my mind."

Then they were able to move apart, and she took his hand and held it in both of hers, both very much aware that the emotions they had experienced before, could have only been subdued by God. "We better head back, but please continue to be patient with me. I know I've treated you abominably, but it was a matter of self-preservation." She leaned her head momentarily against his shoulder.

"You see, when Grandpop died and I learned I would inherit this farm, I would on occasion dream about you, remembering all our good and wonderful times together, and I had no knowledge of you whatsoever. Were you married, divorced, children? At times, I couldn't get you out of my head. You were driving me crazy, and then you called!"

"Jo . . .," he tried to draw her to him.

She resisted, "Please let me finish. Since I had gotten saved through Grandpop's death and a letter he left me, I turned to the Lord, and I honestly believe He put you in my mind, but I couldn't get control until I committed you to Him.

"Then," she looked up to him, "then when I saw you, I about went crazy just looking at you."

She touched his face; he grabbed her hand and held it

there. They couldn't see much but they could feel and hear, as they began walking back to the ranch.

"You are so good-looking, so virile, so ready to love my children and me, that you scared me. I was afraid my kids would idolize you and I knew nothing about you. I was happy for them and scared all at the same time. I wanted you here, and I needed you to stay away. I wanted you near," and with that, the emotions began to rise again. "But I wanted you to leave me alone too." She simply couldn't resist bringing his face down to hers to press her lips to his.

"Oh, but you are so delicious," he cried, as he crushed her to him and kissed her soundly.

"And you are so endearing, and strong," she said, trying to move from his embrace without deflating his aroused ego.

The lanterns were forgotten and John appeared to have fallen asleep when they reached the bonfire area.

"I know I have talked too much, I promise not to do that anymore. There isn't much more to be said, anyway, for Rusty told me that you know everything about us that he knows, which is considerable. But he does not know my feelings unless he is a good guesser, and on second thought, I think he is."

"You're right, count on it, Jo. Oh, how I love your name, Jo, Jo, Jo. Remember?" he asked, as he turned her to the porch. "How are we going to keep him, anyone from guessing what went on here tonight? How can I be judicious in my conduct, now that I have touched your lips and felt your response and heard your, 'I love you'? How can I wait for your mind to tell you what your heart already knows?" He lightly dusted her face with his lips. "How, Jo?"

Burying her head on his chest, "Pray, Gabe, all day, especially when we see one another. We must be prudent for the sake of those we love as well as for ourselves. Personal purity is our first responsibility. We need to be in possession of our lives, our feelings, in obedience to God and as a testimony to those around us, especially to John."

"Right. The floodgates are open and somehow we have to stop the flow. We must do the impossible," he almost laughed, kissing her hair. "I love your hair style, by the way, but then I love everything about you."

"Thank you, my dear man. I can only think of one person who can help. Why don't you talk to Him now."

"Well, I've never prayed with my beloved's head on my chest before, but since this won't be the last time, I'll try."

As Gabe committed them to God's care, honor and love, Jo wondered how long it would be before she could tell Gabe she loved him without reservation.

As he turned to head over to where John was keeping watch, he grinned and said, "Now you know the other reason I needed to give up snuff. I want you to enjoy kissing me and I knew you wouldn't as long as I chewed. And you also know why, when we breed Solomon again, there won't be any problem about who gets what. Good-night, my love."

She laughed, "You were so confident."

"I told you, God told me."

# Chapter 31

When Jo, for that was going to be her name from now on, awoke, she hugged the sheet to her, as the warm afterglow of the previous evening wrapped around her. Here was love such as women hallucinate about, a love that was crashing all around her, a love that she wanted and was hers for the taking. *Gabe, what are you thinking and feeling this morning? I want to bask in your love for the rest of my life.*

Then she remembered that Rusty and Marie were off today. She sat up in bed, to find a blaze of golden glory flooding the room, reflected on the old wallpaper. She hugged herself in an attempt to keep from shouting to the glorious light that promised one more richly warm day.

Dana knocked on her door and rescued her again. "Mom, it's your day in the kitchen, John wants to get going, and if we don't hurry, we'll miss Sunday school."

"Coming, Honey, coming." she called back. "First things first, Mom," she said aloud to herself, as she headed to the bathroom, "and don't you forget that."

Her family were the only ones who responded to the ring of the bell, and when they gathered in the kitchen, the only thing they smelled was coffee. "If there is anyone who can't eat last night's left overs, I'll make you some toast, otherwise help yourself to what's in the fridge, while I pack a box of goodies for John to take back with him."

She thought Gabe would join them for breakfast and wondered why he hadn't. *Can he not face me? Was last night a sham, a one-time thing, an, I'll get even for all your meanness? No, no, I am not heading into another strange relationship, Gabe is different, Gabe is different, I know he is.*

"Did anyone see Gabe this morning?"

"He left the ranch in his jeep, after helping with the chores," John informed her. "Mom, since he isn't here, may I ask you something personal?"

She looked questioningly at him, wondering if he had not been sleeping after all last night. "Of course."

"Did you and Gabe have a thing for each other years ago?"

"Thing?" She was stalling.

Rob jumped in with, "You know, a crush."

She looked at each one in turn. "What's going on here, a conspiracy?"

"Na, but we've been watching you and you're different when he's around, and Rusty won't tell us anything."

"Well, that's the first time he kept something to himself."

"Did you, Mom?" Dana asked.

Perhaps this was God's timing and although they would have to miss Sunday school, it might be best to hang it all out now.

"Yes we did."

"Why didn't you marry him instead of Dad?" John asked.

"Because Gabe was saved. Since I only pretended to be, I couldn't follow God's plan for my life. I was rebellious, a sinner, and didn't care what God wanted. And, we sorta got separated by, *I won't mention my parents,* the miles and different interests between us."

Dana was leaning on the table cradling her chin. "Did you love him?"

"Dana!"

"Well, did you?" Rob and John asked.

"Yes, I did, but didn't know it." She had pretended indifference to their questions by packing John's box, and now as she closed the lid, she said, "but look what wonderful children I have because I met Louis."

"Did you love Dad?" John asked.

"Oh, yes. I couldn't have married him without loving him." That was the truth.

"What happened, Mom? You're such a warm, kind hearted person."

"I don't know John, I really don't know."

Rob spouted out rather strongly. "It wasn't your fault he did what he did."

She laid a hand on his arm. "I'm not sure he could have done otherwise, for he didn't know Christ so he had no power but his own with which to fight." She looked at all of them. "When you're fighting the devil, you had better have God on your side."

She looked at John. "That's why I was so concerned about you and Jodi. She could very easily have accepted Christ into her heart to please you, as I did with Gabe. You must make very certain her decision was real and not based on feelings for you, but as a true awakening of her sinfulness by the Holy Spirit."

"I did, Mom, but I will again."

"Now, about Gabe." She leaned back in her chair. "What do you all think of him?"

"Great, I like him," were their answers.

"I was going to wait awhile before telling you this, but it seems, God has opened a wide path and I had better run on it. So, what if I were to fall in love with him?"

John jumped up and went to stand at the screened door. She quickly pushed back her chair to stand when he turned. "I knew it! I knew it!"

"What? What?" Rob asked, going to stand in front of him.

John ignored him. "You already love him. I could see it. You'd have to be blind not to."

"Just because you're in love with Jodi doesn't mean . . ."

"Oh, Rob, shut up," he said gently. "You think I'm in love with Jodi, but you can't see Mom is in love with Gabe."

Rob turned then to Jo. "Are you Mom?"

"Truthfully, yes, with my heart, but my mind won't release me from your father. And please don't ask me to explain that."

"Has he asked you to marry him?" John wanted to know.

"No. Yes."

"Wow!" Rob explained as if he understood what was going on.

"What kind of answer was that, Mom?" Dana's face and voice questioned.

"He told me several times that he loves me and most of the time, but not always," she reminded them with a shake of her finger, "it means I want to marry you." Glancing at her watch, she exclaimed, "We missed Sunday school and don't have time for church. John, you have to get going and we might as well take the rest of the morning to finish cleaning up outside.

She began putting food in the fridge, and since the kids hadn't moved, said, "What would you think about me marrying again, having a husband, a man around here. Someone who might want to give you directions, advice, and who might even love you too."

John went over and leaned against the table where she stood, grasping the back of a chair. "Are we talking Gabe or someone else?"

Then she knew, she had her answer. It would be Gabe or no one.

She accepted his challenged look by looking him directly in the eyes. "It would be Gabe, or no one."

"Good," he simply stated. "Gabe has been a part of this ranch and the Simpsons ever since I can remember. It's like he's a part of this family anyway, just like Rusty and Marie."

When he threw his arms around his mom, they both had tears in their eyes, and she almost missed hearing Rob's "Yippie", and Dana's "Super", but she felt their hugs and support for her decision.

"Oh, my dear, dear children. What would I do without you?"

"Where else would I find a beautiful woman on such a hot day?" Gabe surprised Jo, as she floated leisurely in the water. He quickly joined her.

His face was radiant as the sun glistened on his water soaked skin. She followed him, until too tired, and swam to a shallow end to catch her breath. When he joined her, she exclaimed. "Gabe, I don't know when I've been happier, when I've felt so exhilarated."

She would only know later what pleasure those words brought him, but they weren't enough. Then she turned and pushed off to float on her back again, her body awash with water one minute and glistening beads from the sun's reflection the next. He floated beside her.

"You talked last night about remembering our past. Were you referring to that summer, when you turned seventeen and came here alone?"

She turned over and swam to the bank. "The kids talked about taking a dip this afternoon."

Gabe followed, taking her hand as they came to the shallow edge and walked up the bank to their clothes.

"Jo?"

She ignored him as she smoothed the water from her body

with her hands, but feeling his eyes on her, simply said, "We were so young then, Gabe, so innocent, so afraid, or, at least I was." She tried to laugh, but when she reached for her blouse and looked at him to see the misery in his face, she realized he needed more explanation.

"All right, Gabe. Yes. I've thought about it many times, especially since I found out you were still around and single. I never swim here that I don't think of you. That's why I came here today." Then she did laugh a little to ease the tension. If he only knew how fearful she had been all day when she did not see him, and how much she had needed to be in the water to think of him and to trust in his sincerity. "You have the body of a young man."

"Jo, quit playing games with me. I am not Louis and I love you, woman. Haven't you allowed that to sink in yet? I love you, Jo, and you never need to be afraid of me or of my true intentions." He was leaning over backwards to give her the space she needed. "I need something from you."

She leaned against his chest with her arms around him. Then she lifted her face, and received his kiss. It was soft and full of love and hope.

"I loved you then and probably never quit, but I loved Louis too and never thought of you; at least I don't have that on my conscience." Taking his face in her hands, I love you now, Gabe with an adult, mature love." Her kiss showed him she wasn't playing games. "Now we need to finish dressing."

Silently they dressed, with their wet suits patterning through. As they walked to their horses, she combed through her hair with Gabe's comb, then took his hand in hers.

As they led the horses, she looked away into the distance, remembering. "Louis was such a disappointment, and I was so hurt, and didn't want, don't want to be hurt again. But you haven't changed, you still take my breath away."

He tried to draw her to him, but she protested. "I'm the

cook on Sundays, remember, and I hope you will join us for more left-overs." She did brush his cheek with her mouth, before continuing. "Remember that first morning when you met me on my morning ride?"

"Yes.'

"Well, you really sent my emotions into a tail spin. Then when I found out you weren't married, I wondered if you were just trying to go back to that summer, to recapture a pleasant memory or something. I didn't want any of that.

"Sky and Brawn Beauty were the catalyst to crack the ice; then you came to work for me, and your presence, your interest in my welfare and that of my children touched me deeply. You have been so gentle, yet forceful, and knowledgeable, that I began to relax and see that you weren't interested in the past, but the present. I knew that if either of us opened up the gate to what we were feeling, a flood of love so powerful would sweep over us that we might not be able to control it."

She turned to him, letting the reins fall to the ground. "Thanks to the children, it has, Gabe. I love you so much, with my heart and my mind, and I want to marry you."

Their eyes searched one another before they were joined in a sweeping embrace, before his lips rubbed along her mouth, searching, seeking, and lifting her emotionally into another world.

Then she happily told him about the children's concerns earlier in the day.

"They saw our love, Gabe, and they approve. They already love and respect you," she told him, with both her hands on his dear face. "I love you without reservations. All the twisting and torment of the past is gone. I feel such a crystal pure, comforted love for you that I can't express it." She drew his mouth to hers for a gentle but thorough kiss."

"Jo," he cried. "When will you marry me: today, tomorrow,

Tuesday? I have loved, waited, wanted, needed you for so many years. I can't wait till you plan some big splash."

With an endearing look, she asked him. "How many days does it take to get a marriage license in Kentucky?"

"Oh, you wonderful creature." He picked her up and swung her around, "Oh, thank you Father, thank you, thank you," he cried before putting her down as they hadn't heard the children's horses approaching.

It was Roy. With absolute radiance and their arms entwined, Gabe told him, "you are the first to know. Jo has promised to marry me!"

"Expected it. Congratulations."

"But don't say anything till we have a chance to tell the children and Rusty and Marie, Okay?" Jo exacted a promise.

"Sure." Then giving Gabe as casual a look as possible, he asked, "Could I have a word with you?"

"Okay, I can take a hint," Jo said, wanting to stay, needing to know why Roy was here and wanted to talk to Gabe alone. "I'll dutifully go home and get a snack ready for supper," she said, as she was helped up on Flora's Girl. Then blowing a kiss to Gabe, she rode off, afraid to look back.

# Chapter 32

When Gabe joined them for supper, Jo watched concern fade away as he looked at her.

"What is it?"

"Just Rocko, riding carefree on your land." She sensed it was more than that, but her great desire to give her wonderful news to her family, pushed it aside and was forgotten.

Rob, Dana, Rusty, and Marie, who were seated at the kitchen table, seemed to be waiting impatiently like "something is different here." Gabe waited for Jo to pour the last of the iced tea, then she went to stand beside him and expectantly looked down as he spoke. "Before we return thanks for our food," he took her arm and drew it within his and held on to it with his other hand. "I would like to ask Rob and Dana a question."

"Shoot," Rob said. Afterward, he said, that when Gabe took her arm in front of everyone, he knew what was coming.

"I have loved your mother since I was nineteen years old. Now that she has learned to love me, too, I would like to ask your permission to marry her. What do you say, may I?"

They hardly heard, "You got it, way to go, and yippie," for the quick scrapes of chairs and shouts and hugs. "Wait till

John hears this!" Rob shouted. There was not a dry eye among them and the napkins were used for wiping those happy tears away and blowing noses.

When a pause came, the inevitable question was, when?

They both laughed and began talking at once, then Jo stopped and let Gabe tell them. "As soon as we can arrange it. Tomorrow if we could."

No one was really surprised and the children were really impressed that Gabe would ask their permission. Then, when he asked the blessing, he also included praise to God for working so fast to bring Jo and him together, and for so much love and support from the family and friends.

Rusty broached the subject of the name of Jo as he held a chair for Marie. "Since you're goin' ta be around here, Gabe, and use the name of Jo, would the two of you have any objections if the rest of used it also, or is it special between you two?"

Jo looked to Gabe as he helped her to sit down, before she spoke. "It has been our special name, but I like it so much, I would love to have everyone call me Jo from now on."

"Mom, that's my name for you, always has been and always will be so: question. We aren't going to have leftovers forever, are we?" Dana asked.

They all burst out laughing and Jo could hardly answer her. This attitude of Dana's was just one more reason to love her so. "This should finish them up, and we better hurry and eat or we'll miss church."

"Mind if I join you at your church?" Gabe asked.

"What do you think? Okay. Right kids?"

The next morning when Jo rode in from exercising Sky, Rusty was in an uproar over a delivery of moldy hay. He was ever ready to impart his wisdom; never forgetting the value of a lesson well learned. He still taught simply, expertly, and plainly.

This load of hay was a small one because their own second cut of hay was being cut now. The first cut went to Jon Altman the farmer who had been cutting it for years and to whom Jo would be eternally grateful, for the cuttings kept the fields from becoming overgrown with thick, unmanageable weeds. It had arrived while Gabe and the rest of the men were busy elsewhere. She had seen Roy wave the truck driver to follow him, and would have allowed the hay to be unloaded, had Rusty not stepped from the barn as the truck passed, and not liking the color, made the driver stop and break a bale open. Inside was mold.

"Looks like it got rained on and baled wet."

Tim, pale faced, for not checking for himself asked, "How could you tell from so far away?"

"Learn ta look at how things should look, then when they don't, you can run a check." He picked up a handful. "Smell." Then he spread it in his hand. "Look, careful now and you can see traces of the mold. This stuff isn't fit ta feed a horse."

Jo stepped up to get a good look too. She was angered by the perpetrated hoax. "Take this back and bring me good rich, selected green hay, with plenty of leaf," she mimicked Rusty, her teacher.

Rusty laughed at her as the trucker turned around. He cautioned Roy to show his men what to look for. "Remember to check everything that arrives here and if you don't know what ta look for, don't be afraid ta go ta Gabe or me."

"Yes, Sir, I will," he replied.

"Rusty and Tim," Jo spoke without allowing her troubled spirit from showing on her face. Before you get back to work, I thought I should tell you that Rocko and someone else was on our land again, down near the swimming hole."

Rusty took off his hat and reset it as he spoke. "That's gettin' brazen and too close ta the stables."

She looked a bit sheepish as she remarked, "Well, I went a

little farther than usual on purpose. But that's neither here nor there. What I'm wondering, is what does he want? Why is he familiarizing himself with the layout of our land?"

"I'm beginnin' to reason it out, so tell Gabe I need ta see him before you two take off for the court house and the preachers."

"And the printers, post office, florists, and on, and on." she laughed at the wonder of it all. "I don't think we'll make it by this Sunday, the next Sunday, maybe."

Tuesday, a mist hung over the fields, as Jo and Gabe exercised two newer horses. It was a sweet moment together of planning for their small intimate wedding and private romancing, before entering into the busy day's activities.

"I can't stand just having these few private moments caught during the day, Gabe," she said, as she snuggled against him in the tack room.

"Jo. I have waited for you for all these years, to hold you close and kiss you and say I love you, and if Rocko doesn't cause us any problems, we'll soon be united. Sooo, my pretty one, hang in there."

At dinner that night, Rob and Dana excitedly talked about school, activities, and new friends. Life at the ranch had begun taking on a regular, more relaxed schedule for the first time since the wedding was announced.

The next day, as soon as the kids were off to school, Jo and Marie went shopping to a jewelry and boutique store. Gabe had some mysterious business of his own to attend to, so he said. Rusty was left behind to ride the range with Roy, Tim, or Josh, checking on water, feed, straw, one of the pregnant mares, or any problems.

The north range had just come into prime pastureland, with the water hole properly drained and cleaned out, and fresh water running in and out of it ready for winter use. A new shelter had been built and installation of wood posts and fence, where needed, had been completed. Wire was strung behind thick brush covering to secure the field in other places.

The good stock: the well-bred mares and Skys' The Limit, Brawn Beauty, and Solomon, were always stabled or in paddocks close to the ranch. The rest of the horses were pastured in rotating ranges preceded by Judd Klein's sheep, and sometimes her own beef cattle and sheep, to reduce worm infestation. Harrowing then followed, to serrate the soil and scatter the harmful dung, thereby encouraging new grass to grow and parasites to die.

Some probably thought she coddled her horses. Having begun with four, she now had over fifty, and had sold nine at private sales and made a nice profit with three more ready for sale. So if getting horses on their feet again, making them well and strong and useful to others was coddling, she would coddle.

A careful record was kept and everyone save Marie and Dana, knew into which pasture or stable to go in search of a particular horse. Roy and his helpers moved horses from field to field, kept check on fences, water supplies and troughs, distributed feed and hay, as well as looked after the cattle and sheep. They were sensible and reliable men and had, or were being taught to have, that patient, gentle quality necessary to work with horses.

Contradicting reason, Sky and Brawn Beauty's return to health was the beginning of having Jo's name spread about. Horses came and went, and people visiting the ranch saw how the horses were handled and treated. There was no problem in reselling; in fact, she now had a waiting list.

Although Rob was in school, he shared a few duties and was always ready with a helping hand in any situation. He counted it a privilege to have Solomon saddled and ready for Gabe and wasn't afraid to saddle and ride Brawn Beauty himself.

Rusty still assumed a lot of responsibility and took over the role of a vet and all that entailed in and out of the sunshine. Jo wondered how he managed to keep things straight, but found he did. Come spring, when the foals began being born, they would probably have their hands full again. Right now a pattern, a routine, had developed to everyone's satisfaction. The only snag was Rocko and the rider on the palomino.

After she and Gabe were married, she wanted to give Rusty and Marie every Saturday off too. Of course, they had a lot of freedom during the day to rest, shop, visit, whatever.

Jo's dismay over killing horses that had years of useful and pleasure-filled life ahead of them, made her a target or an example, it didn't matter which, to would-be-rustlers. Enjoying a kiss in the tack room one afternoon, Gabe warned her that she was not immune to the possibility of rustlers.

"Every meat packer and auction has been visited on occasion by someone searching for a missing horse. It's easy to lead half-a-dozen horses from a field, and once they're hanging in a meat locker, the evidence is destroyed."

"But we keep such careful track of our horses and are always out riding the land. It won't happen here," she wanted to believe.

She tried to dismiss it from her mind as she stood inside her bedroom window that night, thinking about Gabe. He had been mysteriously absent again today for a few hours. She thought he had been some place on the ranch, but wasn't sure. As she made her way to the bed, a streak of lightning cut across the sky and soon rain began to fall. Maybe it would lull her to sleep.

# Chapter 33

The mums hung heavy with blossoms and the squirrels were busier and bolder than usual. It had been an average summer of rainfall, but September had ended with very little rain. They needed the rain, which was continuing from the night before.

Jo lifted her face to it. At breakfast, it was still a steady downpour, pounding the parched earth, so she drove the children to the bus stop.

Gabe had not come for breakfast, and Jo left for the auction without having the chance to find out where he was. She returned at three with a visitor, and seeing Gabe standing just inside the newer barn, motioned for him to come to the house.

Paula Mackey, a recent victim of rustlers, had visited every auction and meat packing plant within the radius of three hundred miles, searching for her thoroughbred, worth fifty thousand dollars, and two other well-bred mares valued at fifteen and twenty-five thousand. Her two weeks' search had been in vain.

Gabe removed his slicker and laid it over a chair before entering the house, eyeing the big white Lincoln in the driveway. Jo poured him a cup of coffee as she introduced him.

"Paula owns a stable in Hanover, Pennsylvania. Rustlers stole three of her horses, one a thoroughbred."

When she handed him his coffee, she couldn't help but look into his eyes. Always, she saw love, and something challenging, insisting, disturbing her thoughts. Today, there was something else.

She laid her hand affectionately on his arm, as she asked with marked concern, "What is it, Gabe?"

He spoke to Paula before answering her question. "Strange that you should be here just now, Mrs. Mackey," he said. Then giving his full attention to Jo, he stated as easily as possible. "Four of our horses from the north range are missing."

For a moment, Jo didn't know what to say, but had found out where Gabe was this morning. "Well, you were right, Paula. They have struck here too," she stated with an air of defeat. She couldn't afford to lose one horse, even if it wasn't a thoroughbred and only worth a couple thousand. She sat down with an air of dejection. "Tell me about it, Gabe."

Gabe sat where he could see Jo's face. "There's not much to tell. It happened sometime during the night, I expect. The rain was used for cover and has washed away any footprints or truck tire marks, although in this case, I don't think a truck was required."

Paula, alert as Jo, asked, "No truck?"

Gabe's eyes didn't leave Jo's. "Rocko's been riding the boundary up there for weeks now. I think he rode over in the rain, took them, led them directly to the slaughterhouse, and by the time I arrived this morning, the four horses were already strung up. Just an early small shipment, the assistant foreman said."

"Do you think Pierce knows?" Her voice was rather placid, as if the truth hadn't quite sunk in. Depending on which horses were taken, her loss was probably under thirteen thousand dollars, but to her it might as well have been one hundred thousand. The prevailing problem was the accessibility of her ranch to Reinhart's, and Rocko's free reign. There was nothing she could do about that.

Gabe answered defensively, "I'm sure he doesn't and I don't want him to, not yet anyway."

Paula was taken back and voiced her criticism of Jo's attitude. "You aren't even angry?"

"Oh, yes, I'm angry, all right." she answered, glancing at Paula.

"Then why aren't you hopping mad? I was and still am."

"Because our situation is different from yours. You stand a chance, however slight, of recovering yours, we don't."

"I don't understand," Paula stated, an understatement of her true feelings.

"You came to Donaldson to check on the horses going through the auction and then to pay a visit to Reinhart's Packing Company. Reinhart is our next door neighbor, so to speak."

"And if you think your horses are there, think again," Gabe remarked gloomily. "I worked there until a few weeks ago, and nothing but horses with papers passed through the plant. I don't think Rocko, the new manager, has reached into Pennsylvania to rustle yet."

"But you think he has reached over the fence, as it were?"

"I do," Gabe answered, turning his attention back to his beloved.

"Call Pierce and tell him," she almost demanded.

Gabe resisted going to her. The fiery demand told him she was strung pretty tight. "He's not home yet, you know that. Wouldn't you like to catch a man like Rocko, and put him where he belongs? It would solve more than one problem with him out of the way."

"It would indeed," she conceded, relishing the thought of not having to deal with Rocko anymore. "What do you suggest?"

"A board meeting, as soon as the children get home from school."

How she loved the way he always thought of them and included them in his plans. Thankfulness in the form of a smile and a light in her eyes, reached across the room to Gabe. She would have rushed into his arms if Paula hadn't been there, but she simply gave him a very expressive look and stated, "Good idea."

Turning to Paula, she said, "I'd like you to stay. Marie prepares the best meals this side of the Ohio."

"I couldn't possibly refuse that offer."

Gabe excused himself and returned to the porch with Jo, to find he no longer needed his slicker. He turned at Jo's touch. She was in his arms before he realized it, squeezing him hard, temporarily shutting out the broader issues of the moment, content in his strength. "Thank you for being here. I love you so much." She kissed him with loving gratitude.

"Now get back in there," he teased, with a glint in his eyes.

She glanced up at the sky; the clouds were clearing, leaving behind a land-washed day. When he picked up his slicker and returned to the barn, she saw a truck with a horse trailer behind it pull alongside the white Lincoln. Another buyer had arrived. "I hope not to buy one of the four missing horses or news will travel faster than a wild fire."

Paula Mackey left right after dinner, and Jo, Rob, and Dana rode out to the north pasture, empty now of horses, on the pretense of looking for something the rest missed. Actually, the children were so concerned, she thought it a good idea to let them ride out to the scene of the crime.

Afterward everyone assembled in the office, ready to hear Gabe's plan. Jo sat at the desk, her back to the triple window. Because of the damp air and mud, Jo had needed to change clothes and work on her hair. She wanted to look more feminine than usual, so chose a peasant blouse and skirt, and had a matching scarf around her neck. As she slipped straw sandals on her feet, she realized it was probably the last time until next summer.

*I must do this more often.* She surveyed herself in the mirror, prior to heading for the office. *I've been dressing like a cowgirl all summer, and although I have loved the relaxed dressing, I am still a woman and a mother.*

She noticed a pleased look spread across Gabe's face when he entered the room, and she felt a rush of love. Every day she learned something new about him, drawing him ever closer, making him ever more endearing and desirous. As it was, she simply motioned for him to be seated near her at the end of the desk.

"I asked Gabe to sit here, so everyone could see him without craning his neck. Roy, welcome to the inner circle. Just kidding. It's just us chickens really. But, seriously, I believe Gabe has a plan. So, My Dear, if you will."

He grinned at that, but fired straight from the hip, nevertheless. "We need more help, full-time help. Men who are able to work shifts. If we can't recruit local men who can go home at night, we'll have to advertise for men, with room and board provided, and fix up the rest of that bunkhouse and then hire a full-time cook."

Jo was flabbergasted and swallowed the lump in her throat. "For how long?"

"Till we catch Rocko red handed!" There was no flirting with his answer; he was all business.

"But that could be a very short time. It doesn't seem logical to hire men and go to all the expense you mentioned, then lay them off."

"It could be a very long time too. How long is it that we have been seeing Rocko riding brazenly on your land, and only last night did he strike?"

Rob asked, "Why can't we all work shifts, and keep the

horses closer to the house and in larger groups? Then we wouldn't need so many extras."

Jo suggested, "Rob you are already taking enough upon yourself. But, Gabe I wonder, haven't you already begun doing exactly as Rob suggests?"

"Yes, and that was a great suggestion, Rob. The horses are safe until we come up with a way to trap Rocko."

"I could do more than cook," Dana declared.

"That you could, young lady," Rusty said, giving her an encouraging wink. He sensed Jo's rejection was financially based, something Gabe may not be considering, and he was searching madly for a different solution.

Jo inquired, "Where would we get men whom we were sure would be sympathetic to our purpose, and, whom we could trust with our plans?"

Rusty spoke up again. "No problem there. Some of those men we hired in June would do. They're old as I am, but might be willin' ta work short shifts. They'd all be loyal. You met most of them an' I understand some of them already told you they would help if you be needin' them for anythin'. I have a feelin' they'd be rarin' ta get in on somethin' like horse rustlin'. It would make them think of the good ole days, in a manner of speakin'."

He stood and walked to the other side of the desk to gaze into the distant darkening land. "Somethin' naggin' my brain." He turned to Gabe. "Do you still have your airplane?"

Jo just shook her head. *Will wonders never cease?* She was sure there were many things about Gabe that she didn't know, and as she glanced toward the children, she saw them look at Gabe with new wonder and admiration too.

"Yes, but . . ."

"If you 're willin' ta trust me, first thing in the mornin' we're goin' for a plane ride."

"Why?" Jo needed to ask.

"If'n I can find what I'll be lookin' for, our regulars an' just a few extras can handle our problem."

"Well, knowing you, my dear friend, we might as well dismiss this meeting. Don't you all agree?"

"Right about that," seemed to be the consensus of opinion.

"Well, let's pray, then everyone but Rob and Dana may go and do whatever, and thanks for the extra hour of your time."

As soon as the door was shut and the men had gone, she threw her arms around her kids and started to cry.

"What's wrong, Mom?" Dana asked.

Taking off the scarf to dry her tears, she tried to reply. "Nothing, nothing at all." Then looking at each one, she said, "How can I ever tell you both how proud of you I am? How much I appreciate the way you have, well, have literally pitched in here? How can I tell you how much my heart overflows with love and pride as I've watched you work your heart out for my dream?" Attempting a smile, "And worked off some skin too."

She took Rob's hands. "Look at them. Louis would have had a fit." Then she did laugh and he put his arms around her and hugged her.

"We've come a long way haven't we, Mom?" Rob stated.

"Indeed we have."

"I can't imagine this happening five years ago."

"Nor can I Rob. Louis, in all his strictness and perverseness, provided well, too well for us, but I am glad you were both young enough to be able to develop into the well-rounded young people that you are."

"Thanks for being what you are, Mom, otherwise, we'd still be back in Jersey, oop's sorry Dana, and John would be going to the university there studying some pre-arranged subject in which he had no interest."

"That's why, brother, I am happier here too. Honest, Mom. I really am, now."

"I guess we're living proof, that if we give God enough rope, He'll lasso us in. Now, I suppose you have homework and a football game tomorrow night, so off you go. Good night Rob," she gave him another hug and kiss, "Good-night Dana," and hugged and kissed her also. "I love you guys."

# Chapter 34

To see the Bluegrass Country from the air was breath taking. The magnificent sweep of undulating terrain, marked by rounded knolls and scenic dales, raced beneath them; the western sky was now clear and bright with the layers of vapor having been absorbed by the sun.

Jo and Roy listened intently as Rusty pointed out various ranches. Finally, Gabe was flying over his old ranch, then the Simpson Ranch.

"Keep west, toward the National Forest," Rusty instructed him, over the noise of the motor and wind. "Now, sweep low and circle around that forested area off to the Southeast."

After a low run over the area, he asked, "What do you see?"

"Nothing, just tops of trees, and beyond, the National Forest," Gabe said.

"Next time around, look straight into it."

Gabe dipped a wing swinging the plane around, and Jo felt her breakfast slide upward. Gabe happened to glance her way and saw the queasy look. He quickly leveled off, then flew back over the rolling fields, until they were once again flying low over the trees.

Jo felt faint, but tried to concentrate on Rusty's words and the forest below.

"Nothing!" Gabe said.

"Exactly," Jo declared.

"I don't see anything either," Roy trailed.

"Now swing around Judd Kleins and the National Forest. See if we can see where he's flaunting grazing rules and ignoring Forest Service orders."

Gabe stated, "He's been served a dozen or more citations, detailing violations."

"Just laughs in Joel Strouse's face," Roy declared.

Even when Gabe needed to turn the plane, he did so with as little dipping as possible. Whatever made Jo uncomfortable, did double for him.

"Down there," Roy pointed. "A whole herd of cattle."

"Thought so," Rusty declared.

Jo trying to be involved, asked, "Why is he pretending he only has a few cattle and using only a few acres of our land. Obviously he could use every acre I own?"

"We may never know that answer," Gabe said, as he easily climbed higher, before turning the plane to fly back over Klein's place.

"Look at those cars and rows of cages." Rusty pointed down. "Looks like chicken pens or rabbit hutches."

Roy volunteered, "Heard he raises and trains birds for cock fighting, and that's unlawful in Kentucky. But, why all the cars? Wonder if he doesn't have cock fights in that building where those cars are parked, and that is prohibited too!"

"I think I'll give Joel a call when we get back," Gabe mentioned.

Seemingly satisfied, Rusty relaxed in his seat. "Good! Perfect! Now before goin' home, swing low like that in several places here an' there in case someone recognizes your plane an' guesses what we're up ta."

"No one at Reinhart's know I have a plane."

"Just the same."

"Rusty, have you lost your marbles?"

"Just hold on ta your britches, you'll see," was all he would say, and no amount of coaxing could drag anymore from him.

Gabe, more used to catching ground movement from the air, kept his eyes on a lone rider, then flew away from the ranch and circled back again, only higher.

"Did anyone see that rider off to the West? It isn't Rocko."

Someone else was on Simpson property in broad daylight who didn't belong there, and it wasn't any ranch hand they knew. No one they knew rode a palomino!

Back at the ranch, according to Rusty's instructions they each rounded up a horse, and with excitement and anticipation mounting, followed him toward the western range and the forested area. The farther they rode, the more dense and thick the brush and trees became.

Undaunted by the over-growth, Rusty continued, for he knew exactly where he was going. They followed silently, and eventually, single-file.

Jo realized she was riding a part of the land she had never ridden before, and apparently, no one else had either, not for a very long time. They rode on between stands of trees set in a line, circling and twisting until each one knew he would not be able to find his way back to open land without a guide.

Finally, in an arena type area, with leafy boughs for cover, but one deep in brush, Rusty reined in and asked, with a glint in his eyes, "Lost?"

"Yes," came the chorus of answers.

"Good. Then this is the perfect place to pasture the horses until Rocko is caught, and you won't have ta' hire any more help nor be worrin' about the bunkhouse and a cook."

They looked around in amazement.

"How did you know about this place? Grandpop and Dad never spoke of it, and Gabe and I in all our adventures as kids never found it."

"It's like that wall of trees in the story about Robinson Crusoe," Roy suggested, with an air of intelligence.

"Exactly like it, Roy. These trees were planted by your great grandpop, Jo. Mostly ta use for the same reason we are wantin' to use them. It worked then, should work now."

"Rustlers?" Gabe questioned.

"The same, only then it was cattle rustlin'."

"This isn't fit for a horse, Rusty." Gabe objected, and it would take a lot of muscle to rid it of this growth, to make it safe for horses."

"T'would, you're right. But then, with hay nets an' an artificial water source, it could be used. One man durin' the day an' one at night could handle every horse we got."

"Wouldn't Rocko think something's wrong when he doesn't see any horses anywhere?" Jo inquired, sensitive to their opinions.

"Not if'n we keep some in the north range, just a few, just enough ta tempt him, and stand guard there too."

"I don't think that would work." Roy was thinking aloud. "Rocko wouldn't dare steal from so few."

Jo pointed out, "We keep buying and selling. No one knows how many we have at one time, but us."

"I wouldn't be too sure of that either," Gabe corrected her. "Someone was checking on us this morning. Is he keeping track? Is he in cahoots with Rocko? From now on, I will sleep in the stable, and for once, I'm glad I am a light sleeper!"

No one protested his decision. Jo felt relieved that there would always be someone close to their best stock. Rusty's house being close by provided extra protection.

Jo looked at Gabe with a studied understanding. He was the first to speak, as he rode to her. "You know what this means?"

She knew, the rest just looked at them. "We have two days before our wedding." She knew he was feeling the same agony over the decision they had to make. It was so difficult to say, so heart wrenching, another week of waiting, but she had to make the decision. "Impossible! We will have to postpone, hopefully for just a week."

Rusty started to ride out of the enclosure, realizing more than the others do, how quickly they needed to get back and prepare the enclosure for use, if it was decided to use it. Roy obligingly lined up behind him. Jo, then Gabe brought up the rear.

"Mom and Dad were to arrive today, some uncles and aunts tomorrow, and others Sunday morning. "I have got to get to a phone!" she cried in alarm.

"Don't forget to call the Inn, the church, the caterer and florists," Gabe added.

*Perhaps it is just as well to have something else to think about. I know the days will go fast and God's presence, ever near, will guide and protect us and enable us to get through this.*

It seemed like a lot of work, but plans went ahead to prepare the corral, dubbed Eden, after the enclosure God made for Adam and Eve. Therefore, after lunch, a group of men returned to Eden with axes, shovels, and saws.

Rob was going to be so disappointed to have missed all this excitement, yet Jo knew deep in her heart, that the boy was stretched to the limit and she needed to be more protective of him. John was coming home for a wedding, or so he thought, and would want to help shoulder some of the workload. How could she get him to just relax one time?

She was carrying a burden known only to her Father. She cried to Him. *Give me the ability to catch a glimpse of how you want to use this situation in our lives. Help me to keep focused on you and what you want to do through our lives as we yield to you.*

Jo was in love: she was also a mother, rancher, and businesswoman. It seemed that love and mothering were taking a back seat as they had done in the past. Only this time, when the storm was over, there would be a rainbow.

Real rustling, a crime she had associated only with old western movies and the cowboy, with his hat at an angle and his spurs a-jingling, was also of gunmen, sod-busters, prospectors, and dance-hall women. It didn't cease in real life, when the inexhaustible pastures were fenced and the cowboy had hung up his rope and pistol.

Rustling wasn't her only problem. First, it had been the loss of Mitsi and Gabe, then Dana not wanting to ride, and Skys The Limit and the trailer accident. Then Brawn Beauty and the sick calf, and always Gabe. Although she now had to be totally concerned with rustlers who drove trucks or flew airplanes, she would not allow this new threat to her security and success of the ranch, to dampen her love for Gabe and her ultimate happiness. Neither would she do it alone. After the men left for Eden, she headed for her bedroom to meet with God.

# Chapter 33

Considering the beehive of activity surrounding the ranch, Jo was appreciative of her aunts, uncles, and cousins' willingness to refrain from overnight visiting until they received a phone call about the 'real' date of her wedding. They were all astounded about her news of rustlers, and actually wished they were there in the thick of things. She issued a "come on along then".

Her mom and dad, Ben and Lindsey Simpson, however, arrived in the afternoon before the kids came home from school. She couldn't imagine what any of her relatives might think, as they would turn into the lane and drive up to the ranch that they had all wanted so badly. "Oh, well, I can't worry about that."

As she hesitantly threw her arms around her parents, she breathed a prayer that she would show how much she loved them and the God they superficially honored.

She tried to talk to both of them as they walked up to the porch. "Mom, I am so glad to have you here. I'm swamped with preparations and cancellations, and Dad, we can use an extra hand, as you suggested. Oh, boy can we use you. I mean, if you're sure you want to assume the role of cowboy for a few days." Then she stopped, "Oh, did you want to get your suitcases or go to your room? Did you have lunch? Are you hungry?" With one look at her mom, Jo started to cry, and threw her arms around her mother.

"There, there, JoAnn, we'll help in any way possible. That's why we are here."

"Absolutely," Ben said, patting her shoulder, but the sound in his voice had a deliberate significance in it. "Where is Gabe?" This time the sound was unmistakable creating a maelstrom of anxiety in her mind. She was in for trouble with a capital T.

"I really don't know." She wiped her eyes with her father's handkerchief, not daring to look directly into his face in fear of what she would see there. "Usually, we know where the other one is because we want to and need to know."

It seemed Ben was relieved that Gabe wasn't around and wanted to question her about something, but Marie, whom they had met at some point over the last year and a half, appeared at the screened door.

After greetings and a refusal of a bite to eat, Ben seemed to take charge and led them straight back the hallway. He stopped with a look of disdain, at the doors to the office and den. They were standing wide open, sun was shining through the windows out into the hall, otherwise nothing had changed.

Jo had to grin at his bold, unreserved vexation, as she spoke over her mother's shoulder to him. "I thought you could use my room, well, I mean your parent's room, if that would be all right." Why did they bring out the worst in her and make her feel so insecure? *I guess I'll need to add "father" to my list of difficulties.*

"That's fine," he said, closing the door to the office before following them, for a moment holding her eyes, testing her will against his to re-open the door.

In her bedroom, Lindsey sat on the edge of the bed, while Jo watched her father shut the bedroom door behind him as he entered. Did they see the shudder pass over her as it clicked in place? It was just like the old days, and it scared her. She looked at her stylish heavy-set mom as she checked her salon styled hair in the mirror. She couldn't think of her as old, just stressed, but as usual, noticed she was in on whatever was going to be discussed. She felt sick and wished with all her heart that Gabe was beside her. But God was closer and she breathed another prayer to Him.

Suddenly, she had a flashback to that other time, and in a split second, remembered that if her parents hadn't interfered, she would never have married Louis. Since God had opened her mind to see it, He would strengthen her enough to face her father, on behalf of her children and her love for Gabe.

With that realization came the power from God to stand and take control. She was not twenty one but forty two years old, and she loved Gabe with all her heart, body, and soul. They might as well know it now.

Her dad was a seventy-four year old bullish sort of man, though just average in build and looks. He still felt he could control her, and before she could get her mouth open to take charge, he began. "About this man next door..."

"For crying out loud Dad, why don't you say, **boy** next door, words I have heard before. That's what you and Mom are still thinking."

She was almost beside herself with anger, dismay, and yet with a more adult, mature understanding of them, than they had of her. She knew in her heart it was God-given, and breathed a quick prayer of thanks.

She shook herself determinedly. "This **man** has a name just as he always had, and in the future, refer to him as Gabe, a name I happen to adore."

Ben started to reproach her with his expansive hand.

"JoAnn, we never . . ." but she stopped him with her outstretched palm-up hand.

"Don't say, you never, because you know you both kept me from Gabe years ago, and as a result I married Louis." The look he gave her was meant to stop her, but it didn't. "Dad, why don't you just sit down in Grandma's rocker while I tell you both how much Gabe and I love each other, and how sure we are of God's will in bringing us together, and how much the children like him and are all for this wedding."

She walked to the door and stood against it, glad now it was shut. They would not walk out this time until she was ready for them to go.

"I don't know when we'll be married now, maybe a week, two weeks, I don't know. But I want you to stay on and watch us, listen to us, sneak around us if you want to. You will not find a kinder, more honest, noble, loving and gentle man this side of heaven. If it hadn't been for you, I would have married Gabe twenty years ago, instead of Louis." They could surely hear the determination in her voice. "I won't have you interfere this time!

"God brought us together in a unique and awesome way, and I can hardly wait to become his wife. I expect you to pay him the respect due him, to help us in any way you can during this very difficult time we are going through, especially so when the children are around.

They happen to love and honor you and the memory of their father, because they have been brought up well. I want them to love you more, by the time you have to leave here.

"By the way, you are welcome here anytime for any length of time you might desire. But Gabe and I are in charge, and with Rusty and Marie, the children and I, are, were doing a first-rate job until the rustlers began taking our horses."

She felt it safe to leave the door and went to sit beside her mother. Taking her hand, she began her story of love. By the time she finished, tears blurred her eyes and Lindsey took off her glasses and reached over to hug her daughter.

"I admit we came here with a chip on our shoulder about..."

"Say his name, for crying out loud, say it, Mom—Gabe, Gabe. It won't kill you."

"Gabe."

"See, that's not so hard," she laughed, but hadn't looked at Ben to see his reaction. "And it's not so hard to say you were wrong either."

"We were, are wrong about both of you, and I apologize and ask your forgiveness."

"You got it," she cried tears as she hugged her mom again. When they looked at silent Ben, still slightly smoldering, they both went to him and each taking an arm, made him stand up. "Well, Dad?"

"Ben?"

Shaking them free, he said, "I'm not a romantic, JoAnn, but..."

"Say it Dad, for once admit you were wrong about me."

He walked over to the door, but before he could open it, Jo beat him to it and leaned against it again, with tears streaming down her face imploring him to understand.

*Dear God help this man, help me.* "I won't let you out until the air is clear."

Standing so near his daughter, watching the torment in her face, the tears on her cheeks, must have been the 'final straw'. "Come here," and she fairly flew into his embrace. "I'm sorry. I was wrong, and I might as well admit it now, I was wrong to fight you about this ranch too."

"Oh, Dad."

"Ben, you stubborn old dear," Lindsey cried, as she joined the circle of love.

# Chapter 36

That night, just as everyone had dozed off, an electric sense of change filled the air; a storm rolled in. Beyond the horizon, noiseless streaks of lightening flared and died. The faint muttering of thunder grew louder as the frightening lightning flashes, grew longer, brighter, and closer.

As a wind charged out of the West, large drops of rain splattered, the first warning of the onslaught heading their way. It swept the fields, pounding the ground. Leaves, discolored by death, ripped away as branches bent to the ground. Anything that wasn't bolted or nailed down well, was ripped loose.

For more than an hour, the storm raged with intensity, before the thunder moved off and the last flickers of lightening flared, but didn't die. Instead, they grew with unbelievable speed, until one was out of control, before Gabe, who had stood just inside the stable doors with the thoroughbreds and better bred of horses, realized that several of the outbuildings had caught fire.

At the clanging of the bell, the few sleeping, were startled awake, and the others, glad for an excuse to get out of bed, ran outside.

With shouts of excitement and questions tumbling over one another, a bucket brigade was begun and hoses pulled into use. Because of the drenching rain, the wood of the old buildings was saturated and the utility shed was the only building destroyed. They had much to be thankful for and to pray about.

Gabe was furious that Tim, who was on guard, had left the horses unattended and sent him high-tailing it back to them.

Much later, wet and muddy, the firefighters, including Ben and Lindsey, had returned to their dwellings to shower and try to get back to sleep. Gabe was making a final check on the fire after making sure Jo had returned to the house. Before going inside, she heard Tim come riding in at a gallop.

"Some horses are missing?" he called, as Gabe appeared on a run.

"Some! Some! How many?" he shouted angrily.

"I don't know. Three, four, maybe more."

"There were only fifteen up there, can't you count that high?"

Tim tried to explain. "When I got back there, I couldn't even find one. So I rode all over the range and only found eleven. They were excited and skittish as if someone had frightened them. They ran from me when I tried to round them up."

"All right, all right!" Gabe grimaced, moving his hand to indicate enough. "Get back up there and stay with those you did find. There won't be any more trouble tonight."

Tim didn't move, and Gabe, who had turned and started to walk away, stopped and turned around.

"May I ask you something? Did you ever find those other horses?"

The single light bulb from the stables was behind Gabe, therefore Tim couldn't see Gabe's face. "No, and we won't find these either, alive, that is."

"You mean..."

"Exactly."

"No wonder you were so mad when I left them unattended," he reflected. "Didn't take them rustlers long, I'll say that for them. They know what they're doing. The rain will cover their tracks this time too, and the fires kept you all occupied."

"Crimeanea, where have I been? The fire! Of course! I didn't see how it could have started by lightning because I didn't see it strike around here."

Gabe was really angry with himself now. "Someone was right here under my nose and I missed him."

Then he looked up at the cowboy. "You know more than anyone in this whole town knows about what happened here. Can you keep it to yourself till we catch them or do we have to lock you up?'

"I'll keep it to myself, and keep my eyes wide open from now on. But in return, let me know what's going on."

"Fair enough," Gabe replied, reaching forth his hand. "Now move along. I'll be right behind you."

After Tim had gone, Gabe heard his name and swirled around to find Jo fighting fear. He drew her to him. "How much did you hear?"

"All of it and it's my fault that you didn't see someone around here. If I hadn't visited you for a good-night kiss and to tell you about Mom and Dad, you would have had your mind on business," she cried softly against his chest.

"I admit I had my mind on you, but the storm chased that all away and kept me occupied, just as they wanted me to be."

"You're not just saying that," she asked, accepting his handkerchief.

"No, my sweet lady. Now there is nothing for you to do but to get John awake before he's fully asleep to come out here and sleep, so go back to bed. I'll give you a full report in the morning."

"Gabe, if you went over there right now, wouldn't you find them alive?"

"I thought of that, but I think they have trailered them somewhere, just in case I did run right over there. Remember what I said about keeping them for studs? There is still a chance the stallions are alive somewhere. If we could find out who is helping Rocko, or who is behind him, we might just find our horses still alive. They'll take them to the slaughter house, maybe one by one when I'm not suspecting."

"Someone else is in on this, like three or four people?"

"That's what I think. I no longer think Rocko is the king pin."

"How do we find that out?"

"I don't know...."

"What about your airplane, first thing in the morning?"

"I thought about that. Mind if I get John and Rob awake early?"

"How about Dad?"

"Trying to put salve on the wound," he teased. "But I'll do it. Set your alarm for five-thirty and do the honors of waking them up."

"Be careful, my darling."

She waited until he rode off, then wandered aimlessly through the barns. *I should have told him what I said to Klein. He could be the kingpin looking for revenge.* She talked to and petted the sleepy-eyed animals, feeling sleep coming over her weary body.

Gabe found her asleep in the aisle on soft hay with saddle blankets wrapped around her.

# Chapter 37

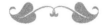

Although the plane ride did put salve on the wound, it was unproductive in turning up any leads. Everyone was sworn to secrecy, but John told Jodi about the rustlers. Jo took Gabe aside and told her story about Klein.

Gabe couldn't believe she had had the courage to accuse him. He kissed her. "You're something else, know that?" He put his finger on her lips. "I know what you're going to ask, and yes, I think you simply added fuel to his already smoldering fire."

"He fits the description of one of the men."

"But, I've never seen that horse before. That's the puzzle."

The following day, Pierce paid a visit, with Gabe, Rusty, Ben, and Lindsey present. Children, crops, and the fire was discussed at length. Finally, Pierce mentioned the real reason for his visit; Jodi had told him about the stolen horses.

Gabe could not accuse Rocko without seeming to say that Pierce had to be aware of the extra pounds of meat or was a poor businessman. So he remained in the background and allowed Jo to meet the challenge.

"Twice, to be exact," she informed him, as she sketched in the circumstances, "eight stolen, altogether."

He looked around incredulously. "You haven't called the sheriff?"

"No, I can't let people know. Who would sell to me when they realized I had a rustling problem?"

"I can see your point. Is there any way I can help?" His manner was formal and correct.

However, Jo sensed his sincerity. "Yes. Keep close watch on the horses you buy and the horses you kill and the amount of meat that goes through your plant. Make sure they are the same horses as the papers show and the weight equals out."

She knew she was almost accusing him, and glanced at Gabe. When she looked back at Pierce, it was to see furious eyes looking from one to the other.

"Are you accusing me of rustling?" He had been sitting foreword, playing with his hat between his knees. Now he jumped to his feet.

Jo, Gabe, and Rusty quickly stood when he did, and she went to him. "Pierce, consider this calmly. You asked, remember. If you had been anyone else, I would have said the same thing. I'm not accusing you, certainly not."

Gabe put his arm around Jo's waist, and said, "It is a dog eat dog world, remember, Pierce. I think you said something to that effect a few weeks or so ago on another visit."

"So I did,' he reflected. "I apologize. If I can be of any help . . ."

"Just keep this information under your proverbial hat for now. Don't even discuss it with your wife and children." Gabe reached out his hand, which Pierce accepted.

"That I will do," he said, making his way to the door.

Rusty followed him out. At the door Gabe told him, "I don't think it will be long before I get in touch with you for your help."

When he was gone, Ben asked Jo if she thought he was innocent. "Yes, I do."

"So do I," Gabe said, putting his arm around Jo. When she looked up at him, she saw a very tired man. Dark circles, rumpled clothing, a day-old beard, late for meals or none at all, were becoming a part of his life.

"Gabe when I asked you to become manager," his face was only inches away. "I never thought we would become involved in such a nasty business, and you would lose sleep and not even have time to eat."

He tried to quiet her, embarrassed in front of her parents.

"Ben, perhaps we should go get a cup of coffee," her mother said.

"No, please stay. We're family, or will be soon," she said to them, and to Gabe she said, "I mean it. I would have quit if I'd have realized my campaign would bring us so much danger and trouble."

"Well, look here, my darling, I am glad I am here. We're in this together and we will catch him."

"When?" She gazed into his eyes as she held his face in her hands. "I want to marry you and I don't want to wait forever."

"You won't my love," he promised her. "Ben, do you mind if I kiss your daughter?"

"Be my guest." he answered sincerely.

He brushed her face with his lips, then paused lightly on her lips with a warm meaningful kiss that said, "I love you", then he pushed her from him, took her hand and picking up light jackets from the back of a chair, said, "Enough of that! Let's go outside." He looked at her parents, "if you'll excuse us?"

"What's this all about?" she asked as they walked to the barn.

"Rocko and whoever is working with him are stupid enough to work on Wednesday or Thursday to correspond with the auction. I want to be sure and turn their hand this week and if there are no horses in the pastures, he'll come to the stables or paddock looking for them."

"I'm with you."

"Good," he gave her hand a squeeze. "So far no one knows about Eden, but we can't put them all in there or we'll never trap him. This will be hard to take, but hear me out. What I'd like to do, is put Bob, Bill, Flora's girl, and Lady in the pasture closest to Reinhart's land, under no apparent guard. He'll appear to be indolent and fall asleep and all the rest will be in Eden, except for those we keep right here under usually tight security."

They stopped to lean on the fence. "Josh will be the only guard in the pasture, but I'd like to use some of those old-timers and their free help in hide outs in the groves around the pasture.

"Then we'll get Jodi to spread the word that you and I are getting married and away on a honeymoon. Rusty will be out buying, John's at college, which will leave only Roy, Tim, Rob and maybe a couple cowboys. Rocko won't bother with those horses in the pasture if he thinks he could have easy pickin's with Sky, Brawn Beauty, Golden Girl, and Solomon, whom he thinks will be in the stable."

"I see what you're driving at. He'll be easier to catch if we can get him closer to the ranch. But, what a chance to take. Why not just put them all in Eden or bring them all here under heavy guard?"

"For how long a duration? Forever?"

"I see. We can't win without blocking his game?"

"That's right. Are you game then? I'm not saying it will work?"

"Yes, but I want to talk to Dad about calling his brothers and nephews to come help now, with our program. I think they would get a kick out of it," she said, reaching up for a hug and kiss.

After dinner, they made the switch, while Ben called his brothers and nephews and scheduled their free help. Rocko was seen riding the fence, first near the pasture observing the horses and guards, then riding off to the West. From the air, Gabe spotted another rider who resembled Klein's build, but for the life of him, he could not pinpoint the horse.

Sunday, John reluctantly returned to school. No one went to church, so Rusty led them in a Bible lesson. Monday through Wednesday, nothing happened.

"He's been scared off. Something spooked him," Rusty had to admit, in discussion.

"Some honeymoon that turned out to be," Jo teased, Wednesday at lunch.

But Gabe was in no teasing mood. "I'm open to suggestions. I have waited twenty-five years to marry this woman and can't wait much longer. You don't suppose someone squealed our plans, do you?" Gabe asked.

"Who?" Jo wondered. "Jodi's the only one we told. I trust her."

"Good question, Pierce, perhaps, inadvertently."

Ben spoke up with words of wisdom. "It seems to me, you need to quit wondering why that plan didn't work, and come up with a new one."

"By the way, if anyone is counting, it looks like the wedding is off for another week." Lindsey stated.

"Mom, I am really sorry, but the Lord has a reason, if nothing else than to teach us patience, and to prove that our love will stand the test of time." She suggested as an after-thought, "Maybe, He just wants you as parents and grandparents around here a little longer," she said, winking at them, then feeling that thumping in her chest again, quickly put her fingers on the artery at her neck, and it quit. Maybe she would say something to her Mom about it. "I know I am enjoying your company."

Ben's words were given consideration and a new plan was put into action.

Bit by bit, horses were taken from Eden, and turned out into various areas, until all were released. When the horses returned from the most northern pasture, another heifer came along. The aunts gladly took charge of this calf. They would not use Eden again, unless matters were not brought under control within the week. Elaborate plans were ready for use, when they were needed, and Jo and Gabe hoped it would be soon.

To all appearances, life at the ranch was back to normal, and her uncles, cousins, and wives were visiting with the purpose of being in the "thick" of things, and to be here for the wedding. They were working shifts, guarding, on the fringes, in hiding, but guarding, none-the-less.

Some of the old-timers who were helping were old friends of her uncles. They all seemed to be having a reminiscing blast, since there was about one man to every two pastured horses.

As one uncle succinctly put it, "Come lightning and high water, there was no way Rocko could steal a horse and get away with it this time." They really were getting a kick out of being put to use on the old place. "Besides, who is complaining about Marie's cooking?"

Jo was so happy they were here, mixing the past and present, to give of themselves in care of the ranch which had meant so much to them as they grew up. She couldn't imagine the discussions they must have been having as they gathered together, reminisced, guarded, and ate and drank coffee. Boy could they put away the food! But, here again, Marie had all the help she could use and then some. Rob and Dana were really enjoying their relatives and some unusual freedom to do what they wanted around the ranch and home.

# Chapter 38

Tuesday night a full moon peeked from behind a cloud, exposing several riders. One was walking his horse on Reinhart land, thinking trees concealed him. Another seemed interested in the pasture recently shut off to the horses, where Judd Klein's sheep now nibbled. A dozen shrewd eyes followed each man along the rolling terrain, the creaking of saddle leather the only sound in the still night air.

Finally, after what seemed like hours, the riders rode off. When the observers gathered back at the ranch at the end of their shift in the early morning, and reported their similar sightings, the group became confused and more concerned than before, this was not going to be a lark!

Were the rustlers going to move into several fields at once?

Tension had built with each successive day. The pressure resting on Gabe's shoulders made him irritable.

"Oh, let it come to an end," Jo prayed selfishly at night, as men were spirited into hiding places to stand guard. Would their plan work with so many people aware of it? "I can't despair, for I know my partner is omnipotent. Help me to lift my eyes to the mountains; for my help comes from the Lord, who made heaven and earth."

Since Pierce would keep rustled horses from being processed through his plant, what happened to hers? Were they still alive or had they been shipped off to another plant? If they were still around, why would Rocko take more, unless he was greedy or angry, and thought her horses were easy pickings. Or, is it all a ruse to scare me from my land?

Because of several sightings of cowboys on and off her land, for whatever reason, everyone felt that since the weatherman called for rain, this Friday night would be the night for Rocko to try again. All the men insisted on being used in some way so they wouldn't miss anything. The women prepared food and guarded the barn and paddock where the best horses were located. Others related messages from the walkie-talkies'. All wanted involved in what could be their last hurrah.

Jo was not going to stay back at the house and miss this either, neither was Rob, nor John who had insisted on coming home. Dana wasn't feeling well and after returning home from the football game, went straight to bed.

All was in readiness by the time dusk had fallen; the rain held off. After sitting and standing for several hours in a thicket of trees and bushes, Jo grew cold and weary. Finally, she dimly saw cowboys appear from several directions. Rocko glanced at his cohorts, who nervously looked around and behind them. She literally shivered with excitement at what was about to take place. *This is the night; I can feel it in my bones.* Flora's Girl, slightly tied to a bush, pawed at the soft ground as they waited, as if she too were anticipating something.

Rocko had been lucky with rain as his cover before, but this night was turning out to be clear and bright. The number of horses left grazing so carelessly would be that much easier to steal.

Tension increased when a palomino appeared over the rolling hill and Rocko motioned his men ahead. The fence was dismantled with a crowbar and wire cutters, and Rocko and three others quickly rode into her pasture, each attaching a rope to several horses. They were going to be greedy. They began leading them back toward the opening in the fence.

An aroma arose from the freshly cut fields. Hay was now safely stored in the barns. Gabe, coming from the opposite direction from the palomino, stole up quietly and joined Jo. Despite Gabe's warnings that she would be cold and should stay home, Jo shivering, stood beside the man she loved and admired.

The October moon, golden and enormous, moved slowly across the sky. The night air had turned keen and cutting before the first rider appeared at the opening in the fence, leading her horses into Reinhart land. There were few whinnies from them; the cowboys knew their business.

Just as all had crossed into Reinhart land and before any could begin to move off, it seemed to arise from out of nowhere, a large circle of men, holding a rifle in one hand and a powerful, glaring flashlight in the other. The night was filled with light, alarm, confusion, like Joshua marching around Jericho, or Gideon surrounding the Midianites.

Word was passed quickly down the line to the house, via walkie-talkies, where Marie dutifully placed the call to Pierce, then to the Sheriff.

Gabe and Jo stood their ground, waiting for the leader to make his move to escape. Even when Pierce and Jodi rode up in a Jeep, and its lights illuminated the scene even more, he remained quiet and hidden.

As Rocko was relieved of his horses and roughly taken down from his, he looked at Jodi, his eyes blazing, and said, "Thanks Jodi!"

John looked from one to the other, and must have thought what Jo was thinking, that Jodi had been the one to tell Rocko of their plans before, and tonight, their plans would have been foiled again if John had told Jodi.

Apparently hurt beyond endurance, John whipped Bill into a gallop and headed for the ranch. Jodi looked at Rocko with his smug grin, then to her father, before realizing what Rocko had insinuated.

"Rob, may I borrow your horse?" He was hardly off of it, before Jodi was on and galloping in the direction of the pounding hoofs in the crisp air.

Pierce almost leaped from the jeep and took several fierce steps to stand in front of Rocko. After moments of a penetrating look, he spit on the ground and turned, and walked away. Then, as if not quite satisfied, he turned again, and in one simple, powerful move, gave Rocko an uppercut to the chin, which sent him spiraling to the ground. Then satisfied, he walked over to Rusty.

Jo and Gabe still hidden, looked at one another with a grin.

The man on the palomino was getting nervous, his horse skittish. It was evident that he would have to get out of there soon or he would be discovered. When Pierce had ridden up, Jo had expected him to ride off then, but perhaps, there hadn't been enough confusion for him to sneak away without being heard, so he stayed his ground.

When, in the distance, everyone could hear a siren and see flashing lights, the rider knew it was now or never, and glanced over Gabe's way, still without seeing him. As the sheriff's jeep roared closer, he prepared to turn his horse and ride away, and when he did, two powerful lights blinded him and Gabe's voice stopped him, as he reached up to catch the bridle of the palomino.

"Going someplace, Judd?" Gabe asked calmly. Jo had been right in her suspicion of the man.

Judd was about to kick his horse into action when Gabe shined his light on the gun Jo held, and demanded tightly as he rode up beside him to check for a weapon. "Don't even think about it, Judd. Let's just turn your horse around very carefully and head toward the little group of your helpers. Jo knows how to use that gun, by the way," he added, "and after the way you treated her dog, she might not mind using it!"

The appearance of Judd caused a stir among the rustlers. When Rocko saw Judd, he pretended indifference, apparently waiting to hear what line Judd would try to feed the sheriff. Jo wondered if Rocko would take all the blame, after all, Judd could give him a job after he got out of jail, if he kept his mouth shut.

Of course, Judd wasn't aware that, although they didn't know who he was because of the distance, he had been observed for the past month, especially the past hour, conferring with Rocko prior to breaking down the fence. So in all bravado, Judd called out, "Reinhart? Sheriff? What's going on here?"

"Couple horse thieves, looks like," the Sheriff answered, "what are you doing here?" His Jeep lights helped light up the situation too.

"Just checkin' on my sheep, been having coyote problems," he lied, trying to watch Rocko out of the corner of his eye. "I saw these young men and waited in the shadows to catch them myself." Then he turned to Gabe. "Gabe here, saw me. He was watching too, and this pretty little woman."

Rocko, fully recovered from the blow, delivered by his boss, was fuming and spit on the ground when Judd looked his way. Jo was surprised that he held his tongue.

"You don't keep track of your men very well, do you Judd?" the Sheriff asked. "Looks like three of these men belong to your ranch, or, am I wrong?"

Judd still full of pretense, looked over the group as if in surprise. "By gum, I think you're right, Sheriff. Glad you caught them before they got into any trouble."

Now, Jo had stood all she could and she was not easily provoked.

"All right, already, enough is enough! Sheriff, I want to get married and this big, wonderful man," she said turning to Gabe, "won't marry me until the rustling problem is all cleared up." She had been walking over to where Rocko, the sheriff, and his deputy, were standing. "If you put these four young men in jail, that won't stop my rustling problem. Oh, it may for a while, but it will start all over again and I'll never get married."

The Sheriff was about to interrupt, when she put out a hand to stop him. "No, it won't, because the ring leader will still be at large." She turned to Rocko to whom she had never been formerly introduced and said, "Gabe tells me that when you get out of jail, you'll head straight to your leader to blackmail him to get work and money, for no one around here will hire you now."

She didn't look at Judd, but from her periphery vision, saw him squirm in the saddle.

"Do you really think he'll hire you, Rocko, and take a chance you'll squeal on him if things don't go your way, or you get him into trouble? And how long will he submit to your blackmail before he kills you, for that would be the only way to keep you quiet."

By now the sheriff, his deputy, Reinhart and Rusty just stood with their arms across their chests, grinning, waiting. Jo saw it, and saw also, that her dear relatives and friends were enjoying it too. Now she was embarrassed, but felt she had to continue what she had started.

She was still holding the gun in one hand and the light in the other and swung it around for emphasis, as she talked.

"It was quite a show," her dad said later, "I was so proud of her, and it was then I knew the ranch rightly belonged to her, that Dad had done the right thing. I think my brothers did too."

Jo questioned Rocko, not only with her voice, but also

with her eyes. She saw him look at Judd and must have seen the truth of her words.

"Rocko, Gabe, Rusty, and I know that Judd Klein is behind this whole set-up, and probably has some of my horses right now in his barn. We have been trailing you men for weeks now, and saw you confer with him prior to entering my land. All these men standing here saw you. All we need is your statement implicating him, and, if you won't, I think one or more of these other young men will."

She sauntered in front of them, flashing her light close to each face. "Isn't that right, fellows? You aren't going to go to jail and let Judd run free so he and Rocko can start up again, for whatever purpose they had of ruining me. I believe he purposely killed my dog and a couple horses." She saw the reflection of that truth on some of the cowboy's faces. "He keeps game cocks, which kill one another. What do you think he will do to you?"

From behind her came a snarling, impatient voice. "He wants your land!" Rocko looked at Judd then, with a final contemptuous look. "And I wanted to sit high and mighty in Reinhart's favor, by helping him meet his quotas, and marry Jodi."

At this ridiculous statement, Pierce spit on the ground before he looked at Gabe, "I can guarantee you that none of your horses have gone through my plant since we talked."

"That's right," Rocko said, "He kept such good track that I couldn't move them in. Most of them are still at Klein's."

Jo thought she was the only one to breathe a sigh of relief, but heard it all around her, and it caused her to drop the gun and light and throw her hands to her face to cry in relief and happiness for the horses and for herself. Gabe and Ben reached her side at the same time. Ben patted Gabe on the shoulder and said, "She's yours, Son." Gabe reached out his hand and firmly clasped that of his future father-in-law, before he drew Jo to him.

The sheriff bristled, and took over. "Okay, Judd, get off that horse." He walked over to put handcuffs on him. "Reinhart, think we could use one of your horse trailers for a temporary paddy wagon?"

"Gladly," Pierce commented, as he put his jeep in gear.

"Okay, you men," the sheriff indicated to the quintet of rustlers, "I'm goin' to put a rope between your hands and tie both ends to the jeep. March ahead of it, and don't try anything funny."

"Now hang on there a minute, Sheriff, you too Pierce, if you don't' mind," Jo had reigned her composure and was grinning from ear to ear, though holding unto Gabe's hand. Then she looked up at Gabe and waited for him to speak.

"The lady is at a loss for words." he grinned. "What she wants is for you all to come to our wedding." He pretended to be thinking or to have finished until she looked at her, and realized the strain she had been under, and didn't need any more teasing to increase that strain. "Let's see, this is Friday, how about a week from Sunday?"

Jo looked over the group and stood with her hands on her hips staring at Gabe. "Make that this Sunday at three in the afternoon. Somehow, someway, we're having a wedding!"

As Gabe swooped her up in his arms, hats were thrown in the air with a roar of approval, horns blew, men continued to shout from sheer relief if for no other reason, and clapped one another on the back. What a kick!

Quietly in her ear before his lips captured hers, he said, "Right, that's exactly what I meant to say, this Sunday."

He laughed as he set her down and the press of men gathered round them with congratulations, before gathering up the reins of the horses. One by one the flashlights beamed their way back to the ranch. What a joyful procession!

There Jo hugged each man and Gabe shook hands with each one, thanking them and begged those who weren't staying at the ranch, to join everyone who was, for some refreshments and hot drinks. It was three in the morning before Jo slipped under the covers next to Dana for a well-earned rest.

There was so much unknown about Judd Klein, but that was the government's problem, not hers. Any which way, he wasn't ever going to get the ranch to pasture his cattle.

# Chapter 39

A small wedding, Jo had said, and with the little time to get it together, it should have been, but with all the female help around, they were well prepared for the many friends of the families involved. It was beautiful, God honoring, and the bride and groom, radiant. It was a wedding where the love of the couple for one another, was so markedly evidenced. When they expressed their love in their own choice of vows, many in the audience had tears in their eyes.

"Where are you going for your honeymoon?" Marie wanted to know, when Jo asked if she would help her mother keep an eye on the children. Marie, nor any of the other women, who had stayed on at the ranch, needed to lift a finger; this was their day too.

"Oh, I'm just going to pitch a tent and move her into it for a week," Gabe teased.

A huge tent with clear plastic sides to protect from any wind as well as to allow light to shine through, had been set up to serve dual purposes—the wedding first, then it was decorated and used to hold the catered buffet.

The caterer had hired extra boys to set up chairs for the

wedding ceremony, and then put up tables and used the same chairs for the wedding seating, for around the tables.

With the tent just a few feet from the porch, and the weather co-operating, under the florist's direction, the tent had a look of ethereal beauty. The tables took on a transformation with the use of white tablecloths, floral arrangements and ribbons. Hundreds of colorful balloons, filled with gas and tied with long silver and white streamers, were brought in from a truck and allowed to float to the roof of the tent.

The catered reception was under way.

Gabe had been more serious than anyone realized. While Jo had been busy with the wedding preparations, and Dana's and her dresses and hair, he had been busy with preparations of his own.

He slipped away to the bunkhouse while she went to her bedroom during the reception. They had eaten, drank, had a small piece of wedding cake, and socialized, until everyone was quite satisfied and pleased. After Jo threw her bride's bouquet, they arranged their slip. After changing clothes, Gabe met her at the side porch with the jeep, grabbed up the suitcases and picked her up to sit her in the seat close to him, but not before melting her with a husband's kiss.

"That's just a promise of more to come," he grinned and winked at her.

"I like that kind of promise."

She wondered at his insistence on the Jeep and watched in amazement as he drove it over one of the implement roads. She could see now why he didn't want the station wagon, which the children had cleaned, washed, and waxed, for the occasion. Turning to him in utter confusion, she asked, "Where are we going?"

"Trust me, this is supposed to be a surprise," was all he would say. "By the way, you look good enough to eat."

His voice was hardly more than a whisper, but it stirred her to remember past experiences when his voice had touched the cords of emotion deep within her. It quieted her and filled her with expectancy at the same time.

"I can hardly wait."

He got out to open a gate to the north pasture, drove through, and went back to shut it.

Then reality set in and she wanted to question him, but held back. He was heading toward Eden!

He realized she was being torn with questions and said, "Just wait. You won't ever be disappointed again." Then he took a moment to lay a loving kiss on her, and looked at her with such hope and love, that she melted back into the seat, forgetting her lovely soft dress and jacket, her new kid shoes. She played with the beautiful ring around her finger, his paternal grandmother's wedding ring.

He maneuvered the jeep, circling and twisting until they were deep within the confines of Eden.

Then she saw it. The largest and most unusually shaped tent she had ever seen. It was colorful, fringed, beautiful, like something out of the Arabian Knights. Pots of greenery and mounds of mums lined the entrance.

"Gabe, it's awesome, beautiful; Eve should have had it so good. When, how. . ." she exclaimed, as he walked around to her side, his eyes never leaving hers.

He took her hand and helped her slide into his arms as he carried her into the tent. It was all satin draped, warm, soft, and alluring. There were flowers everywhere, and candles as well as a wonderful fragrance. It was charmingly and delightfully furnished, like something from a fairy tale. After exclaiming her wonder with oohing and aahing, she finally gave her full attention to her husband.

"Remember the challenge you threw me awhile back, about whose ardor would cool down first?"

"I remember," she said, her eyes holding his, her fingers playing with his ears, his neck, his hair.

"Are you quite up to meeting that challenge?"

"I'm ready, Gabe," she whispered looking at his lips, his eyes. *Can he feel the undulating currents filling her with desire?*

"Then I am about to teach you that there is another side to love."

"Oh, Gabe," she cried, as her mouth sought his.

He carefully lowered her to the wondrously soft, satin covered bed, then quickly returned to the opening to zipper it shut and snap it securely.

Her eyes never left him, and as he returned, she had already taken off her shoes and jacket and started to open her arms to receive him, but instead put her hands to her mouth to stifle a laugh. She was ready to accept and to match the desire seen on his face, in his eyes, and the, "I can't wait moment" as he whisked off his jacket and tie and threw them on the carpet covered platform on which the floor of the tent rested. She really tried not to laugh, as he stood first on one foot, to get off his boot, then the other.

"Do you charge for that dance?"

"Laugh at me will you . . ."

It was only another minute, before she began to experience the other side of love, Gabe's way.

CPSIA information can be obtained
at www.ICGtesting.com
Printed in the USA
BVOW08s0754230717
490029BV00001B/71/P